So Much
It Hurts

Melanie Dawn

Jackie,
Love deeply.
Forgive easily.
Live happily!

♡ *Melanie Dawn*

Copyright © 2013 Melanie Dawn

Cover Design by Brett Fabrizio
Editing by Kathleen Lilley
Interior Design by Angela McLaurin, Fictional Formats
Images used under license from www.dreamstime.com

Permission for use of fictional character, Seth Jordan, and his fictional band, The Rifters, was obtained by Erika Ashby.

Permission for use of book title, It All Started With a Lima Bean, was obtained by Kimi Flores.

Createspace:
ISBN-13: 978-1490962054
ISBN-10: 1490962050

Warning: This book is intended for readers 17+ due to some explicit language and mature themes.

Dedication

To my family
You are everything I need and nothing I deserve.

Prologue

Kaitlyn Davenport
12th Grade English
November 8, 2004

Twisted Nature

A flower stands tall with radiant beauty.

The gentle breeze strokes its petals.

Lifting its face high into the sun,

a fragile butterfly dances on its leaves,

while a fuzzy caterpillar inches its way up the rigid stem.

Soon the sunshine hides away.

Its face cannot be seen behind the tall, majestic mountains.

Darkness fills the warm spring air, as clouds

                    trap

                    the darkness from escaping.

Evil...

Stares from the distant moon, plotting for destruction.

Suddenly, the gentle breeze becomes fierce.

Howling winds sweep the earth, wiping away the teardrops

                                    of

                                        the

                                            rain.

Tornadoes suck up all mankind and spit out the ruins.

Beneath the annihilation, only the twisted skeleton

                    of a once beautiful flower...

                        remains.

Well done, Kaitlyn! You have the world at your fingertips!

A

1

Chapter One

Each thundering crash of the ocean waves in the distance administered a dose of therapy to my soul. With my towel draped across my lounge chair, I reclined by the water's edge sipping a Piña Colada from a hurricane glass adorned by a tiny pink umbrella. My life had all but suffocated me the past few months, and I desperately needed a change of scenery.

Lisa's voice interrupted my thoughts. "Come on, Kaitlyn. Let's go inside and get ready to par-tay," she called, overemphasizing her last word. Lisa's head bobbed up and down in the water as she swam past me toward the pool ladder.

I suppressed a laugh. Only late twenty-somethings remember when it was cool to pronounce it 'par-tay.' There was no need to point out the fact that we were nearly too old to hit the clubs.

Two guys standing at the tiki bar turned to stare at Lisa as she stepped out of the water. She reminded me of a supermodel as she brushed her long brown hair away from her eyes. I met Lisa soon after she found out she was pregnant with her second son. I thought she was the most beautiful pregnant woman I had ever seen. However, Lisa's sweet disposition far outweighed her attractiveness. Like a fair-complexioned cartoon princess, I could almost picture the birds singing to her while they helped her fold the laundry at home. Unaware of the caliber of her beauty, she never seemed to notice when other men were checking her out. She had been happily married to her high school sweetheart for almost seven years.

I watched the two beefcake rubbernecks at the tiki bar gawk at her over their mirrored aviator sunglasses and chuckled under my breath. "Okay, let's go," I replied, before gulping the rest of my drink.

The other girls were toweling off and grabbing their bags to head upstairs to the condo. I looked around my mini-paradise, content with my surroundings. The palm trees swayed against the warm breeze, while the seagulls flew overhead searching for their next meal. The stark white sand glistened for miles under the hot sun, while the swells of the ocean waves toppled against the shore. For the first time I felt a freedom that I hadn't experienced in quite some time.

I left my single life of drinking and dancing behind the day I found out I was pregnant with Eli. Michael and I had no plans of marriage until we saw those two pink lines on that cold November morning. I had set my future of becoming a pediatric psychologist aside while I made arrangements to become a stay-at-home mom. My entire life seemed to have been on hold the last five years. I quickly learned that being a stay-at-home mom was not all picnics and play dates. I felt trapped under the interminable mountain of laundry, lost amid the infinite overflow of dirty dishes, and exhausted from the incessant whine of a tired and cranky child who only seemed to be comforted by the everlasting song of a purple dinosaur. I couldn't remember the last time I had enjoyed a night out; I was actually looking forward to it.

I assumed Michael and Eli were just sitting down for dinner at Burger Land. Michael, the staunch and successful CPA at a thriving accounting firm, was much too busy to cook while I was away. He almost balked at the idea of my weekend escape:

"Kaitlyn, I just can't afford for you to leave right now. I need to go into work the next few weekends to prepare for several upcoming meetings. Work is just more important than some silly girls' retreat right now."

"That's the problem, Michael. Your work. Our lives revolve around your work. You always put your work before your family."

"My work pays the bills. Last time I checked, laundry and dishes don't pay the bills."

"That's just it, Michael. Laundry and dishes don't pay the bills, nor do they create a fulfilling life! I'm worth more than just being a servant for this family! Do you know how depressing it is when your daily goal in life is to sweep up crackers off the floor and dig rocks out of pants pockets before throwing them in the washing machine? I feel like I'm in solitary confinement most of the time. Then, my husband comes home and carries his plate of supper into his office only to disappear for hours on end, coming to bed well after I've gone to sleep. That happens so often these days that sex is barely even in our vocabulary anymore. I've spent the last five years in this unfulfilling life, wiping asses and noses, sweeping crumbs off

the floor, and passing a practically nonexistent husband occasionally in the hallway!" Five years of pent up frustration barreled its way out of me in harsh tones and salty tears.

"We all need a break sometimes, Kaitlyn. Don't you dare think you are the only one sacrificing your needs and wants for this family. I make sacrifices, too!"

"Oh, really? You laugh it up with your coworkers at your lavish dinner meetings, eating filet mignon with lobster tail and drinking three hundred dollar bottles of wine while I sit at home eating chicken nuggets for the third time in a week. When Eli was a baby, you played your endless golf games and slept soundly in your luxurious hotel rooms, while I sat at home breastfeeding until my nipples were raw and cleaning up explosive diapers all night! I never realized those fringe benefits at work were considered sacrifices for you! Please forgive me if I was mistaken!" My seething comments oozed with sarcasm.

Michael glared at me under furrowed eyebrows. He wanted to say something more, but refrained. Instead, he just huffed and stomped to his office, slamming the door behind him.

I stared at his office door, half expecting him to open it back up and say whatever it was he seemed to want to say. But, it remained closed. I could already hear him pecking away at his keyboard on his computer.

What had happened to us over the past few years? It's not that we hated each other. We were still cordial most of the time, but our marriage had become stagnant and downright boring. We worked great together as a team to run a household and raise a child, but most of the time I felt like we were just roommates passing each other in the bathroom, taking turns using the sink. Our conversations used to be interesting and compelling. Now, it seemed like the only thing we discussed was whose turn it was to put Eli to bed. His office was his sanctuary, and my nose stayed in a book. Slowly, I turned around and walked away from his closed office door, in search of my e-reader with its newly downloaded novel.

"If you really want to go, then go. I can rearrange some things at work," he muttered later that night as I lay in bed scouring the beach resort pamphlet that had come in the mail that afternoon.

"You have no idea how much I need this."

"Then go—enjoy your weekend. I'll do what I can to make it work."

With that retort, he grabbed the blanket, rolled over, and promptly fell asleep. On the flipside, I stayed awake for hours, losing myself in the virtual pages of my e-reader.

I felt slightly guilty that he would have to rearrange his schedule, but not guilty enough to stay home. I deserved the break. I **needed** the break before I completely lost my mind.

So there I was at the beach, taking advantage of my much needed getaway while Michael and Eli probably enjoyed a classic burger from Burger Land. Eli would be overjoyed with the idea of a junior meal for dinner. He had been begging for one of the new Space Deputy toys for a week. I looked forward to hearing Eli's sweet little voice on the phone when I called him later that evening to tell him goodnight.

"Hello?"

"Hey, sweetie," I cooed.

"Hey, Mommy! Guess what? I got the new Captain Neptune tonight!"

I laughed. "I figured Daddy would take you to Burger Land."

"Yeah, and it's so cool!"

"I bet," I agreed, envisioning him holding it up for me to see.

"Wanna talk to Daddy?" He was obviously too busy with his new toy to spend another second talking to me.

"Sure, sweetie. Bye. I love you."

"Love you too, Mommy!"

"Hey you! Are you having fun?" Michael asked as he brought the phone to his ear.

"So far I am! We're going out tonight too! Karaoke, I think," I said, a little too exuberantly.

"Sounds fun. I hope you girls have a great time." He didn't sound nearly as enthusiastic as I did.

"Thanks. Well, I guess I better go get ready for our big night out. I just wanted to call to say goodnight and check on Eli."

"We're fine," Michael assured me.

"I'll talk to you later, then."

"Okay, goodnight. Talk to you later." I heard the phone disconnect and I sat there, dumbfounded.

"Love you too," I grumbled at the blank screen. It was a common occurrence when ending my conversations with Michael. In fact, I couldn't even remember the last time he told me he loved me. Most of his sweet nothings and terms of endearment were reserved for Eli…and that bimbo from his office. What was her name? Dollface? Homewrecker? Oh yeah— Bridget. I remembered the first time I became familiar with *Bridget*:

"Hello, Weston and Associates. This is Mr. Thomas's office. May I help you?" A perky voice answered my husband's phone one day from his private office line.

"Who's speaking?" I asked sharply.

"This is Bridget, Mr. Thomas's new personal assistant. How may I help you?"

"Well, Bridget, this is Kaitlyn Thomas, Michael's wife. May I speak with him, please?"

"Sure, Mrs. Thomas. Just a moment, please."

I heard indistinct sounds and murmurings as the phone was being passed to Michael.

"Hey." Michael sounded annoyed. "What's up?"

"I…uh…" I couldn't really remember what I needed. Bridget's perkiness coming from my husband's personal phone had completely messed with my mind.

"Thanks, hon'," Michael's muffled voice echoed through the phone as if he had a hand covering the speaker while he spoke to

Bridget, "Oh yeah, while you're out will you stop by Starbucks for me?"

"Absolutely, Mr. Thomas," she cooed.

God, I hated her.

"Do you want your usual?"

He has a usual?

"Sure thing. Thanks, darlin'."

Hon'? Darlin'? What the hell?! Heat coursed through my veins as I struggled to contain my rage.

"Sorry about that," Michael's voice rang clear as he dropped his hand from the phone speaker, indicating that he, once again, was speaking to me. "Did you need something, Kaitlyn?"

Yeah, I need that tramp to get fired.

"Yeah, I just wanted to remind you that Eli's tee ball game is tonight at six."

Michael sighed. "Sorry, I have to work late tonight."

"Of course you do."

"What was that for?"

I mocked him in the same pouty voice Bridget used to get his attention. "Thanks hon', and sure thing, darlin'." Then anger hijacked my voice as I grumbled, "What the hell, Michael?"

"What? It's totally innocent. Bridget knows that. I just say junk like that so she'll bring me my coffee. It doesn't mean anything."

"Right. I guess that's why when I fix your coffee for you every morning you barely take time to thank me, much less call me darlin'."

Michael huffed. "I don't have time to argue, Kaitlyn. I'm sorry. If it makes you feel better, I won't say it again. Bridget knows I'm teasing her. It's nothing. I swear."

"Okay, Michael. Whatever. I guess we'll see you after the game."

"Fine. See you later."

Michael disconnected, and I gripped the phone angrily as if taking my frustration out on the electronic device would somehow rectify the situation.

"Love you too," I muttered sarcastically, as the words 'hon' and 'darlin' bounced around in my mind like tiny wooden balls tumbling in a bingo cage.

"Who's ready for a night on the town?" Shannon called from the bathroom as she stood in front of the mirror adding the final touches of her makeup. Shannon had been a stay-at-home mom for the last ten years. The epitome of a homemaker, she always left me envious of her organizational skills and her level head. Shannon always seemed to have it all together.

"I know I am!" Tori yelled from the kitchen as she poured some vodka into her glass of orange juice. "I can't remember the last time I've been out with the girls!" Without a doubt, Tori was the most physically fit mom of our group. Almost nothing prevented her from keeping her strict workout schedule at the local YMCA. She had muscle definition in places I couldn't even imagine having muscles at all.

"I'm ready, too!" Lisa's five inch stiletto heels tapped across the tile floor as she walked into the kitchen to grab her purse off the counter.

Together, we were excited to have a few nights of fun without catering to the needs of our families.

The bar was packed with loud and obnoxious drunks. We chose to sit at a table in the back corner of the bar so we could actually hear our conversation over the roar of the crowd and the thumping music from the speakers. The walls and ceilings of the bar were lined with dollar bills that had been haphazardly stapled by satisfied patrons like offerings to a shrine or something. Some of the dollar bills had signatures on them while others had messages and inspirational quotes. Above our heads, about a foot from the ceiling, a small shelf ran the length of the walls. Empty beer and liquor bottles lined the shelves. The wooden floors creaked as people walked by our table on their way to high five the giant claw of the crab statue near the entrance. Our waiter told us that the tradition of fist bumping and high fiving Creighton the Crab started shortly after the bar had opened nearly forty years ago.

I sat with my back to the stage. My friends and I were laughing hysterically at the fools we had made of ourselves during our poor rendition of Aretha Franklin's song, *Respect*. Downing a few drinks prior to our performance gave me enough liquid courage to embarrass myself on stage. I had immersed myself so deeply in the conversation that I barely noticed karaoke had ended and a band had started setting up on stage.

In the background, a voice emerged from the microphone. "Testing…one, two, three. Testing…"

The hair on the back of my neck stood upright. My body seemed to recognize the smooth and soothing voice, but my mind could not recall it. I quickly spun around in my seat and peered at the figure on stage. However, we sat too far away, and the terrible lighting in the bar restricted my view.

"What's the matter, Kaitlyn?" Shannon sounded concerned. "You look like you've seen a ghost."

"That voice…it sounds so familiar. I've heard it before," I stammered.

"Seriously? The sign on the door said this band is debuting tonight. Besides, who do you know that lives at the beach?" Tori asked.

"No one, I guess." But, there was something about the voice that I recognized. I felt sure I had heard it before. I knew it from somewhere, but *where*?

The mysterious voice began to sing. My thoughts drowned out the chatter around me. I dug deeper into my memory as I grasped for any recollection I could muster; nothing sprang to my mind. That soothing melodic voice crept up the back of my spine, tingling and sensuous, radiating through my chest. I just couldn't conjure up the face connected to it. The timbre resonated familiarity, but the perplexity remained.

"Seriously, Kaitlyn, what's gotten into you?" Tori looked at me wide-eyed. "You don't look so good."

I didn't realize it until she said it, but my face felt flushed, and my palms felt sweaty. "I don't know, guys. I just can't explain it. I think I know the lead singer of this band. What was the band's name again?"

"Big Five, or something cheesy like that. Why?" Lisa piped up.

"I don't know…I just can't place it…"

The face connected to the voice remained anonymous as the conversation swirled around me. I considered just getting up and walking toward the front of the stage to get a good look. I needed to quickly solve the mystery; it was driving me crazier by the second. However, to avoid looking like some desperate middle-aged groupie heading to the stage for attention, I stayed seated and half-heartedly listened to Tori talk about her workout routine and her newest 'clean-eating' diet of black beans, edamame, and kale. Listening to her drone on about pairing her meals with an organic strawberry smoothie made with fresh Greek yogurt didn't help divert my attention at all.

Suddenly, someone spoke from behind me. "Kaitlyn?"

The girls at my table froze. Their eyes looked up at the mystery man attached to the voice. I whirled around to see who caused my friends' jaws to drop in awe. My breath caught in my throat while my heart immediately began pounding in my chest. A face from a long forgotten past stood in front of me.

His name immediately sprang from my lips, "Chris!"

"Wow, Kaitlyn. I can't believe it's really you."

"Chris," I said again almost breathlessly. "How long has it been?"

"Eight years and five months, almost to the day," Chris blurted without even taking time to think about it, as if he had been etching hash marks on his wall for each passing day.

"Unbelievable," I said with a hint of nostalgia, as my mind tried to drift back to a time I had tried earnestly to erase from my memory. Immediately, I snapped myself back into reality. "What are you doing here?" I asked, trying to appear collected.

"I live here. I write music by day, and play music by night. Our band, *Fifth Wheel*, is working on our first album. What are you doing here?" Chris looked around the table. The girls stared up at him. I couldn't tell if they were ogling him because he was stunningly gorgeous, or if they were just shocked by the fact that another man— besides my husband—so obviously took my breath away. Deep down, I hoped they didn't even notice my breathless anguish.

"Oh wow, where are my manners? These are my friends…Lisa, Shannon, and Tori. We're here for a ladies' weekend retreat."

The girls continued to look up in amazement. Chris looked as handsome as ever. His breathtaking physique defined itself beneath his tight black T-shirt. They sputtered and stammered their hellos. He politely smiled, but his eyes quickly diverted and caught my gaze. Those same dark eyes that melted my heart more than eight years ago were searching mine. I hoped my friends weren't aware of the pounding in my chest. The awkward, yet intimate moment stirred emotions in me that I had not felt in many years.

"Well, I guess I better get back to the stage. The boys are ready to play again." Chris smiled amiably at my friends. His eyes caught mine, and he beamed that same wide grin that once made my heart turn flips in my chest.

"Okay." I grinned back, trying to suppress the feeling that was welling up inside of me. "I'll see you around."

I watched Chris walk back toward the stage. Shaking my head in disbelief, I looked back at the girls sitting around the table. They all gaped at me in wide-eyed astonishment.

"What?" I blinked my eyes innocently.

"Who. Was. That?!" Lisa asked, emphasizing every word.

I shrugged indifferently. "Oh, that was just a guy I knew from high school."

"No, Kaitlyn," Tori remarked emphatically, looking over my shoulder. "That was not *just* a guy."

"Yeah." Shannon stared in his direction, bewildered. "Wow."

"Guys!" I snapped. "Stop staring, okay? He really was just a guy I knew from high school…who I happened to be in love with at the time."

"Whoa, I bet that was a blast from the past!" Lisa exclaimed.

I sighed. "Yeah, something like that." I looked down at the trembling hands resting in my lap. I had no idea that seeing him would stir up so many emotions in the pit of my stomach.

"Oh honey," Shannon patted my shoulder. Finishing her sentence seemed unnecessary. I felt her sympathy.

The rest of the night blurred by as my mind focused on the tranquilizing voice that poured from the speakers. Once in a while, I would sneak a peek toward the stage. I could feel his eyes settling on me, even in the darkness.

His voice, gravelly and breathless behind the microphone, felt warm and comforting like a soft blanket on a cool night. The quiver in my stomach and the tremble of my hands were evidence of the effect that Chris had on me. Ashamed, I tried in vain to hide my anguish. Occasionally, Shannon would pat my hand, out of sight from the rest of the girls. I smiled meekly at her as she nodded her head with understanding.

"So, are you guys ready to call it a night?" Shannon's eyes looked tired as she sipped her last Cosmo.

We all agreed, began to gather our purses, and stood up to leave.

"Kaitlyn," Chris spoke from behind me again.

The deep sound of his voice startled me, and I dropped my keys.

"Oh, sorry," he said as he quickly bent down to pick them up.

"It's okay. I'm not usually so clumsy."

His fingers brushed mine as he handed them back to me. The tingle from his touch radiated up my arm. I heard a nervous giggle escape from my lips. My hand flew up and covered my mouth, and I immediately felt embarrassed.

"You really made my night," Chris declared with a crooked grin. "I can't believe it's been eight years."

"Me neither."

"See you again tomorrow night?" he asked. "I mean, let's not let another eight years go by."

"Absolutely," I agreed without thinking. "We'll be here all weekend. I'm sure I'll see you around."

"Great!" he replied, flashing his perfect smile at me.

As hard as I tried not to notice, Chris looked absolutely magnificent. His shirt clung to his well-formed chest. His dark hair had been spiked and gelled in a hot sexy mess. The smoldering intensity of his eyes staring into mine sent chills rippling through my body. "I look forward to it," he eagerly admitted.

I could barely contain the elation in my voice. "I just can't believe it's really you." Without thinking, I reached out to hug him. He initially seemed shocked, but welcomed the embrace.

He enveloped me in his arms and whispered into my ear, "I've never forgotten you."

His breath was hot against my cheek. I inhaled the mixed aroma of aftershave and breath mints as I tried to burn his scent into my memory. A breath escaped my lungs and lodged in my throat. *'I'm a married woman,'* I rebuked myself. Quickly, I pulled away from him and practically ran to catch up to my friends.

"Oh my goodness, girl! Tell us everything!" Lisa exclaimed as we walked into the living room of our condo.

I shrugged my shoulders. "What's there to tell?"

Shannon spoke up. "Well, for starters, did you see the way he looked at you? And, did you see the way he looked in that shirt? Wow!"

I laughed solicitously. While these girls were my closest friends, I didn't feel emotionally prepared to rehash the history I had with Chris, nor did I feel strong enough to reopen old wounds I had spent years trying to heal.

"C'mon, Kaitlyn. Give us the scoop," Tori whined. "We want to know about this hot mystery guy."

I sighed, preparing myself for the heartrending wave of emotion I knew I was about to experience by divulging the intimate details of my past. I knew if I was going to tell them about Chris, I would have to start my story from the very beginning—a beginning that I would rather delete entirely from my memory. My history with Chris actually began with Trevor, my all-star athlete ex-boyfriend, who was also known as Jenkins County's hometown hero.

My mind, as it creaked open the lid of the proverbial can of worms, drifted back to a time and place I had only allowed myself to visit in my dreams. It returned to a time and place before that girl I once knew well, but barely recognized anymore, had sped away in her fully packed VW Jetta with hope to start a new life in college.

Chapter Two
Ten years earlier
April 2003

Trevor Kent stood confidently with his friends in his usual spot by the trophy case that would also become known as his throne by his senior year at East Jenkins High School. He was sporting his favorite pair of jeans, a white T-shirt and his letterman jacket. In our school, Trevor was known as a trifecta athlete—a star player on the football, basketball, *and* baseball teams. He and several of the other athletes watched the students mingle in the hallway before school began. Trevor was gorgeous, and being the most popular sophomore at East Jenkins, girls swooned over him. His sandy blond hair was cut high and tight like a marine fresh out of boot camp. Tall and muscular, Trevor could easily bench press two hundred and fifty pounds. His deep hazel eyes had an entrancing power of persuasion. No one could be sure if it was out of respect or fear that most guys looked up to him. Therefore, it came as no surprise to anyone when he was chosen as the forerunner for co-captain of the varsity football team his upcoming junior year.

I fell victim to his hypnotizing, hazel eyes in History class during our sophomore year. He sat beside me in class and pestered me with his immaturity. He and his buddies fervently annoyed the other girls in the class with their desperate attempt at flirting. Most of time I just rolled my eyes at him and his silly antics. However, midway through the year, Trevor hit a major growth spurt, and girls started to notice him. It wasn't long before I took notice also. He lost the chubby baby cheeks, and his face chiseled nearly overnight. He cut the swooping blond bangs that constantly fell into his eyes which caused him to develop the annoying habit of jerking his head to the side to get them off his face. The new buzz cut made him look older and tougher, like a soldier ready for battle. It seemed as though his boyish body grew muscles right before our eyes. His silliness dissipated, being replaced by charm and intrigue. I vividly remembered the day I walked into class, and he smiled at me in a way he had never smiled at me in the past.

"Hey, Kaitlyn," he said shyly, much unlike his usual character as he plopped down in the desk next to me.

"Hi." I smiled curiously at him and wondered what he wanted. *Is he going to ask me to help him study for the upcoming test? Does he need help with his research paper? Will he ask to borrow a pen for today's notes?*

He looked down and tapped his pencil on the edge of his desk. Glancing up at me, piercing me with his glinting, hazel eyes, he asked, "So, are you dating anyone?"

Well, that was the one question I never expected.

"Um…no," I stuttered, suddenly feeling a little shy, and yet incredibly excited at the same time.

"Oh, okay. I was just wondering." He nonchalantly shrugged his shoulders and reached into his backpack for his notebook.

Feeling slightly disappointed by the abrupt end of our conversation, yet thoroughly delighted that Trevor Kent really noticed me, I opened my textbook to the chapter we were studying in class and attempted to look interested. My confusion over Trevor was enough to turn my stomach into a ball of nerves. During the rest of the class I diverted my eyes and avoided looking at him.

"Heyyyy, Trevor," a tall blonde princess-wannabe cooed as she passed him in the cafeteria. Her mousy sidekick snickered and whispered something into the princess's ear. It must have been about Trevor because Princess cackled in his direction like a broody hen and batted her eyes seductively at him. Trevor just ignored the girls and took a bite of his burger.

"Yo, Trevor, my man!" One of his baseball teammates slammed his tray down on the table, flipped a chair around backwards, and plopped down next to Trevor.

"Wassup?"

"Dude, did you see that game last night?"

"Yeah man, I thought the Warriors had it in the bag."

"Yeah, too bad that dude choked in the last inning."

"Par for the course."

"True dat."

"Trevor!" A chorus of his buddies bellowed in unison and sat down at the table, fist bumping and high-fiving like a bunch of club-wielding barbarians.

It seemed as if everyone in the cafeteria was competing for a seat at Trevor's table. A few girls sat behind him, taking turns staring at him and giggling. Several guys sat nearby vying for an opportunity to include themselves in the potent exchange of machismo.

I sat a few tables away with Allison and Rachel trying to avoid the boorish nonsense. We talked about upcoming tryouts for the Varsity cheerleading squad while I picked at the mystery meat on my plate, glancing up only when Rachel gasped and grabbed my arm.

"Oh my gosh, Kaitlyn. Trevor Kent is looking at you."

"What?" I looked up just in time to see his hazel eyes settling on mine. A coy grin spread across his face. My cheeks burned crimson, but not before I returned a bashful smile.

I avoided making eye contact with Trevor the rest of the week. Occasionally, I would sneak a peek from the corner of my eye, and would sometimes catch him staring at me. I could feel my cheeks flush as I quickly looked away. I couldn't be sure, but I felt like Trevor was burning a smile into the back of my head. On Friday of that week, he finally spoke to me again.

"Hey Kaitlyn, are you coming to the baseball game tonight?" He sounded hopeful. "I'm pitching tonight," he added.

I hadn't planned to go, but since Trevor specifically asked me if I was coming, I knew I wanted to do everything in my power to get there. "Yeah, my mom said she would bring me," I lied. I assumed I would have to do some major sucking up that afternoon to get my mom to drive me back to the game.

"Great!" Trevor said with a grin, then turned his attention to the assignment written on the chalkboard.

After doing all of my chores and a lot of begging, I finally convinced my mom to drive me to the baseball game. I would be so glad when I didn't have to rely on my parents to drive me around. Although my mother would never admit it, I knew she enjoyed going to the ballgames with me. It was actually kind of fun to have mother/daughter time. My mom was never really the embarrassing kind of mom; she was actually pretty cool. All my friends thought so too.

I couldn't tear my eyes away from Trevor throughout the entire game. He looked spectacular in his baseball uniform. His muscles were well defined as his red and white jersey clung to his body. He swung his bat with such ferocity that it wouldn't surprise me if the birds ducked for cover when he made contact with the ball. I was spellbound by him; most girls, at the very least, were intrigued by him. I could have sworn that once during the fifth inning, when he rounded third base, he winked at me right before he slid into home plate. The whole game seemed to play in slow motion as I savored Trevor's every move. At one point my mom asked me which player had me so hypnotized.

"Number five," I replied. "Trevor Kent—but it's nothing, Mom. I mean, he barely even notices me."

After the game I hung around the bleachers talking to a few friends in the warm spring air. It was the first evening that week we didn't need a jacket after sunset. I secretly hoped Trevor would walk out of the dugout and come over to speak to me. My mom decided to wait for me in the car. I casually chatted with my friends until my cell phone vibrated in my pocket.

"Where are you?" my mom asked hastily.

"I'm coming. I'll be there in a minute."

Reluctantly, I walked to the car feeling bummed that I didn't get to talk to Trevor. I could see my mother waiting for me, impatiently drumming her fingers on the steering wheel of her white Yukon Denali. Just as I got into the car and shut the door, out of nowhere, Trevor ran up to my open window.

"Hey Kaitlyn," he said breathlessly, as if he'd sprinted to get there.

"Oh, hi!" My smile widened at the sight of him, but I immediately pursed my lips. I didn't want to look or sound too desperate…like that Princess chick in the cafeteria.

Trevor glanced at my mom and flashed his charming smile. "I was wondering if I could drive Kaitlyn home tonight, Mrs. Davenport."

My mother looked at me as her eyes filled with wonder and curiosity. I turned my back toward Trevor, out of his sight, and pleaded silently with her. *Pleeeease, Mom.*

She nodded her head with approval. "Okay. Is this the Trevor Kent I've heard so much about? It's so nice to meet you," she said with a smile.

My cheeks flared.

Trevor grinned. "Yes, ma'am, the one and only," he said in his sweet southern drawl.

Wow, he really knew how to turn on the charm!

"Thanks, Mom." I couldn't tell by my own tone if I was thanking her for letting Trevor take me home, or for humiliating me in front of him.

Trevor's red lifted Toyota truck roared to life as I buckled my seatbelt.

"So," he began, "you've been talking about me, huh?"

I think my heart stopped for a second. My words caught in my throat, causing me to silently suck in my breath.

He laughed. "I'm just teasing you!"

'Breathe,' I reminded myself. I was eager to change the subject. "You did great pitching tonight."

"Thanks." He shrugged and made a futile effort to sound humble. "I try." His confidence exuded sexiness, a trait that melted most teenage girls' hearts. I was no exception. The conversation flowed easily the rest of the ride to my house. I hated that the ride home had to end. I could have talked to him for hours. It seemed as though I blinked my eyes and we were parked in the driveway at my house.

"So," I asked with a devilish grin, "when you asked me in class if I was dating anyone, what exactly did you mean by that?" It was his turn to blush.

"Oh yeah…about that…" he stammered.

"I'm just kidding. You don't have to answer that." I playfully punched his shoulder. He grabbed my hand and held onto it. Caught by surprise, I stared up at him. His beautiful, hazel eyes accented by delicious specks of caramel and dark chocolate held mine captive for a few seconds.

"Kaitlyn, you have no idea how pretty you are," he told me.

I could feel my cheeks burning, but I didn't care. He leaned toward me, and my breath hitched as his lips touched mine. His soft lips stirred my senses. Kissing him came so easily, as if we had done it a hundred times already. He lightly caressed my cheek with his fingers as he moved his lips in rhythm with mine. His tongue caressed the seam of my lips, gently prodding my mouth to open. I gladly complied. His gentle touch and swirling tongue awakened the butterflies in the pit of my stomach. Then, he pulled away quickly, leaving me breathless. My lips burned for more.

"Sorry—"

"No, don't be," I said, cutting him short.

"There's just something about you, Kaitlyn."

I leaned into him and flirted, "There's just something about you, too." Giving him a quick kiss on the cheek, I hopped out of the truck.

"Hey, what's your screen name?" he asked.

"Cheerchick88. What's yours?"

"Str8ballin05. I'll IM you."

"Okay," I said eagerly, and bounded up the stairs toward the front door.

"He hardly notices you, huh?" my mom snorted when I walked into her bedroom to tell her goodnight.

"Well, maybe I was wrong…"

She shook her head knowingly at me. "I remember my first crush."

"Mommm," I whined, rolling my eyes at her.

Chuckling, she turned her attention back to her book.

Sleep didn't come easily that night. I lay awake for a long time just thinking of the possibilities. *Trevor Kent kissed me!* I felt like I floated into dreamland as I drifted off to sleep. Our kiss occupied my dreams the rest of the night.

Only a few short weeks lingered on the school calendar. Summer break started shortly after the night he took me home from the baseball game. Since Trevor had his driver's license, I knew it would be easy to see each other over the summer break. Trevor surprised me with his good manners considering what a pest he had been earlier in the year. He was a most gracious gentleman. Unlike most guys, he was not in a hurry to rush things between us physically. He opened doors for me; he pulled out chairs for me. He even asked permission from my parents before he asked me out on our first *official* date. He completely mesmerized me.

It had been exactly two months since we shared our first kiss in his truck. I could hear his loud, muffler-less truck barreling down the road miles before he got to my house.

"Hop in. I've got somewhere special to take you." He gave me a tantalizing smile as he opened the door for me.

"Where are we going?" I asked curiously.

"You'll see…" He just grinned mischievously at me, like he had something up his sleeve.

I crawled in and squeezed into the middle of the truck cab so I could sit as close to him as possible.

"You look stunning," he said, finding my hand and curling his fingers around mine.

"Thank you." I gave him my best flirty grin.

We pulled into the parking lot at dusk. The sunset painted the sky with varying hues of pink and orange clouds. A dark and empty wooden picnic shelter overlooked the lake. The water glistened as the sailboats created white-capped ripples that lapped up onto the shore. In the distance, I could see a blanket spread out under the trees by the water's edge. The tall oak trees hung their heavy branches over the spot Trevor had chosen for our romantic picnic by the lake. It was perfect.

He gently kissed my hand. "Happy two month anniversary."

"Wow! You planned all this by yourself?" I couldn't believe that Trevor would go to such lengths for me.

"Well, I had a little help," he confessed. "Allison helped set it all up before we got here."

Allison was my co-captain on the varsity cheerleading squad. We had been friends since elementary school. She and I got along pretty well. We squabbled a little, as most friends do, but in the end we always seemed to work it out and keep our friendship intact. Allison was short and sassy, and she seemed to be loved by everyone. A natural born leader, Allison could tame the masses. She was never afraid of a challenge. She would toss her auburn hair around her head as she gave her pageant queen smile and could convince even the famous groundhog that he did indeed see his shadow. She drew people in with her spunky attitude. I was always a little envious at her ability to captivate an audience.

"This picnic is better than anything I could have imagined," I said, trying to convince myself I wasn't dreaming.

Trevor led me down the path toward the picnic blanket. "I hope you like Antonio's."

Duh! Antonio's is only the best Italian restaurant in town!

"I love it!"

We sat down on the blanket, and Trevor lit a candle. We ate in silence, savoring every bite of Antonio's special entrée of baked ziti. I didn't realize how hungry I was until I saw that I had devoured mine. Trevor just smiled as he opened a box with a delicious looking slice of vanilla bean cheesecake. Handing me a spoon, he winked at me and said, "Enjoy!" Trevor watched me as I relished the first bite.

"What?" I asked, suddenly aware that he was staring at me.

"I don't know. I guess I'm just thinking about how perfect things are between us." He pressed *play* on the portable CD player he'd carried with him from the truck. *Wonderful Tonight* by Eric Clapton started playing softly through the speakers. "Wanna dance?" he asked as he held out his hand to me.

I grinned as he grasped my hand and helped me to my feet. Wrapping my arms around his neck, I nuzzled into his chest. I breathed in the cool, refreshing scent of his cologne. He held me close as we swayed back and forth under the moonlight. The feeling of warmth spread throughout my body as I cuddled up to him. I held my breath so I could hear his heartbeat; the constant rhythm was soothing. Melting into his arms, I felt my feet sweep right out from under me.

"I hope things will always be like this…perfect," I whispered.

"Me too," he said. His breath in my hair sent shivers down my spine, and the butterflies came back. Trevor gently cupped my face with his hands. I could feel his breath sweep across my lips. He leaned in and touched his lips to mine. His kiss started gently, but it quickly became more urgent as he pulled me closer. I let myself melt into his body. He slowly pulled away and looked into my eyes. "Kaitlyn…" He seemed apprehensive to continue. "I think I'm falling in love with you."

I knew it had only been two months, but I couldn't help the way I felt. I gave him a crooked grin. "I've been there a while, waiting for you."

That night was magical—forever etched into my memory. I think the remembrance of that night is why I held onto Trevor for far too long.

Chapter Three

The rest of the summer flew by at record speed. Trevor and I saw each other every day. We couldn't get enough of each other. Every day felt more intoxicating than the day before. I dreaded seeing the summer come to an end, although I was excited about a new school year. I couldn't wait to walk down the halls of East Jenkins High School with Trevor Kent by my side.

I spent most of my time that morning deciding what to wear. Having bought a few new outfits over the summer and loving all of them, I stood at my closet longer than normal trying to decide. I finally settled on a cute denim skirt, a pink form fitting T-shirt from my favorite SoCal-inspired store in the mall, and my trendy brown flip flops that I had to break in by wearing them in the hot shower. I checked the mirror several times to reassure myself. The first day of school was always a big deal, regardless of your age.

Arriving a little early to pick up my new schedule from the main office, I recognized several people who were waiting in line. Already hot and stuffy from the heat of mid-August, the office buzzed with excitement of a new school year. The secretary answered phones as quickly as she could, while the assistant principal gave important announcements over the loudspeaker. After getting my schedule, I took a moment to check it out. I was thankful for what seemed like a fairly easy semester. As I was trying to memorize my class list, I heard someone call my name.

"What's up Kaitlyn?" a male voice greeted me.

I looked up, catching a glimpse of baby blue eyes and a wide grin smiling at me under a bright red zip-up hoodie. While it was nearly one hundred degrees outside, some classrooms tended to get chilly from the air conditioning. *Hmmm… too bad I forgot to grab a hoodie in my rush out the door this morning.*

"Hey," I said. It was a guy from my English class last year. I couldn't recall his name, but I remembered he was pretty funny in class—a practical joker.

"So, who do you have for homeroom?" he inquired.

I checked my schedule again. "Mrs. Hamilton."

"Cool! Me too. I'll see you in class." He turned around and walked down the hall toward the cafeteria.

Breakfast. I had forgotten about breakfast. Oh well, my stomach felt too jittery to eat anything anyway. The first day of school always got the best of my nerves. "Okay, see you later!" I called after him.

Just then, a hand grabbed my shoulder from behind. I spun around. "What are you doing?" Trevor asked.

"Um…getting my new schedule?" I answered, more in the form of a question, confused by his tone of voice.

"No, who were you just talking to?" He glared down the hall at the kid walking toward the cafeteria.

"Just some guy from my English class last year. I don't remember his name." I wondered what he was getting at, and why he was frowning.

Trevor scowled down the hallway as the kid disappeared around the corner, and then he looked back at me, scrutinizing me from head to toe. "Kaitlyn, go put some clothes on!"

"What do you mean?" I asked, confused.

"Do you want every guy in the school checking out your butt in that short skirt? And look at that T-shirt. You can practically see right through it."

I immediately felt defensive. "My mom bought this for me. Trust me. If it were inappropriate, she never would have let me leave the store with it."

"Well, I think it's inappropriate, and I'm your boyfriend."

I sensed his frustration.

"Here. Put this on," he barked as he handed me his lettermen jacket.

Stunned by his insistence, I complied with his request.

"And, I'd really rather you not talk to that guy again." His demeanor became more pleasant after I'd put on the jacket. "I don't want some other guy trying to steal my girl," he said, winking at me.

I swooned....*he called me his girl.* Trevor wrapped his arm around me as he walked with me toward my homeroom. I sensed every girl staring at us as he escorted me past them. Murmurs rumbled down the hallway like the domino effect.

"You and Trevor are still dating," Eva said, sounding somewhat disappointed. Eva was in my homeroom class. She was also on the varsity cheerleading squad with me. I was fully aware of her disdain for me; it began a year ago when I had been voted captain of the junior varsity cheerleading squad. I felt her contempt for me growing as she realized that Trevor and I were still a couple. I couldn't understand why it mattered since she was dating Caleb, the rising star quarterback of the varsity football team.

"That's great!" Eva smirked. "You guys make a cute couple." She patronized me with her fake, sticky sweet grin. If she smiled a little wider, maybe I would have seen her fangs. I wondered if she was considering sinking them into my throat.

When homeroom ended, the guy I had talked to before school walked up to my desk. I remembered his name from the morning roll call; it was Logan Canterbury.

"Oh, hey Logan," I said.

"So, you and Trevor are a thing, huh?"

"Yeah, we've been together almost three months."

"Oh." His smile disappeared for a moment, but he quickly recovered. "Cool. Well, see ya around." He waved as he headed toward the door to his next class.

"Bye, Logan!" I waved back. My hand was still in the air when Trevor sauntered through the door just as Logan ducked out. Trevor glared at me. He didn't have to say anything. I could see the disappointment on his face. *Or was that anger?* I couldn't be sure.

"Come on," Trevor said flatly.

I quickly obeyed. *What was his deal?* "What's wrong?" I asked innocently when we arrived at his locker.

"I thought we talked about this. I don't want you talking to that guy. I watched him checking you out like you were a piece of meat."

"Who? Logan? He's perfectly innocent, and besides," I said, flirtatiously bumping my shoulder against his arm, "you're the only one for me. No one is going to steal me away from you."

"Whatever," he said emphatically, slamming his locker door shut. "I'll see you after class."

I reached up to give him a quick hug, but he brushed me off. *What's gotten into him?*

The summer had been so perfect for us, but the first day of school that year was the beginning of the downward spiral. It was such a gradual process, like the 'boiling frog' analogy. If you throw a frog into boiling water, he'll jump right out. But, if you place him in a pot of water and slowly bring it to a boil, then he will sit in the water until he dies. I guess I was sitting in a pot of cold water and Trevor was slowly turning up the heat.

"I'm so sorry," Trevor pleaded with me one day after school. We had been arguing about my new lab partner in Biology, a guy on the soccer team, and Trevor insisted that I request a new female lab partner. I had flat out refused; the teacher would think I had officially lost my mind. I knew exactly what Mr. Hendrix would have said as he glared at me with his beady eyes over his wire-rimmed glasses. *What difference does it make, Miss Davenport, if your lab partner is male or female?'* No way! I was not going to comply with Trevor's ridiculous request. My stubbornness sent Trevor over the edge. It was the first time he had ever raised his hand at me.

He immediately apologized, his eyes wide with shock over his own actions. "Oh my god. I'm sorry, baby. I know you don't really have a choice about who your lab partner is. I didn't mean to hurt you."

I rubbed my cheek where he had slapped me across the face in anger during the argument. Tears welled up in my eyes.

"Please," he begged. "I love you. Please forgive me. I'm so sorry. I can't live without you!" He tentatively reached out to touch me.

I recoiled from his hand.

"Oh, Kaitlyn," he cried with tears welling up in his eyes. "Please don't be afraid of me." His hand caressed my bright red cheek. "I'm sorry. I love you," he pleaded.

Cautiously, I let him draw me into his arms. He smelled so good. He was wearing the new cologne I had bought him for his birthday. His warmth enveloped me, and the memory of this past summer when things were so good between us flashed into my mind. He seemed sincerely regretful. Resistance seemed futile.

"I love you too," I whispered.

After the first incident, it seemed easier and easier for him to raise his hand in anger toward me. Our arguments always ended in the same scenario. He begged for my forgiveness, professed his love for me, and held me in his arms until I caved. Every single time I surrendered to his pleadings, I scolded myself for being so weak. *When did I become such a pushover? Why did I let Trevor walk all over me? Why couldn't I just walk away from him? Why did the thought of letting him go terrify me so much?*

I laid in the bed at night and argued with myself about the reasons why I bothered to stay with Trevor. First, there was the Trevor that I fell in love with in the beginning. We had a history. He was my first date, my first kiss, and my first love. The world viewed him as a hero—a god. He was the junior co-captain of the varsity football team, gorgeous, popular, headed to a great college on a scholarship, raised by a good family…the list went on and on, *ad nauseum*. Everyone expected me to be with him. People constantly reminded me of what a cute, great, wonderful, 'add your own adjective' couple we were together. No one knew that he hit me, shoved me, or bruised me. No one knew that he threatened to kill me if I ever broke up with him. No one knew that under that façade of godliness, he was a monster. I felt like a scared kitten on the edge of a bridge in the middle of a busy freeway. Either way I turned I was sure to meet with doom. Staying with Trevor would cause more pain and heartache. Breaking up with him would only cause more of the same. I felt scared and lonely. Fear apprehensively clutched the key that would unlock the real truth about Trevor.

Late one night while my parents were out to dinner with some friends, we were in my bedroom arguing about my instant messenger chat activity. He insisted that I log in so he could search my chat history. While I knew I had absolutely nothing to hide, I refused to yield to his demand. Searching my history and invading my privacy was a line I was unwilling for Trevor to cross. He ranted and raved, clenching his fists and pacing the floor like a crazed lunatic, accusing me of cheating on him. I stood my ground and insisted he was imagining things. His faced hardened with frustration while his eyebrows furrowed in a deep crease. He demanded me to log in immediately, which I adamantly declined.

"Log in now, or you will regret it!" he growled and grabbed my arm, leading me toward my computer.

"No!" I yelled and attempted to jerk my arm free of his tight grip. "If you don't trust me, I'm sorry, but that's your problem!" I managed to slip away from him and took a few steps backward.

"How can I trust you if you won't let me see your history?" Gritting his teeth, his jaw muscles twitched while the veins of his neck bulged on each side.

"I'm just not going there, Trevor. This is just something you are going to have to deal with, or else."

"Or else, what?" Trevor's eyes held fast with a menacing glare.

"Or else…" I hesitantly fumbled for the words, but I'd had enough of his possessiveness and the constant arguing. Gaining my composure, I shouted with brazen fury, "Or else, it's over. We're over. I'm done!"

"Oh yeah?" he hissed as he came at me with fire in his eyes. Grabbing me by my throat and shoving me backwards, his tense arms held me tight against the wall of my bedroom. Shallow breaths fought against the choking sensation in my throat. My hands desperately clawed at his fingers that were wrapped tightly around my neck, struggling to break them free. His words seared themselves into my memory. "If I can't have you, then no one else can either! I've got a 9mm pistol with a magazine full of bullets. I'll give you one guess as to what I'll do with them."

"Please," I gasped, panicking under his suffocating grip.

He spat more words into my ear before he finally loosened his grip. "And if you even dare to breathe a word about this conversation to anyone, I'll hunt you down. Don't worry, sweetheart, *trouble* will find you."

I felt sure it was just a threat. He would never actually do it, right? I was too terrified to tell anyone. That night I slept with my closet light on and double checked all the locked doors. Nightmares of dark shadows and gunshots plagued my dreams all night. I woke up sweaty and out of breath several times, crying into my pillow until exhaustion overcame me. I never threatened to break up with him again, nor did I ever find the courage to tell anyone.

Chapter Four

Our senior year was no different than our junior year. I was still a frog sitting in extremely hot water, but for whatever reason I couldn't will myself to jump out of the pot.

"So, I guess I'll take you home after practice today." It was more of a statement than a question. Trevor had a presence about him that kept most people from questioning him.

"Okay," I said. "I'll meet you at my locker after school." Trevor had picked me up earlier that morning to take me to breakfast before school started. It was a nice gesture, but I wondered if it was more for him to keep tabs on me than for anything else.

"See you later," he blew me a kiss as he walked into his class.

My last class came and went in the blink of an eye. I was so ready for the day to be over.

Arnold stood by my locker as I took out the books I would need for homework that night. "So, have you finished the science project for the county science exhibit yet?"

"Nah, but I'm working on it," I told him.

Arnold was in several of my classes. Always friendly, a bit overweight, and unbelievably intelligent, he held the title of Valedictorian of our senior class. He and I had worked on a few projects together in the past.

"Just let me know if you need any help with it," he offered as he picked up the pencils I had accidently dropped on the floor while getting out my books.

"Thanks," I said.

"See you later!" He waved as he walked down the hall toward the library.

Out of nowhere, a fist punched into the locker beside me. Startled, I flinched causing me to bump my head on my open locker door. "What the hell were you talking to that guy for?" Trevor's eyes burned with anger.

"That was just Arnold," I said, stunned. "He was asking about our science project."

"I don't care what he was asking you. You better not be talking to him again," Trevor barked at me. Trevor's anger always made me uneasy. Attempting to calm him down only made him even more furious.

"Okay." I chided myself for backing down so easily.

Trevor grabbed me by the arm and tightened his grip. Blood pulsed in the veins of my hand. He glared at me, his face inches from mine. "It better not happen again," he practically growled.

Storming away, he slammed the door on his way outside to football practice. I stood there, rubbing the tender spot on my head caused by my open locker door.

Tears sprang to my eyes as I finished getting my stuff from my locker. I caught a glimpse of Amanda out of the corner of my eye. Amanda was a girl from my Spanish class. She sat a few rows over from me. I barely knew her, but she seemed really nice. "You really shouldn't let him treat you like that," she whispered.

I knew she meant well, but those words were just not the ones I needed to hear at that moment. I smiled politely at her and said, "I know." I quickly turned to face my locker just as the first tear rolled down my cheek.

I changed into my cheerleading practice clothes in the upper hallway bathroom; no one ever went into that bathroom after school. I just needed some time to compose myself before practice began. The other cheerleaders were well aware of how Trevor treated me, but blinded by his popularity, they had a tendency to overlook his temper. Maybe they were secretly jealous that I was dating the newest captain of the varsity football team. How lucky I must have looked in their eyes. *Little do they know...*

I finished getting dressed for practice and walked outside toward the football field. Just as I rounded the corner, I saw a group of guys skateboarding near the gym. I recognized a few faces from my senior class, but several of them were underclassmen. A couple of guys were sitting around the base of *Bruiser*. Bruiser was the statue of our school mascot, the bulldog, that was erected outside the gymnasium and dedicated by the graduating class of 1995. The guys who were sitting around Bruiser were strumming their guitars and singing while the skateboarders jumped the curbs and rode the rails.

"Hey Kaitlyn, what's up?" One of the skateboarders tossed his hand up and waved.

I waved back. "Hey Allen."

Allen was never really part of the so called in-crowd, and I was only part of the social elite by default. I was popular because I was a cheerleader. However, I loved cheerleading more for the sport of it than in what social class it placed me. I loved the tumbling and the stunts. I always challenged myself to push harder when running or lifting weights. Cheerleading was a natural high for me. I think I was in the minority, though. Most of the cheerleaders cared more about how cute they looked in their short skirt than how far they could throw a basket toss. I tried to be friendly to everyone, which usually got me dirty looks from the other cheerleaders. They didn't try to understand why I would even bother talking to someone beneath us in the social hierarchy. To me, standing outside of the elite circle felt more comfortable. I never really felt like I quite fit in with the in-crowd, anyway.

"Yo Kaitlyn, is your man Trevor gonna carry us to the championships this year?" Allen asked with admiration in his voice.

It never failed. Trevor seemed to have followers everywhere.

"Hopefully!" I answered with fake enthusiasm.

"Tell him I said good luck."

"I will. See you later, Allen."

My last word stopped short as I caught a glimpse of the deepest, darkest eyes staring at me. One of the guys I had heard singing was staring at me as I walked past him sitting on the brick retaining wall. He had the most beautiful dark brown eyes, with eyelashes that cast shadows onto his cheeks. A gray Hurley hat sat cockeyed on his head with a few soft curls flipping out around it. His black hoodie draped carelessly around his shoulders. He wore a stud diamond earring, a coned barbell in his eyebrow, and a silver hoop in his lower lip—but all that cold hard metal didn't take away from the softness in his eyes. He held my gaze as the butterflies awakened and began fluttering in the pit of my stomach. His hand stopped strumming and dropped down by his side. Ever so casually, he pulled the corner of his mouth up in a half grin. I caught myself shyly smiling back, and our eyes locked. Slowing my pace, I tried to relish the moment between us. I had never felt so enraptured, and yet so…addled. Quickly, I tore my eyes away from his gaze and rushed toward my destination. I was afraid to look back at the mystery guy with the dark, enchanting eyes and the guitar in his lap. I could almost feel him staring at me as I continued walking toward the football field. When I finally got far enough away, I heard the music start again. *Who was that guy?!*

"Kaitlyn, there you are!" Allison called to me as I reached the group of girls. They were all stretching out and awaiting my arrival.

With not a cloud in the sky, the track around the football field where we normally practiced was scorching hot under the blazing sun. Our school was the only school in the county that still had an asphalt track; all the others had the springy latex resurfaced tracks. We hoped our Booster Club would foot the bill to resurface our track soon. Instead of roasting on the asphalt, the girls had chosen a patch of grass at the edge of the end zone to stretch out for practice.

"Yeah, sorry I'm late. I got caught up."

"No problem." Allison jumped right into what she does best—leading. Occasionally, I was so thankful she was the co-captain; I was no good at being the boss. "We're going to start with the dance from the routine. Then we are going to work on the new cheer for homecoming this year. Is that okay with you?"

"Sure, whatever." I had too much on my mind to care. However, the new cheer for homecoming did pique my interest a little. From a distance, I could see Trevor working out with the football team. In the few minutes I had been there, I hadn't seen them stop doing push-ups yet. I could tell he was taking his anger at me out on the second string. Those poor guys—I knew they would be sore the next day.

Completely distracted, I stumbled through practice. I could still see the guys skateboarding by the gym. My eyes casually searched for the mystery guy.

I fumbled through the motions while Allison counted out the dance. "1, 2, 3, 4, 5, 6, 7, 8...1, 2—"

"Hey! Ouch!" Eva yelled. I'd bumped into her, nearly knocking her down when I took a step in the wrong direction.

"Sorry," I apologized, throwing my hands up and shrugging my shoulders.

Allison confronted me. "What's gotten into you, Kaitlyn?"

"I said sorry!" I said defensively.

"Look, I'm not accusing. I'm just asking. What's your deal today?" Allison backed off a little.

"Caleb told me that she and Trevor got into a fight today," Eva said with a smirk.

I fought tears as I rolled my eyes at her. *Why did Eva have to hate me so much?* She had never liked me. I felt like she had been competing with me from the first day we met. For her, it was a never ending battle, and once I started dating Trevor, she had pretty much declared war. I think she would have reduced me to ashes if she had her choice. I tolerated her for the sake of the squad. "Don't worry about it," I practically hissed.

"Kaitlyn," Rachel interjected. "Why do you let Trevor treat you like that?" I had known Rachel as long as I had known Allison. Rachel and I shared Allison. We were friends, and we got along well. However, friendship triangles never work, and we always battled for Allison's attention. Rachel was a few inches taller than me, with fiery red hair and bright blue eyes. She was brilliant and usually the teacher's pet. Rachel was well on her way to an Ivy League school. Cheerleading, to her, was just an extracurricular activity that looked good on her college applications.

"Everything is fine," I lied. "It was just a…misunderstanding. Trevor loves me and that's all that matters." I had lied more times than I could count about our arguments. He was far more controlling than I let other people believe. I never told anyone the real reason why I had to wear leggings under my cheerleading skirt and why I couldn't wear tank tops anymore. "Let's just get back to practicing," I ordered. *This conversation is over.*

I managed to get through practice without knocking anyone else down.

After practice, I saw Trevor leaning against his truck waiting for me. I walked cautiously up to him, unsure of his mood. "Hey baby," he said sweetly. "How was practice?"

"Good," I said. "Yours?"

"Pretty good. I couldn't take my eyes off you the whole time. You looked so beautiful."

I was taken aback by his pleasant mood.

"Hey," he said as he hugged me closely and kissed me softly on the forehead. "Sorry about that thing after

school. I guess I didn't realize you guys were talking about a science project. Can I make it up to you?"

"Okay." I eyed him warily. "What did you have in mind?"

"I could take you to see that movie you wanted to see—the chick flick."

"Great," I tried to sound enthusiastic, but our most recent argument still felt fresh in my mind, and the bruise he caused still looked fresh on my arm.

We drove home in silence. I looked away from Trevor, ignoring him as he held my hand and caressed my skin with his thumb while we cruised down the road. Confusion and fear continued to plague me while I stared out the window at the scenery as it blurred by me.

Chapter Five

I was startled awake at two in the morning. The deep penetrating brown eyes in my dream felt so real. I could not get those dark, intriguing eyes of the mystery guy out of my head. There was something about them that felt so…comforting.

That morning, my excitement to get to school overwhelmed me. As I walked into the building, I scanned the clusters of students gathered outside. I figured I could pick those eyes out of a crowd by then, since I'd seen them all night in my dreams. I searched the hallways as I walked toward my locker. Trevor caught up with me just as I reached it.

"Hey you," he teased. "You're a hard girl to catch up with." His wink entranced me like a snake charmer's flute.

He was so hard to resist. I grinned at him. "That depends on how fast you run to catch me," I teased back.

Suddenly, his eyes turned stone cold. "Don't worry. I'd hunt you down."

I wasn't sure if he was still teasing me or not. But, he seemed dead serious. *Was he threatening me? Did he know about the mystery guy? Maybe Allison told him how distracted I was at practice yesterday. Maybe he had figured it out. Surely not. How could he?* I hoped I was just being paranoid.

Classes seemed to drag by. Between each class I scanned the crowds to find the mystery guy. My next to last class of the day was Theatre Arts. I had chosen that class as an easy elective. It turned out to be my most challenging course.

When I walked into the class, I caught my breath. There he sat—the mysterious guitarist who had kept me swooning the past twenty-four hours. He glanced up at me just as my eyes and smile widened with pleasant surprise. I looked away, bewildered, trying to compose myself. Walking as casually as I could manage, I took my assigned seat right next to his.

"'Sup?" he said, acknowledging me with a slight nod of his head.

My breath hitched at the sound of his voice. The burst of adrenaline caused my heart to pound in my chest. He leaned toward me. The scent of his cologne awakened my senses with its crisp and refreshing aroma that reminded me of the sandalwood and cedar scents from my favorite clothing store in the mall.

"I'm Chris," he said, introducing himself. "Chris King."

"Hi," I said as my mouth fumbled for words. "I'm Kaitlyn Davenport. You must be new here." *Well, genius, that was a brilliant observation. Duh!*

"Yeah, I stopped by yesterday afternoon to get my new schedule and to check out the school. I just transferred here from Fairbanks."

His deep brown eyes searched mine as I mentally struggled for the next thing to say. "That's cool," I managed. "Fairbanks is a good school."

"Not the school," he corrected, without even as much as a hiccup. My expression must have shown my confusion because he clarified his statement by whispering, "Juvie." Glancing around, he slouched down in his chair and stuffed his hands deeper into his pockets. He claimed his space by spreading his legs wide and placing one foot on each side of the desk in front of him. He let one knee angle out into the aisle between us. I couldn't tell if it was a sign of his insolence toward school or if he was just a typical guy declaring his territory.

"Oh." My cheeks flooded with embarrassment, turning several shades of pink as I shifted my eyes away from his confident gaze. *So, this was the guy I had heard rumblings about throughout the school.* Rumors had flooded the halls about all of the possible reasons why he had been in a juvenile detention center. I wondered if they were true.

"Whoever he is, we'd better stay away from him. He might be dangerous," Allison said solemnly one day after practice. We were standing outside the field house waiting for our boyfriends to finish with football practice. Several of the cheerleaders were talking about some guy they had heard about who was going to transfer to

our school after spending some time in jail. None of us had ever known anyone our age who had spent time behind bars.

"You're right," Rachel agreed. "We probably shouldn't associate ourselves with troublemakers like that anyway."

"I agree with Allison and Rachel." Eva nodded. "You just never know…"

Looking at the guy sitting beside me in Theatre Arts, he didn't look dangerous. For once, I agreed with Eva. You could never be too sure about a person. I averted my eyes and pretended to look busy as I began rummaging through my backpack. Chris didn't say another word to me the rest of the class. I forced myself not to look in his direction. Each time I caught myself wanting to, I could feel the blood rise to meet my cheeks while my heart pounded out of my chest. I just hoped he didn't notice my uneasiness. When the bell finally rang, it saved me from my personal torture. I jumped up and instinctively ran to my last class without even looking back.

That night, my dreams were plagued by those deep, haunting eyes again. I woke up more exhausted than I had been before I had gone to bed. The dark circles that encompassed my eyes were proof of my restless night. I stood at the bathroom mirror longer than usual trying to hide my fatigue with my liquid makeup concealer.

"Kaitlyn!" my mom yelled up the stairs. "You're going to be late for school!"

"Coming, Mom!" I put on the finishing touches of my makeup and flew down the stairs; I didn't want to be late for school. Not only would Trevor get angry and question my whereabouts, but I also didn't want to miss an opportunity to catch a glimpse of the face that infiltrated my mind, keeping me up all night.

That afternoon in Theatre Arts was much the same as the day before. Ms. Carducci lectured us about the history of the Globe Theater while I tried my best not to stare at Chris. My anxious heart refused to stop pounding, causing red blotches on my chest and cheeks. About midway through class, I caught Chris looking down at his desk. He was scribbling furiously on a piece of paper. Lost in thought, I knew he wasn't paying any attention to me stealing occasional glances at him. Relief flooded me and the pounding in my chest subsided. I reveled in the pleasure of watching him as his eyes gazed down at the paper. Clearly, he was in deep concentration. His fingers made their way to his temples and pressed as if they were trying to squeeze out a thought. His eyes narrowed as he studied the writing on his paper. Leaning ever so slightly toward him, I tried to peek at the paper in front of him. Just when I thought I saw what looked like musical notes, he quickly began scribbling again. I stared at him, memorizing every detail of him.

He was dangerously handsome. His dark eyes were set deep beneath jutting eyebrows, and his black hair was tousled on his head in total disarray. His shoulders were broad, and his muscular arms peeked out beneath the sleeves of his taut T-shirt that only showcased them even more. The scent of his masculine cologne wafted toward me, and I inhaled a deep, staggering breath. At that moment, he glanced up at me, and his gaze caught mine. *Crap!* I could feel the blood surging adrenaline throughout my body again. My stomach quivered at the sight of his delectable, chocolate brown eyes settling on me. One corner of his mouth tilted upward in a half smile as he gave a slight nod in acknowledgment. As if in a trance, I smiled back at him unable to tear myself away from his stare. As quickly as he looked up, he returned his attention back to the paper and continued scribbling.

I literally felt breathless. *How could a guy I barely knew have that kind of effect on me?* I spent the rest of the class period trying to concentrate on the teacher's lecture. When the bell finally rang to end our time in class, I noticed that my notebook paper was filled with pictures of dark irises and question marks. Shamefully, I ripped the paper up and tossed the shreds into the nearby trashcan on my way out the door to meet Trevor.

"So," Allison asked at cheerleading practice that day, "do you know anything about the new guy?"

"Not really," I said, trying hard to remain casual.

"Well, I heard that he escaped from juvie in another state and transferred to our school under a new name," Rachel piped up.

Eva nodded. "Yeah, I heard he ran a drug ring in his old school, and when one of the kids from a rival gang showed up dead in a nearby lake, they pinned it on him."

"Guys," I said, exasperated, "come on. Do you really think all of that is true?"

"Well, that's what I heard." Eva's eyes were wide with worry.

"I seriously doubt it," I said defensively.

They didn't sit next to him in class. They didn't rush to school each morning to see if they could find him in the crowd of students. They didn't watch him while he poured his heart onto his paper during class. Their dreams weren't saturated with his enchanting eyes.

Every day felt like the same old scenario. Trevor and I continually argued, and our heated disputes became more and more frequent. I tried everything I could to avoid Trevor's fiery rage. The harder I tried to squelch his anger, the less happy I became. I realized I was becoming a doormat. Trevor stomped all over me and left me feeling dirty and used. My bruised ego and suffering self-esteem drifted aimlessly down the hallways of the school as I somehow managed to get through each day while trying to keep a smile on my face. After all, a cheerleader was always expected to be happy...and peppy. I miraculously faked them both.

Chapter Six

The only time I felt in control of my life was on Friday nights at the football games. I was in my own world as I yelled at the top of my lungs in front of the crowd. The onlookers roared along with us in support of our football team's first big game that year. Our team, the East Jenkins Bulldogs, was playing our arch rivals, North Wingate Patriots. It was the biggest game of the season. Everyone was expected to come out and root the Bulldogs to a victory. The cheerleaders anxiously stood by the field house to cheer on the team as they trotted out onto the field. Excitement coursed through my veins. I knew this was a big game for Trevor. He would never admit it, but he was nervous. Several scouts from colleges had come to check him out that night.

Being captain, Trevor led the team out onto the field. He looked like a champion already in his football uniform. Resembling a warrior, he headed into battle with black stripes painted below his eyes. His head held high, he proudly trotted across the field holding his helmet above his head while the other football players bellowed their battle cries. The crowd roared to life as the players rallied around Trevor on the sideline. I knew it was Trevor's night to shine, and although I would

never admit it, I felt incredibly proud that I could call myself his girlfriend that night.

The game was in the third quarter, and the score was 20-14, with our team in the lead. Trevor had scored two of the three touchdowns for the night. Eric, our kicker, did not seem to be on top of his game. He had already missed one extra point. Except for a few minor injuries, the game had been fairly uneventful. The humdrum of the game didn't prevent the crowd from continuously thundering with excitement. The frenzy never subsided.

We were in the middle of a cheer when I caught *him* out of the corner of my eye. At the top of the bleachers, Chris was sitting amidst a group of guys, but his eyes weren't on the game. They were on me. I almost lost my train of thought as I struggled to keep my mind in focus. I couldn't look at him. I didn't want to be too obvious. Involuntarily, my smile widened at the thought of him watching me.

After the game, I waited by the field house with Allison. Trevor's third touchdown of the night had won the game for our Bulldogs, 33-28. Eric had missed another extra point, but that didn't seem to matter to anyone except him. The cool night air buzzed with excitement. I always loved when our team won because Trevor was in a great mood the rest of the night.

He jogged out of the field house in faded jeans and his lucky Bulldogs T-shirt. "Hey, babe!" He greeted me with a huge smile. Hugging me, he lifted me off the ground and swung me around full circle.

"Trevor, you were awesome tonight!"

"Man, that was the game of my life! We almost didn't make it, though. I couldn't believe they almost had us down by one point!"

"I know!" I cried. "But, you did it! Those scouts are sure to love you!"

"Man, that game rocked!" Putting his arm around me, he walked me to his truck. "Wanna meet some people at Spud's?" he asked as he opened the door of his truck for me.

"Sure!"

Spud's was a local diner where a lot of kids hung out on Friday and Saturday nights. The owner, a former Bulldog, always gave free food to the football players after home games.

When we got to Spud's, we found Allison and her boyfriend already seated. The greasy scent of fried food filled the air. Flashing signs in the windows beckoned customers with *'Eat Here'* and *'Open Late'* in bright neon colors. The black and white checkered floor, the laminate table tops, and the retro lights hanging above each table made me feel like I'd stepped out of the twenty-first century back into a 1950s diner. Several other football players and their girlfriends were hanging out in the booths nearby, while others hovered around the vintage juke box in the corner choosing songs from its meager selection.

"Trevor!!!" several guys yelled in unison as we walked through the door. The hero had arrived. I hung back as Trevor received some high fives, a few punches to the shoulder, and a couple of tackling bear hugs.

Spud, a nickname the owner went by, came out of the kitchen with a tray full of burgers and fries. "Good game tonight, boys!" he bellowed as he placed the tray in the middle of the hungry football players.

"Thanks, Spud!" several guys said, and the feeding frenzy began.

Trevor was lost in conversation, recounting the plays of the game with his teammates when I slipped away from the table and headed toward the bathroom. While I was as happy as I could be at that moment, I just needed a minute to myself.

A shadowy figure sat at the back booth in a dimly lit corner of the diner. A few other guys nearby were throwing darts at a dartboard that hung on the wall.

"Hey," a deep male voice stated.

"Hey." I squinted my eyes to adjust to the darkness. Just as my eyes focused, I realized it was Chris. My heart immediately began to pound. I glanced back at Trevor, but he was still lost in conversation and hadn't even noticed I was gone.

"You're a cheerleader," Chris said flatly.

"Yeah..." *What's he getting at?*

"Humph." Chris let out a disapproving grunt.

I immediately felt defensive. "Don't go making judgments," I told him.

"I'm not," he backed off a little, tossing a French fry dripping with melted cheese into his mouth. "Just surprised, I guess," he said with his mouth full. "Cheerleaders like you don't talk to guys like me."

"Cheerleaders like me?" I had never really put myself into the 'snobby cheerleader' category before.

"Didn't you get the memo? Cheerleaders don't give guys like me the time of day. I just—"

"No, don't explain. You've made yourself perfectly clear. Obviously, cheerleaders *like me*," I said, using my fingers as air quotes for emphasis, "shouldn't talk to convicts like you, period." I glared at him, more hurt than angry.

"Ouch," he said, looking genuinely upset.

My face immediately softened. "I'm sorry," I quickly apologized, embarrassed by my thoughtless jab. I wasn't usually so confrontational. Trevor had kept me under his thumb so long, I had almost forgotten what it felt like to take up for myself. I stepped toward the bathroom door trying to escape from the awkward moment.

"It's no big deal. I deserved it," he said, looking down at an invisible spot on the table. He looked up again and caught my gaze with those dark brown swirling irises that whisked my insides to a pulp. A bashful grin spread across his face. Shyly, I glanced down at the floor, but slowly looked up and locked eyes with him again. I secretly prayed that he couldn't read the emotions on my face like a book. Inching my way to the restroom to escape his entrancing stare, I quickly swung open the bathroom door and rushed inside.

I stood at the sink and looked at the mirror. Sitting in the diner, two very different guys had my attention. I chided myself for letting one of them control my life. I just wasn't sure exactly which guy that was at the moment. I took a deep breath then stepped out through the doorway, back into the diner.

Chris was still sitting at the same spot he was when I had walked into the bathroom. I tried to ignore him. I hoped he didn't see how much he affected me.

"What I meant was…you're a lot nicer," he said as I walked past his table, "and a lot prettier."

I froze. *Did he say pretty?* "Uh…thanks," I choked out.

"It's just…well, you're not like any of the other cheerleaders I've ever met before. You're nice. Most cheerleaders wouldn't even acknowledge me, but you were so friendly to me on my first day here. Thank you for that."

I stared at him sitting there in the darkness of the diner. His chiseled jaw line perfectly framed his beaming smile. Wisps of his brown hair flipped out from under his gray, billed beanie. His sculpted biceps bulged beneath his black T-shirt. He looked even more gorgeous than I remembered from class. I could *not* will my feet to move. I was perfectly content standing there, becoming infatuated with everything about him. Oh, how I wished I could slip into the booth with him and talk the night away!

"Chris," one of the guys, a few feet away, called out from the dart game. "Come on, dude. Let's hit some corks."

"I'm being summoned," Chris said with a smile as he stood from the booth. I must have looked confused because he laughed and added, "It means let's throw some darts and hit some bull's-eyes."

Nodding, I replied, "Okay, see you later."

"I'll see you around!" He tossed up his hand, waved, and winked at me as he walked away.

I caught my breath, suddenly realizing I hadn't been breathing regularly the entire time I stood there. Quickly, I hurried back to join Trevor and his crew. I sat in silence as the football players continued endlessly recounting the moments of the game. Trevor completely ignored me as he regaled countless tales of his experiences that night. My mind wandered to the dark figure in the back of the diner.

"You ready to go?" Trevor finally asked.

"Yes," I said gratefully.

Trevor kept his arm hugged around me as he walked me out to his truck. Once inside, he looked longingly at me. "It's been a great night," he whispered, carefully brushing a strand of hair away from my face.

"It has," I agreed, although I felt sure it wasn't for the same reasons.

Caressing my cheek, Trevor leaned toward me. He gently brushed his lips across mine. I could feel the energy surging from him as he began to kiss me. Surrendering to him, I let myself kiss him back, welcoming his tongue as it encircled mine. Reaching up, he slipped his hands into my hair and tugged me closer to him, eagerly sucking and nipping at my lower lip. I could feel an urgency in him that made me uncomfortable. "Let's go...celebrate," he said, his voice thick with desire.

I pulled away from him. "No, Trevor, not that." I grew weary of his constant badgering for the one thing I kept sacred.

"Come on, Kaitlyn," he said impatiently as he grabbed my face and kissed me harder.

I jerked my head back. "No," I insisted.

"Why do you always lead me on, Kaitlyn? You always do this. We've been together almost two years. Not many guys would wait that long," he growled.

"I didn't. I mean, I'm not. I—" I stammered, taken back by his sudden anger.

"You. Are. Such. A. Tease!" He spat every word in my face, then shoved me away from him toward the passenger door. He turned the key in the ignition as his truck roared to life. The tires squealed, leaving black marks, as he sped out of the parking lot.

I hugged the passenger door. I couldn't believe how quickly my perfect night had come crashing down around me. Trevor flew down the road, taking sharp turns much faster than he should have. I spent the ride praying all four tires would stay on the road. Pulling onto my street in my neighborhood, he grumbled profanities since he was forced to slow down over the speed bumps. Finally, my heartbeat returned to a normal rate knowing I would be safely home soon.

"Get out," Trevor practically growled when we pulled into my driveway. "Call me when you aren't so stuffy and uptight."

He nearly shoved me out of the passenger door. Blinded by my tears, I stumbled to the front door. I quickly wiped the tears away on the sleeve of my jacket. I didn't want my parents to question me. My mom wouldn't understand. She still believed Trevor hung the moon and walked on water.

My parents were sitting in the living room watching the local news when I got home. "Wasn't Trevor great tonight?" my mom asked with admiration.

"Yeah, that last touchdown was miraculous!" my dad exclaimed, sounding star-struck.

"Sure," I said, feeling less than enthusiastic. "I'm going to bed. It's been a long night." I trudged upstairs to my bedroom.

"Okay, goodnight sweetie," my mom called to me when I reached the top of the stairs.

I stared at my ceiling for a long time that night before going to sleep. Renae, my best friend from middle school, and I had spent hours one weekend researching constellations and strategically placing hundreds of glow-in-the-dark star stickers all over my ceiling. Although she and I had grown apart once we got into high school, I smiled at the reminder of our fun memories together—a time of innocence and happiness. Staring at the glowing "night sky" that Renae and I had created somehow brought peace to my broken spirit.

I regretted not slipping into the booth with Chris. If I had, I felt sure my night would have ended differently. No one suspected my heartache. No one knew the longing I had in my heart to be rescued from the nightmare of Trevor. I felt trapped, like a caged animal, desperately clawing at the metal rods. Finally yielding to my futile efforts for escape from the cage that I so willingly had walked into, I gave up all hope of freedom by lying listless in the corner. I was a pawn in Trevor's game of chess just waiting for his next move. I never thought of myself as a coward. I had always been strong-willed and never viewed myself as a weakling, but for reasons I didn't understand, Trevor had a power over me that I felt like I couldn't overcome. As soon as I tried to walk away, he would pull me back with his pleading declarations of love. If that strategy didn't work, he'd remind me of his 9mm handgun. I kept hoping that things would change and get better, but they didn't. My fear of Trevor kept me running like a hamster on a wheel going nowhere; I hated myself for it. I was too scared to do anything about it. No one grasped the pain that I felt as I forced myself to look happy on the outside, while a war on the inside raged out of control.

Chapter Seven

The following Monday, I found Trevor waiting for me by my locker before school. He grinned. "There's my girl."

I never knew from day to day what kind of mood Trevor would be in when I saw him. "Hey," I said dryly.

He caught me in a hug and held me close for several seconds. "I'm really sorry about what I said the other night. I love you so much, and couldn't imagine my life without you. Are you still mad at me?" he pouted, looking like a lost puppy.

"Yeah," Caleb teased from a few lockers down. "Don't be mad, Kaitlyn. Trevor would be lost without you."

I looked at Caleb who shot me his best puppy dog look also, and then grinned.

Ugh. "I guess not," I caved.

"Good!" Trevor lured me with his enchanting smile that got me every time.

I smiled half-heartedly at him as he headed off to class. When he got halfway down the hall he turned around and blew me a kiss. I reprimanded myself immediately for forgiving him so easily. I decided that Trevor had some kind of magical power over me. His mystical power was the only explanation I had for his ability to change my mood, and my mind, in one instant.

When I got to Theatre Arts class that day, I was relieved to see Chris sitting in his usual seat. A couple of students were gathered around him while he strummed a guitar. Ms. Carducci kept a variety of instruments in her classroom to use for props and accompaniment during our rehearsals. Chris's fingers strummed effortlessly while he sang the words to a song I had never heard. His voice was soft and smooth like velvet. I sat down in my seat, mesmerized by the sound of his tender voice. The tardy bell rang just as his song ended, and everyone quickly rushed to their desks.

Leaning toward me, he whispered, "I wrote that song while I was in juvie."

My eyes grew wide. There's that word again—juvie. I remembered Eva's warning. *You just never know…*

"It's okay," he laughed as if he could read my mind. "I'm not a psychopath. I'm not going to hurt you." His deliciously smooth, dark chocolate eyes found mine, and I instantly felt comforted.

"It was stupid," he explained. "I burned dov some old lady's barn by accident. We were m around with some firecrackers when some ha the barn caught on fire. When it started r control, we got scared, hot-wired the parked nearby, and took off. They got me for trespassing, arson, and grand theft. But, don't worry, the barn was empty, and the old lady got her car back. It was just a stupid mistake, and I got caught. Definitely learned my lesson though."

I felt relieved—at least he wasn't some psycho serial killer. "You're a really good singer," I told him.

"Thanks," he said. "I hope to make it big someday." He winked at me, causing my heart to skip a beat. His voice was so soothing when he spoke. I would have loved to hear him sing again sometime. I stayed lost in my thoughts the rest of the class period.

Allison caught my arm as I floated past her in the hallway. "Kaitlyn," she hissed. "Eric told me that you were talking to that convict in drama class. Were you really talking to him?"

"Yeah, I guess," I felt a little defensive. "Chris is not all that bad, Allie."

"Chris? His name is Chris? Kaitlyn, girls like you shouldn't even know his name," Allison chided me with a blatant look of disgust on her face. "Besides, why would you even talk to someone like him?"

I glared at her. "Because he's *nice*," I said curtly, hoping she would take the hint.

"Oh." She spoke the word as if it left a sour taste in her mouth. "Well, you won't catch me talking to him," she huffed.

I rolled my eyes at her just as Trevor walked up at that exact moment. The look in his eyes told me he was not happy. "Hey," he barked. "I told you to meet me by the water fountain after class."

"Oh, sorry," I apologized quickly while I immediately reprimanded myself.

"Did you get caught up by another guy again?" he asked sarcastically.

Allison coughed loudly beside me. I pinched her arm where Trevor couldn't see. "Well, I guess I'll see you guys later," Allison announced. She had taken my hint as she rubbed her arm where I had pinched her.

"Bye," I called as she walked down the hall.

"Next time, be where I tell you to be," Trevor commanded. "I'll see you at your locker after school." He practically stomped away. He got angry so easily these days. I just didn't understand him anymore. Maybe I had never understood him in the first place.

I turned to go to my last class. Chris King was leaning coolly against the wall. Several other guys were talking to him. Clearly, they admired him for his recent encounters with the law. I could tell by the look on his face they annoyed him merely by the way they idolized him. He looked at me over his ravished audience. Tilting his head up to acknowledge me, his eyes settled on mine. Waves of excitement pulsated in my stomach, and I could almost feel a sense of longing in his stare. I wondered if my eyes gave him the same feeling. He held my gaze for several seconds as if he were silently pleading for me to deliver him from his minions. I shrugged apologetically, wishing I could rescue him and sneak into a janitor's closet just to have a moment alone with him.

I couldn't wait for school to end that day. My last class went by...ever...so...slowly. I watched the minutes tick by on the clock; every second seemed longer and longer. The class dragged on forever while Mr. Abernathy droned on about the women's suffrage and the ratification of the 19th Amendment. I barely paid attention to the lecture. Maybe Rachel would let me borrow her notes; then again, I highly doubted it. To Rachel, getting into college was a rat race, so she would do just about anything to keep her competitors down.

The school bell rang and I jumped from my seat. Maybe I would bump into Chris again.

"Where are you going in such a hurry?" Rachel asked inquisitively.

I tried to sound casual. "I gotta meet Trevor."

"Okay, I'll see you at practice," she said. I was relieved she didn't interrogate me any further. I might have spilled my guts about secretly hoping to bump into Chris.

The hallway was packed like sardines as people tried to make their way to the exits, but I could still see Chris coming down the hallway toward me. I panicked as I scanned the crowd for Trevor. Thankfully, I didn't see him. Chris smiled as he got closer to me. His crooked grin made me blush. I lowered my chin and peered up at a him through bashful lashes.

"See you later," he said covertly.

"Bye," I responded quietly.

Just as Chris got within inches of me, he reached out and touched my hand as he brushed by me. I could feel the energy pass from his fingertips to my palm. My heart rate quickened as a rush of adrenaline surged through my arteries. His eyes held mine hostage for a few extra seconds. Then, his fingers fell from my hand the minute he was pushed forward by the steady flow of people rushing by us. My hand still tingled from the sensation of his touch. I felt myself longing for more.

Somehow I made it to my locker. Trevor was already waiting for me. I swallowed hard, detecting that he was ready for a fight. I could see his jaw muscle clenched as I got closer to him. "Eric told me you found a new boyfriend," he said flatly.

"Who?" I asked, although I already had an idea.

"The convict," Trevor stated, narrowing his eyes at me.

"I was just being friendly to a new student," I replied.

"Well, like I've told you before, you better not ever talk to another guy. Ever."

"That's not fair, Trevor! How is that even possible?"

Without hesitation, he grabbed me by the shoulders and slammed me into the lockers. My head bounced off the cold hard locker door. The sound of clanking metal seemed to echo down the hall. I caught my breath as he hissed, through clenched teeth, into my ear, "You'd better make it possible."

A few other students slinked to the other side of the hallway to avoid our confrontation. Others quickly ducked into empty classrooms with open doorways.

"Please stop, Trevor. You're hurting me," I said as the tears stung my eyes.

He loosened his grip a little. "I mean it, Kaitlyn. If I ever catch you even looking at another guy, then you can guarantee there will be *trouble*."

At that moment, I didn't want to even think about what he might have meant by *trouble*. The night of the death threat immediately sparked my memory.

"I'll see you after practice," he said sharply as he released me from his painful grasp.

"Okay, okay," I said trying to keep my composure.

He headed out the door for practice just as my eyes opened the flood gates.

The tears continued to flow, despite my efforts to stop them, as I walked down the hill toward the track where the cheerleaders held practices. Unfortunately for me, the track encircled the football field where Trevor would be working out with his teammates.

"Kaitlyn!" a familiar voice called out.

It was Chris. He was sitting on the sidewalk listening to his mp3 player. A notebook and pencil were in his hand. His backpack had been slung onto the ground next to him. I glanced around nervously, looking for any sign of Trevor, even though I knew he was probably in the locker room getting suited up for football practice.

"Oh, hi Chris," I said, smiling through my tears.

"Whoa! Are you okay?" he asked, concerned.

I'm sure my face was a mess with my mascara running down my cheeks. Embarrassed, I tried to wipe it away on my sleeve. "Yeah, I'm fine."

"F-I-N-E. Feelings Inside Not Expressed." He pretty much nailed it.

"You wouldn't understand," I replied.

"Try me," he prodded.

I considered his offer for a moment. "Have you ever been afraid of someone?" I asked cautiously, resisting the sudden urge to confide in this guy I barely knew.

"I guess," he admitted, eyeing me warily. Shutting the notebook and cramming the pencil into the spiral metal binding, he stuffed them into the backpack that was sprawled out beside him.

"Well," I said, glancing apprehensively toward the ground and kicking at an imaginary pebble, "I'm afraid I wouldn't be alive tomorrow if I did what I wanted to do." I looked up, just in time to see him narrow his eyes and tilt his head to the side.

Hopping up onto his feet, he met me at eye level. "What exactly do you mean?" he asked, clearly concerned by my statement.

I shook my head at him. "Never mind. It's nothing. Forget I ever said anything." I internally scolded myself for opening my mouth to a near stranger.

Chris took a step closer to me, attempting to close the gap between us. "Kaitlyn, it can't be nothing. If it were nothing, you wouldn't be crying right now." Chris's eyes probed mine, searching for answers.

"Really, Chris, it's nothing. Don't worry about it," I insisted, peering up toward the clouds in the sky. I couldn't look him in the eye anymore. He already knew too much.

"Well, if you're sure…" he said hesitantly. I could feel his eyes on me as he stared at me, unconvinced.

"I'm sure," I nodded, glancing back at him and faking a smile, "I'll see you tomorrow."

Waving to him, I quickened my pace toward practice. I wasn't sure which one I regretted more— telling Chris too much or not telling him enough. Part of me wanted to tell him the truth, but the other part wanted to protect him from the wrath of Trevor. Although I felt sure Chris could handle any fury Trevor tried to dish out, I was just afraid that Chris would be sent back to the detention center if he got mixed up in any trouble. Fighting with Trevor Kent would surely cause the school board to boot a "trouble-maker" like Chris straight back to the juvie. *No!* I had to protect

Chris from going back to jail. I could *not* let him get involved.

Chapter Eight

I sat beside Trevor at his kitchen table on Thursday of that week. He had a paper due in his English class the following Monday and needed help editing it. Having spent hours helping him, I actually found myself writing his paper more than proofreading it. Technically, I should have gotten credit for the paper instead of Trevor. I found myself in that situation a lot during our senior year—completing Trevor's assignments for him. None of his teachers questioned the fact that Trevor had gone from a teetering 2.5 grade point average our sophomore year to being well on his way to graduating with honors by our senior year. Maybe they thought his brain matured like his body had—overnight.

"Thanks for your help," Trevor leaned over the paper and tried to kiss me.

"You're welcome," I said and leaned away from his kiss. I just wanted to finish the paper. I had been working on it for at least three hours straight.

"Come on," Trevor whined. "Give me a kiss."

I ignored his request. "I'm almost done."

"Okay," he pouted, but couldn't stop the smile that quickly overcame his lips. "After this, I'm taking you somewhere. Anywhere you want to go. You deserve it!"

I thought about the possibilities…limited by a small town. Still, I could really take advantage of Trevor and his promise of "anywhere."

"Let's go to Millennium with Allison, Eric, Eva and Caleb tonight," I grinned at him.

Club Millennium was a dance club in town. On Thursday nights, they closed the bar and opened the doors to all students ages fifteen to nineteen. Club Millennium was just about the only hang-out location in our small town. Most students lived for Thursday nights. Of course, the school board tried to shut down the club for years because so many students were useless on Fridays. To no avail, the club remained open and students flocked to Millennium in droves. Trevor rarely graced the doors of the club because he detested dancing. I knew his promise of "anywhere" was my only chance to get him to go there.

He rolled his eyes at me. "Kaitlyn! Ugh! Club Millennium? That's not exactly what I had in mind," he groaned.

"You promised," I pleaded.

"Okay," he mumbled. "Whatever."

"Yes!" I squealed with delight.

Soon, we were speeding down the highway on the way to the club.

"Hey man, I brought the booze!" Caleb said proudly as he tossed a beer in Trevor's direction. Trevor caught it and popped the top.

"Good," Trevor said. "I'm gonna need it!" Guzzling it down in a few seconds, he belched loudly and asked Caleb for another one.

I rolled my eyes at Allison. "Ugh," I groaned. "I hate it when Trevor gets drunk. He's such a mean drunk."

"Awww, girl, what fun is the club without a little alcohol? Lighten up!" She elbowed my ribs and giggled. "We're gonna have fun tonight!"

"Yeah," Caleb added as he tossed Trevor another beer. "The fun has just begun!"

Several beers later we headed toward the entrance of Club Millennium. Trevor was already buzzing and obnoxious when we walked in.

"Baby, you are so beautiful!" Trevor grabbed my waist and staggered beside me. "Let's dance!" He dragged me out to the middle of the dance floor and began making a spectacle of himself.

"You need to chill," I whispered harshly into his ear. "People are going to suspect you're drunk. They're going to call the police."

"Okay, baby," he slurred. "I'll do better."

We danced through a few songs, and then I decided that I needed something to drink. Trevor and Caleb went to the men's room to sneak a few sips from the flask Caleb had stashed in his jacket pocket. I stood at the bar and ordered a soda. Allison came up behind me and bumped my hip with hers.

"Hey, girl! Are you having fun?" she yelled over the loud, thumping music.

"Yeah! I wish Caleb would stop trying to get Trevor plastered though," I told her.

"I think Trevor can hold his own," Allison said with a smile. "You two make such a cute couple! Trevor is a good catch! You better hold onto him!"

I gave her a weak smile and turned to pay for my drink. Two guys walked up to the bar beside us. Allison gave them her flirty grin and they smiled back.

Allison looked at me wide eyed and innocently. "They're cuuuute!" she dragged the word out for emphasis.

"Allison," I reminded her. "We're both taken."

"So!" she teased. She turned to the guys and waved.

"Hello ladies," one of the guys called. "Would either of you care to dance?"

I glared at Allison. I wanted to see how she planned to get out of this one.

"I would love to!" Allison disappeared into the crowd with the strange guy.

I stood there in shock. I wondered what Eric would say when he found out. It didn't take me long to get my answer. There, in the middle of the dance floor, was Eric. He was dancing with another girl, tall and blonde. Allison grinned and waved at me. If her arms were long enough she would've picked the chin of my gaping mouth off the floor. Apparently Allison and Eric had some sort of open relationship. It was a strange way of maintaining a relationship, but I guess it worked for them. Trevor would never be open to that way of dating.

The other guy leaned toward me. "So, do you wanna dance, too?"

I sipped my soda and fumbled for the words. "My boyfriend might not like that too much."

He looked around the room. "Well, your boyfriend isn't here right now, is he?"

I pointed toward the men's room. "He's in the bathroom." *He'll be staggering out any minute*, I thought, *and it won't be pretty if he catches some guy chatting it up with his girlfriend.*

"Well, when he comes out, you can tell him you found someone better." His arrogance was irritating.

"Thanks anyway," I told him, hoping he'd take the hint and find someone else to annoy.

Trevor stepped out of the bathroom just in time to see the nuisance flirting with me.

"Oh," the guy stopped short. "You didn't tell me your boyfriend was Trevor Kent."

"You didn't ask," I said flatly.

Trevor strutted up to me and wrapped his arm around me, taking ownership.

"Uh…hey, man," the guy stammered. "Sorry…I wasn't trying to steal your girl. I mean, I didn't know she was yours. Sorry, dude."

The music blared while the thumping bass reverberated in my chest. My stomach clenched into a ball of nerves, fearing the worst from 'drunk Trevor.' I looked around the dim club, praying for a bouncer in a black security shirt to be standing nearby. Lights bounced and flashed across the faces of unsuspecting dancers. Didn't they realize a fight was about to break out? I frantically searched for the emergency exits, hoping to make a quick getaway once the first punch had been thrown. However, what happened next didn't end in a bloody brawl. I couldn't have been more shocked, but I welcomed the exchange.

"Hey, aren't you the quarterback from Templeton?" Trevor asked.

"Yep," he nodded. "Joe Cockerham."

"I thought so!" Trevor stuck out his hand to the guy. "I've heard a lot about you. It's good to meet you!"

"Oh, yeah," Joe seemed relieved. "I've heard a lot about you too! With your stats, you're probably headed to Ohio State or Michigan on a scholarship."

"I hope so. I've heard you're probably headed to Georgia."

"Probably. I have a couple prospects, but Georgia is my first pick."

Trevor nodded his head in agreement. "I feel ya."

"Well, man, I'll see you around." Joe tipped his cup toward Trevor and walked toward a few of his buddies standing nearby.

"See ya!" Trevor said with a smile and then turned his attention toward me. His pleasant demeanor dissipated, and a look of pure unadulterated anger replaced his fading smile. "So, you thought you could sneak around behind my back, huh?"

"No, he came up to me. I told him I had a boyfriend," I looked at him wide-eyed with fear. Being drunk and angry was a scary combination with Trevor.

"What did I tell you about talking to other guys?"

"Trevor, I—" I squeaked.

Before I had a chance to finish my sentence, Trevor grabbed my arm. Pulling me close to his body so no one would see the pain he was causing me, he hissed into my ear, "Well, let me put it this way...if you ever talk to another guy again, you'll wish you hadn't." He was squeezing my arm so tightly I could almost feel the capillaries popping under my skin.

I winced from the pain. "Ouch. Let go, Trevor. Please," I whispered. I didn't want to cause a scene. Things might get a whole lot *worse* if I caused a scene.

"I just want to make sure I'm getting my point across." He glared at me with his nose only inches away from mine.

"Okay, okay. Please, just let me go," I begged quietly.

"I mean it Kaitlyn," he growled into my ear. "You're just asking for trouble."

There's that word again—*trouble*. To me, trouble translated to a 9mm handgun.

He turned to Caleb who was kissing Eva on the bar stool next to us. "Come on, man. I need more alcohol!" Trevor grabbed Caleb by the jacket and dragged him off the stool away from Eva. The two of them faltered toward the men's room.

"I love it when Caleb is drunk," she grinned. "He's so kissable!"

"I wish I could say the same about Trevor," I muttered. Unfortunately, Trevor had gotten really good at camouflaging his abuse in front of people.

I decided to take some time to get a little fresh air. Although Club Millennium was strictly non-smoking on Teen Night, the smoky smell from the rest of the week still lingered in the air. I clutched my tender arm, sore from Trevor's death grip, and walked toward the exit. Sobs caught in my throat, but my frustration and embarrassment restrained my tears.

Stepping outside, I breathed a sigh of relief. The cool night air was refreshing. Cars of all shapes and sizes lined the parking lot. Blazing street lights brightened the night sky so much I could barely see the stars in the distance. The full moon shone brightly like a giant flashlight in the sky. I could still hear the thumping from the music inside the building; the constant rhythm had a calming effect. Kicking the gravel under my feet, I casually stepped around the corner of the building and out of site of the main entrance. A quiet bench beckoned me. Graciously, I sat down to enjoy my moment of peace.

A group of students had gathered farther down the side of the building. I could tell by their murmurings and laughter that they were probably up to no good. Trying to ignore them, I made myself look busy by looking at my cell phone and pretending to text someone. The sound of a familiar voice enticed me to look up. I could see Chris standing in the middle of the group that was obviously enthralled by his presence. He was engrossed in telling his story to them. I only caught bits and pieces, but it sounded like he was recounting his miserable days behind bars. I think he hoped to deter others from making similar mistakes. Instead, I could tell the others were deeply fascinated by his experience in juvenile detention. A break in the crowd caused him to catch a glimpse of me. For an instant, he seemed to lose his train of thought, searching my eyes for an explanation.

"Sorry, guys," I heard him say, "I gotta go." Looking curiously at me, he walked toward my bench. His sexy swagger had me eyeing him from head to toe. He wore saggy jeans that hung loosely off his hips. A white T-shirt revealed the taut muscles of his chest. A gray, zip-up hoodie carelessly cloaked his shoulders. His silver piercings glinted under the light of the street lamp. His black billed beanie sat cockeyed on his head, while his thick tongued sneakers, loosely tied, flopped around on his feet as he sauntered toward me. His chestnut eyes stayed fixated on me, while the others from the group stayed engrossed in conversation. No one from the group seemed to notice me. I breathed a sigh of relief. "Hey," Chris smiled with a quick nod of his head. "I'm surprised to see you here."

"Yeah, I don't come here often," I admitted.

"Did you come here alone?" Chris glanced around. "I expected to see your entourage following you."

"Haha," I retorted. "You're a real comedian." I rolled my eyes.

He laughed. "I'm kidding! I just came over here to make sure you were okay. You look lost."

"Yeah, I'm okay," I said. "Everyone else is inside. I just needed some fresh air, that's all."

He eyed me suspiciously.

"Seriously, I'm fine," I lied. "Thanks for checking on me."

He hesitated. It seemed as though he were debating sitting down next to me on the bench. I wished he would sit down. I wanted him to—no, *needed* him to sit down. He chose to stand instead. "There's that word 'fine' again. Kaitlyn, are you sure you're all right?" His voice sounded so protective, much unlike the asshole in the club drowning himself with Caleb's flask. Chris stared at me, probing me for an answer. I feared his eyes would burn holes through mine and he would see the truth I tried to hide behind them.

"Really, I'm fine," I lied again. Tears threatened to escape my eyes. I looked down at my throbbing arm, already bruised, and hurriedly covered it up with my jacket.

Chris's eyes narrowed; I could tell then that he knew I was lying. "Listen," he said, "I realize you don't know me very well, but something tells me there's more to the story than you let on."

I stared down at my jacket, willing my tears back.

He pulled a Swiss Army knife from the front pocket of his jeans and grabbed a small piece of paper that looked like a wadded up receipt from his back pocket. Flipping out the tiny ball point pen from the knife, he wrote something down on the back of a gas station receipt and handed it to me. "Look, here's my phone number and my screen name. Call me or IM me if you ever need me. Ever. Even if it's three in the morning. I mean that." He looked at me solemnly.

I looked at the receipt, glancing at his screen name:

Ha! Brilliant play on words. I managed a smile. "Thanks. Mine is Cheerchick88."

"Good to know," he said and looked down at me, grinning. His eyes penetrated mine, melting my heart. After a prolonged moment, he turned and walked around the corner of the building out of sight.

As I made my way back into the club I stuffed Chris's phone number and screen name into my jacket pocket. Trevor must have still been in the bathroom. There was no sign of him or Eva anywhere. Caleb was standing by the bar holding onto a bar stool to steady himself. Allison and Eric were dancing in the middle of the dance floor. A slow song was playing through the speakers, and they didn't seem embarrassed to make out in front of everyone.

"Where's Trevor?" I asked Caleb.

"I don't know," he slurred. "Where's Eva?"

"I have no idea," I told him.

Just as the words came out of my mouth I saw them staggering toward the bar together. Eva was giggling while Trevor leaned on her for support.

"Hey guys," she said as they got closer to us. "Trevor wanted me to help him find you, Kaitlyn."

"There's you are!" Trevor announced, nearly incoherent from the alcohol. "Lessgo home….I'm think I drunk."

"That's an understatement," I muttered, annoyed by how the night was turning out. I wrapped my arm around him and helped him as he stumbled to my car.

"Thanks, babes," Trevor smiled that drunken stupor smile that nearly churned my stomach as I climbed into the driver's seat. His head clumsily bobbled back and forth as he slurred, "You're da best!"

I just rolled my eyes and started the engine. About halfway home, in the middle of a sharp curve, Trevor bunglingly leaned out the half-opened window and puked. Vomit streaked down the window and onto the car door. "Sorry," he sputtered as he wiped his mouth on his sleeve.

"Oh gross!" I shrieked. "Trevor, good grief! That's disgusting!"

I sped to his house and ushered him to his room. Flopping down on his bed, jeans and all, he immediately passed out. I didn't even bother to take off his shoes. Instead, I hightailed it out of there to escape the disgusting stench of bile and beer that burned my nostrils.

On my way home I drove through an automatic car wash. The nauseating scent of alcohol and vomit still lingered inside my car. I couldn't wait to escape to my bed, my safe haven of fluffy pink pillows and plush microfiber blankets. The four walls of my cozy bedroom served as my sanctuary. The white eyelet comforter that I'd had since I was four draped carelessly over my bed. Pillow shams stacked around my head like a soft barrier against the harsh reality of life. The sooner the night ended, the better.

I wanted so badly to pick up the phone and call Chris just to talk to someone. His soothing voice would calm my nerves and help me sleep soundly. I restrained myself from dialing his phone number and spent the rest of the night in a fitful sleep.

Chapter Nine

Trevor came to school the next day reeking of stale beer and cigarette smoke with a faint hint of vomit.

"Good grief, Trevor, did you shower today?" I asked him when I got close enough to really get a whiff of him.

"Not yet," he groaned. The hangover was evident by the dark circles under his eyes. "Coach Harrison is going to let me shower in the locker rooms this morning. He told me I better shape up before class starts. He didn't want his star player getting a bad rep and making him look bad. I'm headed down there now. I'll see you later." He grabbed his bag and headed down toward the locker rooms.

The school day could not have crept by any slower. The minutes felt like hours. I was so tired from my restless night of sleep. I had too much on my mind to care about school. Trevor avoided me most of the day. I didn't know exactly what was going on with him, but he seemed to wear a guilty look all day. His avoidance suited me just fine. I needed some time to think anyway.

Trevor met me at my locker when the last school bell rang. He definitely looked and smelled better than he had that morning. The scent of his cologne reminded me of dry woods with a hint of musky leather. My stomach did flips when I saw him. He looked as gorgeous as ever when he gave me his award-winning smile. He had some kind of hypnotic ability with those hazel eyes. I scolded myself for being spellbound by him.

"So," he asked, "are you ready to see the movie tomorrow?"

"Really?" I squealed with delight. I couldn't believe he was actually making good on the promise he made after practice that day to take me the 'chick flick.'

"Sure. I promised I'd take you."

"All right, I guess I'll see you tomorrow evening then." I looked at him suspiciously, wary of his sudden kindness.

"Oh, by the way," he leaned toward me, whispering, "some people were telling me that you were talking to some guy outside the club last night. You better pray I don't find out who it was, and you better hope to God I never hear of you doing that again—for your sake." Narrowing his eyes, he patronized me by patting me on the shoulder as he walked away.

I stared into my locker and tried to process what had just occurred. Tears worked their way to my eyes as I fought hard to keep them from falling. I wish I could've just walked away from Trevor and never looked back, but I knew that couldn't happen; his death threat was always in the back of my mind.

On my way to practice that day, I saw Chris standing by the vending machines. I used the excuse that I wanted a soda to go over and speak to him.

At our school, mostly drug dealers and gang members hung by the vending machines in the quad. It was no surprise that most school fights took place out there. Members of the so-called popular crowd never ventured to that area, and cheerleaders *never* bought snacks out of the vending machines. Purchasing tiny packages of sugar coated, saturated fat was against some secret diet code. I planned to buy *two* packs of Marshmallow Dream Cakes; I was feeling rather rebellious.

"Hi," I said shyly as I dropped the coins into the slot.

"Hey, you," he grinned. "What brings you out here?"

"I didn't eat lunch," I fibbed.

"Well, it's good to see you." Chris winked, stuffed his hands in his pockets, and leaned back, propping one of his feet against the brick wall behind him.

"Thanks. Actually, I'm glad I bumped into you, too," I offered sheepishly.

"Really? Why? Is everything all right?" he suddenly sounded very protective.

"Yeah, at the moment…" my words trailed off as I turned to look at the snack choices in the machine. I knew he was staring at me, burning holes into the back of my head with his glare.

"Kaitlyn," he said, "you're the nicest, prettiest girl I have met at this school. Yet, there is something about you that seems…off. It just feels like you're hiding something. I have seen you crying several times now, and the dark circles under your eyes tell me that you aren't getting enough sleep. I don't know, you just look like you could use a friend right now—someone to talk to that could help you. I could be that person, you know. I could help you."

I whirled around, narrowing my eyes and giving him a look of adamant determination. "No. I can't let you get involved."

Reaching over my shoulders, Chris placed his hands against the vending machine behind me. He towered over me, but leaned down to look me square in the face; his forehead nearly brushed against mine. The heat of his breath against my face caused my own breath to hitch as he almost closed the gap between us. My heart skipped a beat under the intensity of his stare. The longing in his eyes said everything and nothing in the exact same moment. With pure conviction he whispered, "I already am."

A rush of relief spread over me. Tears dripped down my cheeks. Maybe I would finally be able to admit how terrified I really was of Trevor because at that moment it seemed I had a protector—someone who could see through Trevor's charm and deception. I couldn't believe I was outright crying in front of him. This guy. This stranger. I just couldn't stop myself.

Chris hesitantly wrapped his arms around me. My heaving sobs became stronger as I buried my face against his chest. "It's going to be okay," he assured me. He held me until my crying subsided.

"Thank you," I whispered.

Cupping my chin in his hand, he looked directly into my tear-filled eyes. "You are so sweet, and damn, you're beautiful. You are worth it, Kaitlyn. Keep telling yourself that."

My lip quivered and the tears threatened to fall again. "I have to go. I have practice," I said, even though I didn't want to leave him. I felt secure in his arms. I couldn't believe this guy I barely knew and had only spoken to a handful of times, this ex-convict, could make me feel so safe—so free to be me.

His eyes searched mine. "Do you want me to wait for you?"

"No," I instinctively covered the bruise on my arm. "I'm meeting my boyfr—Trevor, after practice."

Chris glanced down at my arm as I made futile efforts to hide the bruise. It seemed obvious that he heard me hesitate on the word 'boyfriend.' Chris took a step back and glared at me with piercing eyes. "Is that what this is about? Your boyfriend? Has he been hurting you?" The anger immediately rose in his tone. "Don't tell me that I'm going to have to fuck up some punk who thinks he can lay a hand on a girl?"

"No, it's not like that…not really," I attempted another lie.

"Oh, really? Well, then what's this bruise on your arm?" He looked at me accusingly as he lifted my arm to point out what I already knew was there.

"I—" I couldn't formulate a lie fast enough and dropped my eyes in shame.

"I knew it," he yelled, punching the side of the vending machine with his fist. The noise echoed like a gunshot.

Startled, I flinched.

Before I had time to think, his arms were around me, hugging me protectively. "I'm sorry," he whispered. He held me there, trying to swallow back his anger.

"It's okay," I assured him.

"No, it's not okay. I didn't mean to scare you. It just pisses me off to see some asshole treating you like that. It's not right, Kaitlyn. Don't worry. This," he declared, pointing to my bruise, "won't be an issue any more."

I wasn't sure how he planned to fix it, but I felt secure knowing that somehow I would be protected from Trevor once and for all.

I nearly floated to practice. The other girls looked at me inquisitively. They wondered what had me looking so aloof. They would never understand. I knew they wouldn't even try to understand. I didn't bother to explain it either. To them, Chris was a convicted felon crouched around the corner waiting for his next victim like some kind of monster. They would never give him a chance to prove himself otherwise. They would never

believe that the monster I dated was far more dangerous than the monster they saw in Chris King.

Chapter Ten

Trevor came by my house that Saturday. "Hello, Mrs. Davenport," he said, dazzling my mom with his cheesy smile and charisma when she answered the door.

"Hi, Trevor," my mom responded, obviously fooled by his act.

I never talked to my mom about the arguments Trevor and I had. As far as she knew, he was still as wonderful as that night two years prior, when he impressed her after the baseball game. "I hope your parents are doing well," she said.

"Yes ma'am. My mom is almost finished with her nursing degree, and my dad is as busy as ever at work."

"That's great," she said warmly, "I'm glad to see your dad's business hasn't suffered during this recession." She walked into the kitchen to wash the dishes from dinner. I was just finishing some homework at the dining room table as he made his way over to where I was sitting.

He beamed at me as he plopped down at the table beside me. I half-heartedly grinned back at him; it was the best I had to offer.

"Ready for the movie?" he asked.

"Yep, just finishing up." I was actually kind of excited about seeing the movie I had been begging to see for weeks. Trevor, like most guys, didn't really enjoy chick flicks.

When I'd finished my homework, he walked me to his truck and opened the door for me. "Such a gentleman," I commented.

"I do my best, babe!" he said, flashing those pearly whites again. He still managed to make me melt sometimes.

I waited in the lobby while he bought the tickets and popcorn. The aroma of fresh buttered popcorn caused my stomach to growl.

"Oh, hi Kaitlyn!"

Hearing Arnold's voice characteristically caused me to scan the lobby to see if Trevor was nearby. If Trevor caught me talking to Arnold, things could get ugly. Thankfully, Trevor was nowhere to be found. "Hey, Arnold," I said, peering around to determine if he was with a date. "Are you here by yourself?"

"Yep. I wanted to see *Alien Invasion* again. What movie are you guys seeing?"

"*Times Gone By*. It's a movie based on a popular romance novel," I replied.

"Trevor's willing to watch it again?"

My eyes narrowed. "Again?"

"Yeah, you guys were here last night. I saw Trevor walking into the theater and…I thought that was you with him," he expounded, suddenly sounding slightly distressed.

I guess the look on my face explained it all.

"Oh," he said quietly and bit his lower lip like he knew he had said too much.

I nodded, immediately aware that Arnold had just inadvertently slipped me the truth of Trevor's deceit.

Eva! The thought exploded in my head like an atomic bomb. Everyone was always getting us confused. From the back, she and I looked like twins. My blood boiled. I felt like my body could burst into flames. To be honest, I wasn't sure if I wanted to kill Trevor, find Eva to rip her apart limb by limb, or just run away crying and sulking in my own foolish despair.

"Sorry," he whispered apologetically. "I'll see you around."

"It's okay. Enjoy your movie." I forced a smile. After all, it wasn't Arnold's fault. He had actually done me a favor. I might have never known otherwise.

"One popcorn, one Coke, and one ticket to a chick flick," Trevor beamed as if he had just handed me a million dollars.

"Thanks," I said flatly. I still wasn't sure if I wanted to cuss him out right there in the middle of the theater lobby, or pretend like nothing was wrong and seize him when he least expected it.

I decided to lay low for a little while. I deserved to see the movie. He owed me at least that much. The

fading bruise on my arm was proof enough as far as I was concerned. I fought the tears back with all my might. He'd probably never notice anyway. He was too busy checking out the other girls standing at the popcorn counter. *How had I never noticed that before? Was I too blinded by him that I missed the signs?* I reprimanded myself for trying to take the blame. This was Trevor's fault. He was the guilty one. Not me. A soothing voice reminded me in my head, *"You are worth it."* Trevor, on the other hand, was not.

I couldn't concentrate on the movie at all. The whole time I plotted my next move. I hardly laughed at the funny scenes. Even the sad scenes barely struck a nerve. I noticed that Trevor didn't flinch like everyone else during the surprisingly loud parts. It was almost like he already knew it was coming. My blood boiled inside of me.

"So, what did you think of the movie?" he asked once we were sitting in his truck.

"It was pretty good," I said. "Fairly predictable."

"Yeah, I thought so too," he agreed. By then, we were pulling out of the parking lot and heading down the highway toward my house.

"Oh really?" I asked innocently. "So, was there anything you saw tonight that you didn't catch last night?" My plan was intact.

"Nah," he said absently. "I wasn't really paying attention last ni—" Suddenly, his words caught in his throat. His eyes widened, burning with the reality of being caught, and he swallowed hard. As usual, anger fumed from him.

Ha! I got him!

"How did you know?" he screamed. "Who in the hell told you?" He stomped on his brakes and swerved into the parking lot of an old abandoned gas station. Yanking the emergency brake into position, he barely avoided slamming his truck into the gas pumps. *I should've known better than to bring it up in the truck. I should've waited until we were at a safe place.* He got in my face and growled, "Who. Told. You?"

I was not about to rat out Arnold. "I saw you," I reactively spat out, covering the truth.

"Liar!" he shouted.

My eyes were wide with fear as I stammered, "I saw you…with Eva. I followed you."

"Tell me the truth, Kaitlyn!" he roared even louder. "Whoever told you—I'll kill them!"

That is exactly why I was not about to tell him the truth. "Take me home, Trevor."

He glowered at me. "I'm not taking you home until you tell me who told you."

"Fine," I scowled at him. "I'll walk." I jumped out of the truck into the dark parking lot.

He flew out after me. "You'll do no such thing. Now get in this truck right now." He snatched me by the wrist.

Shit! Why did I confront him like this? Stupid, stupid, stupid…but, I can't take this anymore. I can't keep going like this! That's it, this is over. I have to stand up for myself. God, please don't let him hurt me! I stomped my foot and tried to jerk my hand away from him. "No, Trevor. Let me go, now! We're over!"

He gaped at me in horror, refusing to release my wrist. "No!" he snarled through clenched teeth. His grip tightened as he twisted my arm behind me forcing it upward.

I let out a gasp. I had to be strong. I would not let him get to me. "I'm not going anywhere with you! Break my arm if it makes you feel more like a man, but I can tell you now, we are over!" I screamed the last word as loud as I could with hope that someone passing by would hear me.

"You'll regret this," he loosened his grip on my arm. "I can promise you. You *will* regret this."

I turned my head to glare at him. "I doubt it."

At that moment, with all of his strength, he shoved me onto the pavement. My arm was weak from being held in such an awkward position behind my back, and it buckled under the weight of my body. My face hit the pavement with such force, I quickly tasted blood on my lips. Within seconds, Trevor's truck roared to life. His spinning tires spewed loose gravel all over me as he sped out of the parking lot.

I laid there for a minute trying to assess my situation. No bones seemed to be broken. I could tell my face was bleeding, but that was all. I began to shiver. I wasn't sure if it was because I was cold or because I was terrified. I suddenly realized I was in an empty parking lot, in a bad section of town, in the dead of night. *Alone.*

I fumbled for my cell phone. I didn't dare call my mom and dad. Allison was with Eric, celebrating with her family for her grandmother's eightieth birthday. Rachel went to her dad's house for the weekend, which was nearly fifty miles away. Oh, and I would have rotted there alone before I would have called Eva.

There was only one person left to call. I searched frantically in my jacket pockets for that wadded up piece of paper. *Chris King.* Nervously, I dialed the number.

Someone picked up on the fourth ring. "Hello?" a groggy female voice answered. My phone call must have woken his mom.

"I…I'm sorry," I stumbled over my words, trying to find a way to hang up quickly. "I must have the wrong phone number."

"Are you looking for Chris?" she asked.

"Yes, please," I said through anxious, panting breaths.

"Hold on," I could hear muffled sounds as the phone was being passed.

"Hello?" Chris's voice came on the line.

"Chris!" I suddenly lost control and sobs claimed my speech.

"Kaitlyn?" he asked. "Is that you?"

"Yes." I took a deep breath. "He drove away. He's gone! I'm by myself! It's dark. I'm bleeding!" The words tumbled out of my mouth like a rushing waterfall. I wasn't even sure if I was making any sense.

"Whoa, Kaitlyn. Slow down. Where are you? What's going on? You're bleeding?" Chris pumped me for answers.

"I don't know. We left the theater and headed back to my house. We got into an argument and he drove into the parking lot of the old Mobil gas station. He pushed me down. He left me here. I mean, I told him to leave, but now he's gone," I said, taking a breath. There would be more time for explanations later. "I'm scared, Chris." That's all I needed to say.

"I know exactly where you are, Kaitlyn. I'll be there soon."

Relief flooded me. "Thank you!"

I crouched down behind a gas pump and waited for Chris. Just in case Trevor drove by again I didn't want him to see me. My face was swollen. It hurt pretty badly. I could tell one of my eyes was almost swollen shut. My arm was sore, but I was so thankful it wasn't broken.

Suddenly, a black souped-up Honda CRX swerved into the parking lot. A silhouette jumped out of the driver's seat. "Kaitlyn?" Chris's voice sounded worried.

"I'm right here," I called out. He rushed over to me. I tried to smile through the pain on my face. "Thanks for coming to get—"

"Oh my god!" Chris interrupted. "What the hell did he do to you?!" He lifted my chin up and to the side to get a good look at the injuries on my cheek. I could tell by the look of horror on his face that it had to be bad.

Shaking his head, he wrapped me in his strong, comforting arms.

I collapsed into his chest. "It was my fault. I shouldn't have pissed him off…" I apologized into his shirt.

"Don't, Kaitlyn. Don't you fucking say that! He's the one who did this. This is *all* on him. I'm gonna kill that motherfucker!" he growled.

"Please, Chris, you don't understand. You can't do that. He's got the whole town in his back pocket. They won't think twice. They'll send you back to juvie. Please, don't do anything. I need you *here*," I pleaded with him as my tears threatened to fall.

He held my gaze and pulled me tighter against him. Brushing a strand of hair off my forehead, he assured me, "Only for you, Kaitlyn. If it were up to me, I'd put that asshole six feet under, but just for you, I swear I won't touch him." He held me there while I tried to compose myself. I held my breath to keep the sobs from coming. I knew the salty tears would sting my face. "It's okay." His voiced soothed me as he gently stroked my hair. "I'm here now. He's not going to hurt you again." I wasn't strong enough. My sobs got the best of me and my chest heaved under the pressure. "Come on," he said. "Let's get you out of here."

We drove by the drug store on the way to his house. I couldn't go home looking like I did. What was I going to tell my mom? Maybe once I got cleaned up a little I could conjure up a convincing story of tripping down the stairs.

He ran in and out in record time. I think he was afraid to leave me alone for too long. Thankfully, Trevor wouldn't recognize his car even if he did see it.

When we got to his house, he helped me up the stairs to his kitchen. At that point, my eye was swollen completely shut. He pulled out a chair from under the table.

"Dr. King, at your service," he said with a grin. I flinched as I tried to smile back at him. "Don't," he whispered. "Let me get you cleaned up. Maybe the medicine will help with the pain." He withdrew some antiseptic, a few bandages, a roll of tape, and some tweezers out of the plastic drug store bag.

"Tweezers?" I asked, perplexed.

"To get the gravel out." He winced empathetically. Within minutes he had it all removed. The tears falling from my eyes burned my face. "It will be over soon," he assured me. His dark eyes comforted me. The antiseptic stung when he touched it to my cheek. I flinched. "I'm sorry," he whispered.

"It's okay. Go ahead. Do it quick, though." I held my breath.

The burning was over after a few seconds. Chris had me bandaged up in no time. "Almost good as new…and just as beautiful," he lied.

"Yeah, right," I looked at my reflection in the window.

"Well, at least you have a pretty convincing story, right?"

Just then, we heard feet shuffling into the kitchen. "Chris!" his mother's voice boomed. "What have you done?"

"Nothing mom. I was just helping her out," he said truthfully.

"Chris," his mom repeated accusingly.

I practiced my story on her. "It's not his fault. I called him to come help me. I was out shopping and I tripped on a curb and landed on the pavement. My eyes were too swollen to drive myself home so I called Chris to come get me."

It worked.

"I hope you're okay," she told me as she grabbed her reading glasses off the kitchen counter and disappeared into the dimly lit living room.

"Well, at least you've had some practice in getting your story straight," Chris said half-jokingly.

"Yeah, I'm not a very good liar," I admitted.

He winked at me. "I can tell."

"There's just one more big favor I need," I told him.

"You name it," he said whole-heartedly.

"Okay. I need to sneak home, get my car, take it to the Stop-n-Shop, and have you bring me back home again." I felt sure my parents were already asleep in bed. They felt comfortable going to bed even when they knew I was out with Trevor. I guess they thought Trevor would keep me safe. *Ha!* "I'll just tell my parents that Trevor dropped me back off at home after the movie and I hopped in my car and headed back out for a little

shopping. That's convincing, right?" I asked, not certain I even convinced myself.

"I guess. You don't really have a choice, right? I mean your mom saw you leave with Trevor. She's going to wonder why you needed me to come pick you up," he reasoned.

"I'm just not ready to tell her the truth. I'm not sure she would believe me. She thinks the world of Trevor." Quite honestly, I wasn't sure if anyone besides Chris would believe me if I told the truth. Trevor was the Golden Boy, the star athlete, the model student, and every underclassman's hero. Everyone loved him.

It didn't take long to sneak my car out of the driveway and drop it off at Stop-n-Shop. I was a little disappointed that my night with Chris was coming to an end. In the meantime, my cell phone had rung off the hook. I finally put it on silent mode after the tenth time. Chris and I sat in his car and listened to the many voice mail messages Trevor left for me. They ranged in emotions from angry death threats to pleading declarations of love.

"Save those," Chris suggested. "You might need them later."

"Good idea," I agreed.

We pulled into my driveway a little after one in the morning. My curfew was normally midnight, but my parents had gone to bed long before that. They would never know what time I actually arrived home. When they thought I was with Trevor, they never enforced the curfew.

"Thank you again for coming to my rescue," I stated, staring at Chris in the driver's seat.

"Anytime. That's what I told you, and that's what I meant. I'm glad you called me," he said. "Under different circumstances, I would tell you I had a great time tonight."

"It's okay," I assured him. I understood what he meant, because I felt exactly the same way.

Chris watched me in the darkness. "He doesn't deserve you, Kaitlyn. You deserve to be treated with kindness and respect." Chris reached over and took my hand in his, lacing our fingers together. The touch of his hand ignited a warmth upon my skin. It burned its way up my arm. A sensuous longing permeated throughout my body. My heart jump started in my chest as pounding adrenaline coursed through my entire body. "I would never hurt you, you know," he continued, rubbing his thumb across the soft flesh of my hand. "I mean, if you were *my* girl, I would never do anything to hurt you. *Ever.* You would mean too much to me. Trevor should feel the same way. It's not fair the way he treats you, and he *still* gets the girl."

"I know. You're right," I said sadly, staring at the interlocked fingers of our hands in my lap. "I can't explain it. Trevor and I have been together almost two years. He was my first real boyfriend. I was in too deep

before I realized what he was capable of doing to me. I broke up with him tonight, but this fight isn't over. He might have left me alone in that parking lot, but I'll have to face him again. What scares me the most is that he'll *convince* me to take him back." I winced at the memory of Trevor's death threat, but continued, "For reasons I can't explain, I can't seem to get away from him. I know you don't understand. No one does…" my voice trailed off. The shiny black 9mm that I knew Trevor kept in a locked box under his bed was the reason I couldn't explain; it was the reason no one understood. Fear kept me tied to Trevor. Fear alone.

Reaching upward, Chris tenderly grasped my chin in his hand and tilted my head up to look at me. "You're right. I don't understand. I don't understand *at all*, but I hope whatever happens, you'll do what's best for *you*. You're amazing, you know that? You're smart and funny. He's too selfish to appreciate what he has. He shouldn't get to wrap his arms around you or kiss your beautiful lips. God, Kaitlyn, I wish like hell you were *my* girl, not his. He isn't worthy of you. Please wake up and realize there's someone right here in front of you that would treat you the way you deserve to be treated."

I peered into his chestnut brown eyes. Feeling dizzy with the tempest of emotions swirling in my mind, I tried to quiet the bedlam of feelings that he had just created inside of me. Chris looked intently at me, pleading silently for me to reason with him. His dark, stormy irises stirred up complete pandemonium inside my heart. I couldn't speak. I could only gaze at him through the darkness that surrounded us while he gently removed his hand from my chin and cupped the uninjured side of my face. The warmth of his hand sent yearning pulses of desire through my body, echoing their way down to the tips of my toes.

"Well, I hope you can get some sleep tonight," he whispered as he brushed a strand of hair behind my ear, then ran his thumb down the length of my jaw line and caressed my sensitive skin. My breath caught in my throat. I wished I could think of something brilliant to say.

"Thanks. You too." It was all I could muster. I quietly stepped out of his car and tiptoed my way to the house. With one single glance back in his direction, I caught him watching me as I made my way up the walkway toward my front porch. Knowing his eyes were glued on me, I felt a spring in my step as I ascended the stairs toward the front door.

My phone rang and alerted me with texts the rest of the night. Thankfully I left it on silent mode, serving Trevor right. I had no desire to speak to him—especially not after my emotionally charged conversation, and strangely glorious night, with Chris.

Chapter Eleven

The next morning I awoke to muffled voices coming from the living room. Sleepily, I walked into the room. Sitting in the recliner, along with my mom and dad who were sitting together on the sofa, was Trevor. *Trevor!*

"Oh my god!" he screeched, jumping up at the same time my mom and dad sprang to their feet. "When I didn't see your car in the driveway, I got worried!" He sounded convincing to anyone who didn't know the truth.

I glared at him.

My mom gasped when she saw my face. "What happened to you?!" She rushed over and put her arm around me.

I never took my eyes off of Trevor as I spoke, "Well, after Trevor dropped me off at home I needed to run out to the Stop-n-Shop. I had to get some tampons. You guys were already asleep and I figured you wouldn't mind since I didn't plan to be there for long. While I was there, I tripped on a curb and fell onto the pavement. It's okay; it looks worse than it feels," I lied.

"Where is your car?" my dad inquired. "How did you get home?"

"I called a friend." There was no need to tell them about Chris.

Trevor looked relieved. I glowered at him. I didn't lie to protect him. I was just too afraid to admit the truth, so I lied to protect myself.

"Thank you," he mouthed when my parents weren't looking.

Whatever. I rolled my eyes at him. "I'm still tired…and sore," I added. "I think I'm going back to bed. Goodbye Trevor." I hoped the look I gave him got my point across. I wanted him to leave.

"Okay, sweetie," my mom cooed. "You go back to bed. I'll fix you something to eat when you get up." I knew she was worried about me.

"Trevor can call you later," my dad piped up.

"Whatever," I muttered under my breath as I headed back upstairs to my room. Thankfully, my bedroom was on the second floor, or I would have been worried that Trevor would try to climb through my window.

It was two o'clock in the afternoon when I finally got out of bed. I crept downstairs hoping to avoid my parents.

"Oh, there you are sleepy-head!" my mom said, eyeing me over the novel she was reading. "Are you hungry?"

"No, thanks," I said. My mouth hurt too bad to chew anyway, but I didn't tell her that.

"Okay," she stated, looking back at her book.

Good. She looked engrossed. Maybe I could get Allison to drive me to the Stop-n-Shop to pick up my car. I wasn't terribly confident that my story would work on her though.

"Hello?" Allison answered.

I tried to sound happy. "Hey, Allie. What are you up to?" I asked, attempting to rearrange the shoes on a rack in my closet.

"Not much," she sighed with boredom. I heard what sounded like her cat bumping his head against her phone and loud purring echoed into the handset.

"Wanna go to the mall?"

"Sure!" she perked up. "I need a new shirt to wear to my cousin's birthday party in a few weeks."

"Can you come pick me up, though?"

"Yeah, where's your car?"

"It's a long story," I explained as I placed the last pair of shoes neatly onto the rack.

"Okay, you can tell me when I get there," she said.

"See you later," I told her.

"Okay, bye!"

"Oh! Hey, Allie!" I exclaimed, fearful that she was close to hanging up the phone.

"Yeah?"

"Don't freak out when you see me."

"Okay…" she sounded intrigued.

I decided that I would explain it when she got to my house. Not long after we got off the phone, Allison pulled into the driveway. Grabbing my purse, I bounded down the stairs and opened the passenger door of her silver Prelude.

She gasped. "What happened?" I could tell she was trying hard not to freak out.

I told her my fabricated story as I settled into the seat next to her.

She eyed me suspiciously. "Kaitlyn. Do you really expect me to believe that garbage?" Allison asked when I finally buckled my seatbelt. If anyone would've guessed the truth, it would have been Allison. She knew more about Trevor than she let on, so her questioning comes as no surprise.

"What do you mean?" I asked nervously.

"Look. I'm your best friend. I have known you most of my life. We grew up together, remember? You are an awesome cheerleader who can tumble and stunt with the best of them. Clumsy is not a word I would use to describe you."

Gulp. "Seriously, Allison. I really did trip. It was dark, and I had my hands full. I just didn't see the curb. People make mistakes, Allie. Geez, get off my back."

"Okay, okay." She held her hands up, surrendering. "Whatever. You tripped. I get it."

I immediately reprimanded myself. What was so hard about admitting the truth? Deep down, I knew the answer to that question. I would have to acknowledge the way I have allowed Trevor to treat me for so long. I would have to confess my weakness in letting myself become a doormat. I'd have to proclaim my failure to stand up for myself and declare to everyone else, that I was a victim. I was *not* ready for that. "I know," I softened my tone. "I'm sorry. I didn't sleep well last night. I'm a little cranky."

"It's all right. Nothing a little retail therapy won't help."

"Yeah…" I said, glancing out the window.

She changed the subject. "So, Eric and I…well, we…uh, we finally did it."

I reached down and pressed the power button on the radio to silence the loud raucous music blaring from the speakers. "What? You did the deed? Oh my god, Allison! Why didn't you tell me?"

"I'm telling you now," she beamed.

"I meant, like, when it happened."

"Geez, Kait, it's not like I could text you from the bed or anything."

We both laughed. I felt myself relax a little.

"So? When did it happen?" I inquired.

"The night we went to Club Millennium."

"And?" I asked with expectancy.

"And what?"

"And give me details, Allie! Best friends need details!"

"I don't know…he was nervous. I was scared. It was painful and awkward. Definitely not all it's cracked up to be, that's for sure."

"I'm sure it will get better."

"I sure hope so."

"Did you use protection?"

"Like, as in a condom?"

"Of course," I said.

"No," she replied shamefully.

"God, Allison! You didn't use protection? What the hell? Do you want to get pregnant your senior year?"

"No. I mean, we got caught up in the moment. I wasn't thinking."

"Seriously, Allison, it only takes one time. You better not do that again unless you want to be barefoot and pregnant before graduation."

"I know, I know. We promised each other we wouldn't let it happen again."

"Good," I insisted.

"So," Allison, the Queen of changing the subject, inquired, "Where do you want to go first?"

"How about McAlister's?"

"Sounds good to me." She laughed as she turned the radio on and twisted the volume up just in time to catch the tail end of *Hey Ya!* by Outkast. We rolled the windows down, and I listened to Allison sing at the top of her lungs. I would have enjoyed singing too, but the pain from my injury kept me from joining her.

We spent the rest of the day trying on clothes and shoes in every department store in the mall. I tried on more than I bought since it seemed as though every cashier eyed my face peculiarly while I paid for my purchases. However, I was certain Allison maxed out her dad's credit card.

"Thanks for going shopping with me," I said gratefully as Allison parked her car next to mine at the Stop-n-Shop, "and thanks for the ride."

"No problem," she smiled. "Call me anytime. I'm here if you need me."

I knew she meant it, but I also knew she was trying to probe me for more information. I kept my secret locked up tight.

"Thanks," I waved goodbye to her. "See ya."

I hopped into my car and sped off. I would be glad to get back home. I thought maybe I would give Chris a call when I got there. For all the help he had given me the night before, I at least owed it to him to tell him that I was still alive.

"Hello?" his smooth voice liquefied into my ear.

"Chris?"

"Hey, Kaitlyn!" I could almost hear him smiling through the phone. I smiled back, wincing in pain from the scrapes and bruises on my face.

"I just wanted to thank you again for last night," I told him, "and wanted to let you know that I'm feeling better today."

"I'm so glad to hear that. I've been thinking about you all day," he confessed.

I radiated through the pain. I was just so happy to hear his voice. I don't think I had felt that kind of happiness in almost two years.

"Guess who was at my house when I woke up this morning?" I dared him to guess.

"Are you kidding me? Bastard!" he muttered angrily.

"Don't worry. He didn't stay long."

"What nerve! Are you okay?" He changed his tone back to a more soothing one.

"I'm fine. Trevor knows I lied. He thinks I did it to protect him."

"Whatever...he can think what he wants. You're sure you're okay?"

"I'm fine," I answered as I savored the sound of his voice.

"Good. Well, my little brother is hounding me to use the phone to call his *girlfriend*," he teased.

"Shut up, Chris!" I heard his brother say in the background, followed by what sounded like a slap.

Chris laughed. "Okay, I'll see you at school on Monday, Kaitlyn."

"Hey, Chris," I added, internally punching myself for what I was about to say. "No one really knows that we talk. Maybe we should keep it that way. I don't need more drama in my life right now...Wait, I didn't mean that as awful as it sounded." *Crap! I need a mulligan.* "I'm sorry. I'm not as superficial as that came across. It's just that...well..." *God, I suck at this. How do I make him understand what I'm trying to say?*

"Trust me. I understand. You have a lot going on with school, Trevor, your parents, and planning for college. I get it. I really do. You have a lot riding on the line right now. I'm not here to cause more trouble for you, and I understand that everyone knowing about me will only be stirring up a hornet's nest. It's no problem. Keep *us* a secret…I can do that. No worries." The sincerity in his voice told me that he truly understood what I had failed so miserably at trying to explain.

"Thank you, Chris. I really appreciate you. I'll talk to you later."

"Bye, Kaitlyn."

I hung onto his last word. My name slid off his tongue like silk. I felt my heart skip a beat at the sound of it.

My mother was folding laundry in the living room while she watched television. As I was passing through that room on my way to the kitchen to grab a bottle of water, she asked, "Hey, who were you talking to?"

I was tired of lying. I figured she wouldn't care if I told her a little bit of the truth. "Just a friend…a guy from school," I stammered as I tried to explain.

My mom looked at me accusingly. "Kaitlyn…a guy? Are you sure you should be chatting with other guys on the phone while you are dating Trevor?"

Ouch. Really, Mom? She might as well have slapped me across the face. At least a smack across the face would have hurt less than the sting from her words. "Whatever, mom," I rolled my eyes. "You wouldn't understand anyway."

Abruptly, I turned around and stomped back up to my room. Besides coming downstairs to eat during meal times, I stayed in my bedroom the rest of that day. I used the excuse that I was giving my face time to heal, which was half true. The other half was trying to avoid Trevor. So far, it was working.

Chapter Twelve

Monday morning came all too quickly. I dragged myself out of bed and stood in front of the mirror praying for a miracle to heal my face. A deep purple bruise fanned across my cheekbone. Ugly scabs covered the same side of my face from the corner of my eye to the corner of my jaw. I didn't feel like lying anymore. Then again, who would believe the truth? Begrudgingly, I managed to make it to school on time.

Several students stared at me while I made my way down the hallway to my locker. No one bothered to ask what happened or even if I was okay. Maybe deep down they already knew.

I retrieved the things that I needed for my morning classes, hoping to avoid curious stares—and Trevor—just a little bit longer. As my luck would have it, Trevor came up behind me and gently nudged his shoulder into mine.

"Hey beautiful," he flirted.

Ugh! "Hey," I rolled my eyes and avoided looking at him.

"You know I love you, right?" Trevor asked.

"Whatever," I muttered under my breath.

"Listen, Kaitlyn," he pleaded. "I'm sorry. Really, I am. I overreacted the other night. It's all my fault. I made a stupid mistake. Can you please forgive me? I promise I will never cheat on you again, and I swear on my life that I will never hurt you again! Please!"

His begging sent a wave of nausea through my whole body. I wasn't sure if the nausea set in because his lies literally sickened me or whether I felt repulsed by the urge to forgive him.

I looked up at him. I stared deep into those wonderful hazel eyes. I remembered the Trevor I knew he could be. I did love him. I loved him more than anyone I had ever known. I wanted to kick myself for not being able to run—run away as fast as I could and never look back.

"Trevor, I'm going to have to take some time to think about it," I finally told him.

"Take all the time you need, baby," he whispered. "I'll still be here waiting for you when you realize we're meant to be together."

He walked away toward his first class of the day. I stared after him. My heart felt like it weighed a hundred pounds in my chest. After all we had been through, and despite it all, I really did still love him.

I struggled to get through the day. A few people asked me about my face, and believed the story I told them. I kept to myself mostly, lost within the confines of my own thoughts. The internal conflict threatened to implode my heart.

"You can't break up with Trevor," Blake whispered to me during Advanced Math. Blake was on the football team also. He and Trevor had been friends since Kindergarten.

"Why not?" I asked.

"Because no one else will go out with you. They are all afraid of what Trevor would do to them. Think about it, Kaitlyn...Prom, Senior Night, every weekend...You'd be alone."

Alone. His word exploded and echoed inside my head as though he had thrown a string of firecrackers into a metal trash can. Why did the thought of being alone frighten me so much? Blake was right; no one would ask me out ever again. I would be the social outcast, the loner who sat by herself in the cafeteria, the hermit who never got invited to parties, and the loser no one would even ask on a date because they were too afraid Trevor would annihilate them.

I saw Chris from a distance a few times throughout the day. I wished I could just run up to him and let him hug me with his safeguarding arms. A reassuring hug was exactly what I needed. A few times, he glanced at me and winked through the oblivious crowd. I grinned at him. Theatre Arts class could not come fast enough.

"Ahem!" Ms. Carducci clapped her hands to get the attention of the class. "In the coming weeks, we are going to be working on some scenes from the musical, *Guys and Dolls*. We still need a guy to play the part of Sky Masterson. Anyone up for the challenge?"

Chris's hand shot up. "I'll do it!"

"Okay, Chris," Ms. Carducci appeared uneasy, but agreed. "Are you familiar with the play?"

"Yes, ma'am" Chris replied. "Sometimes, the guards in juvie rewarded us for good behavior by letting us watch movies; most of them were old black and white films. There were a few musicals, too. *Guys and Dolls* was the house favorite. There's just something about a no-good troublemaker winning over the straight-laced goody-two-shoes." He winked at me. I hoped no one else noticed.

Ms. Carducci laughed, sounding a little uptight. I guess the word *juvie* struck a nerve with her like it did with everyone else. "All right, Chris. The part is yours. Come in tomorrow prepared to sing Sky's part from the song, *I'll Know*."

"Not a problem," Chris boasted.

Ms. Carducci quickly prepared a video for us to watch for the rest of the class period.

Once the lights were turned off and the video had begun, Chris whispered, "You okay?"

"Yeah, I guess," I responded softly.

He stared at me in the dark. I guess he was trying to decipher whether or not I was telling him the truth. A few seconds later he looked away and continued to watch the video.

Chris kept his promise. He barely acknowledged me at school. No one knew that we talked or how he'd helped me over the weekend. It was probably better that way.

We spent the rest of the class watching varying clips from several different productions of *Guys and Dolls*. I couldn't help but think Chris would make the perfect Sky Masterson.

When I got home that afternoon, my mom greeted me at the door with a vase full of a dozen red roses. "These came for you today," she said excitedly. "Somebody must really love you." She winked.

"Thanks mom," I replied emotionless. I took a moment to read the card:

Gag.

I tossed the roses into the trashcan on my way up to my room. I heard my mother gasp behind me. "Kaitlyn, that wasn't very nice," she declared sternly. "Trevor went to a lot of trouble to send you those roses."

"Butt out, Mom," I seethed.

She glared at me with frustration. "What's gotten into you?"

"Nothing," I muttered and escaped to my room before she could say another word.

I couldn't talk openly with her like I used to when I was younger. Ever since I had become a teenager, she would inevitably conjure up some reason to ground me each time I confided in her. I found myself telling her less and less until she barely knew me at all. My mom just didn't understand me anymore.

I sent an instant message to Chris as soon as I flopped down at my desk. To hear from him would have been such a relief. With Chris, I could be myself. I was tired of wearing a mask. Everyone expected me to have it all together. My English teacher had written, '*Well done, Kaitlyn! You have the world at your fingertips!,*' at the top of my poetry assignment that afternoon—a poem I had written out of desperation for my situation with Trevor, hoping she would understand my metaphor. She didn't, and at the current state of my life, I felt like my world was crashing and burning around me.

Eventually, I talked myself into finishing my homework. I constantly checked for an IM response from Chris, to no avail. Around six that evening, I made my way downstairs for dinner. My mom and dad eyed me silently throughout the meal. I made no effort to explain my sullenness. I figured they would never understand anyway.

Later that night, my mom softly knocked at my door. "There's a phone call for you," she said.

Opening the door, I realized I must have left my cell phone sitting on the dinner table.

"Some guy named Chris." She looked at me disapprovingly as she handed me the phone.

"Thanks." I gave her a sheepish smile and shut my door again. "Hello?" I said as I brought the phone to my ear.

"Hey, Kaitlyn."

"Hey, Chris."

"I'm sorry. Did I call at a bad time? I just needed to hear your voice."

"No, it's okay. I'm glad you called." I wondered if he could hear me smile through the phone.

"I'm glad too." His voice cracked; it was the proof I needed that, yes indeed, one can hear a person smile through a phone.

We chatted for several minutes about random, unimportant things before I finally got my nerve up to ask him deeper, more personal questions.

"So, tell me about your family," I inquired.

"Well, for now, it's just my mom, my brother, and me. We do okay. My dad is in prison. He went to prison three years ago for dealing drugs." He supplied no more explanation, and I didn't press the issue.

"I'm sorry," I offered, meekly.

"Oh, it's okay. He was a great dad though. He taught me how to play the guitar; I get my musical ability from him. He once told me in a letter he wrote that when I become a father I will understand why he did what he did. Desperate times call for desperate measures. Sometimes, he had to do things he wasn't proud of just to put food on the table for his family. I have forgiven him for not being here the last three years, though. I know he was just trying to provide for us, but I want a different life. I screwed up with that stupid prank that sent me to jail, but I'm different now. My dad wrote me while I was in juvie and begged me not to make the same mistakes he did. He insisted that I had already started down that same path. I made a promise, from that moment on, to try to do the right thing. Make something of myself. *Man up*. Know what I mean?"

"Uh huh," I said, hypnotized by the sexy, confident tone of his voice.

"Sorry, I'm boring you, aren't I?"

"Not at all. I think it's great that you are trying to do the right thing. I know your dad will be proud of you."

"Thanks. So, tell me about your family."

"They're nothing exciting. My dad travels a lot. He's a top salesman at Nusco International. He travels to different states across the country and is hardly ever home. You'll almost never see him at the games to watch me cheer. It's sad, really. I barely know him."

"Yeah, I know the feeling," Chris expressed sadly.

I continued, "My mom is lonely and depressed. She takes her frustrations out at the gym. Sometimes I feel like she wishes she were married to her Yoga instructor instead. Most nights she's drowning herself in her box wine and losing herself in her racy romance novels. It's pathetic. I mean, we have a good relationship, but sometimes, I feel like she is so out of touch with reality." Wow. It was the first time I had ever spoken so candidly about my parents. Chris just had a way of making me feel safe enough to speak openly. By doing so, I let him burrow himself a little deeper into my personal life.

"I know what you mean," Chris responded. "My mom mostly seems more angry than she is happy. She walks around in her robe all day and insists she can't get a job because of her back pain. She spends most every day catching up on her soaps and watching reruns of Jeopardy. Since dad went to prison, we've been living off of government assistance and disability. There are weeks our meals consist of nothing but instant oriental noodles, but we survive. That's why I want to make it big with my music. I'm tired of struggling with money. I want to get out of this town."

"Me too. That's why I plan to go to college. I don't want to be like my mom, stuck at home, relying on my dad's income. I want to have my own money—my own life. My parents have pressured me relentlessly to apply to college. They know it's my ticket out of here, and I'm ready."

"Me too. Let's go. We got this!"

His fierce passion was contagious. With my tenacious drive and his effervescent enthusiasm, I felt like together we could conquer the world.

"Kaitlyn, I don't know what it is, but there's something about you…some kind of magnetism that draws me to you. It's crazy, but true. Logically, I think we both know we live in two different worlds, running in two different circles. But, somehow, some way, we collided. I don't get it, but it's amazing. *You're* amazing. You have no idea how beautiful you are, and sweet, and…amazing."

"I don't get it either, but I like it. I don't want it to end. Thank you for being there for me. I honestly don't know what I would have done without you Saturday night."

"Speaking of Saturday night," he blurted. "The next time that prick lays a finger on you, I'm obliterating him. That douche bag needs someone to cut him down to size."

"It's okay. I'm done with Trevor."

"Good. Like I told you before, he doesn't deserve you." The sound of his voice felt so refreshing, so reassuring. I could have stayed on the phone all night. What I would have given just to be sitting in his kitchen with him right at that moment. I imagined his brown eyes locked on mine, his comforting arms holding me

close against his warm chest, and his strong, capable hands gently running his fingers through my hair. I took a deep breath and could almost smell the scent of his cologne through the phone. I hated to have to say goodbye.

"I'll see you tomorrow, Kaitlyn," he promised me. "Go get some rest. Remember, I'm here for you if you need me. G'night. Sweet dreams, beautiful."

Sweet dreams indeed. "Thanks, Chris," I whispered. "See you tomorrow." I hung up the phone and sighed, flopping my head back onto my pillow. I just had the most amazing phone call of my life.

It wasn't long before my mom was knocking softly at my door again. "Kaitlyn, can I come in?"

"Sure, mom," I sighed, still delirious from my exhilarating phone call.

She opened the door and tiptoed inside, the floors squeaking beneath her feet. Sitting down at the edge of my bed, she smoothed invisible wrinkles and picked nonexistent lint from my comforter as if she were giving herself time to debate how to begin the conversation. Finally, she clasped her hands in her lap and looked up at me as she spoke. "That Chris…who is that guy? Is he the one all the parents have been talking about? The kid whose dad got busted for selling dope? The kid who just got out of prison himself?"

"Mom," I said, exasperated. "He's not like that, okay. Chris is a good guy. Just misunderstood."

"Kaitlyn," my mom spoke resolutely, "I forbid you to have anything to do with that boy." She wrinkled her nose in disgust, unable to even call him by his name.

"No, mom!" I cried.

"Is that understood, young lady?" She glared at me.

"You don't even know him! That's not fair!"

"I'm sorry, but I'm not having my daughter associating herself with some ex-convict, drug dealer's son. I completely forbid it, Kaitlyn!" My mom stood up, turned on her heel and stomped out the door.

Blinded by my rage and frustration, I lunged at the door and slammed it behind her. Surrendering to my tears, I fell onto my bed. Why did everyone have to be so judgmental? Why couldn't they see Chris for how wonderful he was, rather than for his stupid criminal history? Why did they turn a blind eye to Trevor and the monster he had become? Why couldn't I just tell my mom the truth about Trevor? I already knew the answer to the last question. I would have to admit what a doormat—a weakling—I had let myself become. Besides that, Trevor had everyone completely snowed. I cried myself to sleep yet again that week. I needed those eight hours to escape from reality.

Chapter Thirteen

"You guys wanna go hiking with us this weekend?" Allison asked me at lunch the next day.

"Who? Me and Trevor?"

"Of course!"

"I don't know, Allison," I shrugged as I twisted the cap on my water bottle to open it.

"Awww, come on!" she begged, puckering her lip out with a pout. She looked at me with her innocent doe eyes and sweetly batted her eyelashes.

I firmly shook my head. "Trevor and I are not even on speaking terms right now."

"I know he's not perfect, Kaitlyn. I know he could tone it down in the anger department sometimes, but you and Trevor are meant for each other. I can't even picture you with anyone else. He really does love you. Eric says he talks about you all the time. He even told me that Trevor was crying in the locker room yesterday before practice. I mean, for a guy to cry in front of his friends, you know he's totally whipped. Besides, it will be a lot of fun. We were thinking of taking a picnic lunch and hiking up to see the waterfalls. The weather will be perfect."

Stunned, I nearly let the water bottle slip from my hand. "Wait. He was crying?" I asked, cocking my head to the side and cutting my eyes suspiciously at her.

"Yeah. Eric said all Trevor kept saying was 'I lost her, man. I screwed up! I lost her!' He's got it bad, Kaitlyn."

I couldn't believe it. Trevor was crying over me? My heart pricked a little at the thought of it.

"So, about this weekend? Are you guys in?" Allison asked hopefully.

After the comment Blake made in math class about being *alone*, and my argument with my mom about having no contact whatsoever with Chris, what other choice did I have? Deep down I didn't want to, but I could feel myself caving. You can't just spend two years of your life with someone and walk away that easily. I didn't know *how* to live without him. Hell, I didn't know how to be alone *at all*. Letting go wasn't as simple as it sounded. Why couldn't I just walk away? Trust me, it was a question I'd asked myself more times than I could count. That's the thing about an abusive relationship— it's a vicious cycle that you feel like you can't escape. It's similar to getting toppled by a wave in the ocean and sucked into its strong current. You're tumbling out of control just below the water's surface while you scramble to get your footing. No matter how hard you writhe and kick, you just can't seem to free yourself before your lungs start burning for oxygen. Eventually, you lose the will to fight; it's easier to ride the current than fight against it. I felt myself slipping back into the same old routine of riding the current, and I despised myself for it. "I guess," I said with an exasperated huff.

Allison pumped her fist into the air. "Yes!" she said happily. Within an instant she was texting Eric with excitement. "Trevor will be one happy guy today!" she exclaimed.

I sighed inwardly. *At least one person would be happy today.*

Trevor grabbed me up in a big bear hug as soon as he met me at my locker. "I knew you'd come around," he said. "Kaitlyn, you just made me the happiest guy in the whole school. I love you so much!"

"Remember your promise," I reminded him.

"Scout's honor," he said solemnly. "You are the only girl I want. I promise. I swear I will never lay a hand on you again. You mean too much to me."

Trevor walked me toward my next class with his arm around my waist. I caught a glimpse of Chris standing at the water fountain as we rounded the corner. A look of disappointment immediately spread across his face. I couldn't take my eyes off him as he stared at me with an unexplainable look of— sadness? Hurt? Anger? *Oh, how I wish I could make him understand!*

I knew it had been my choice to take Trevor back, but how could I explain to Chris that I didn't really have any other option? Everything was at stake! The whole school was waiting for me, the captain of the varsity cheerleading squad and All-American girl-next-door, to screw up. I could *not* let my parents down. They had already forbidden me to have anything to do with Chris, and would be disappointed if they found out I disobeyed them. My teachers were all busy writing my letters of recommendation for college. How would I explain to everyone, who wouldn't take the time to understand anyway, why I was hanging out with Chris King, the ex-convict whose dad went to prison for dealing drugs? No, I had no other choice.

Chris held me captive with his stare as I walked toward the classroom door. I held onto his gaze as long as possible imploring him to see my silent explanation. I longed to go talk to him—to beg him to understand. He stood motionless by the water fountain. At that moment, I felt like we were the only two people in the world. Tearing myself away, I reluctantly walked into my Advanced Math class and took my seat. Trevor blew me a kiss as he walked away. My stomach lurched with nausea. *What have I done?*

Later that day, I considered ditching Theatre Arts class. My heart couldn't take seeing Chris again. The only thing that kept me from skipping was the possibility of being able to explain everything to him. I walked into Theatre Arts with my head hung shamefully. I was so afraid to

face him. When I sat down, his seat was empty; I waited anxiously. Chris was laughing when he stepped into the class.

"Later, man!" he called to one of his buddies. Turning his head, he caught a glimpse of me; instantly, his smile faded. Recovering quickly, he coolly took his seat next to me. "'Sup?" he mumbled with a slight nod of his head.

"Hi," I said nervously, feeling totally unsure of myself and scared to look him in the eye.

Leaning back in his seat and claiming his space as usual, he asked, "You okay?"

"I guess," I answered with a shrug of my shoulder. Couldn't he see that I was completely broken inside— existing as a hollow shell of a person, just trying to live my life peacefully?

"Good," he said. A tiny smile reassured me that at least he didn't hate me.

"Chris, are you prepared to sing Sky Masterson's part of *I'll Know* today?" Ms. Carducci asked, putting him on the spot.

"Absolutely, Ms. Carducci!" he affirmed with a wink. Chris sauntered to the front of the room, grabbing a guitar from the corner of the room. He pulled up a stool and plopped down, propping the guitar on his lap.

Looking directly at me, he began his song. His soft tone caressed me like a mink blanket snuggled against my cheek. He sang from the deepest corner of his heart, crooning about knowing when his love came along. His eyes bored holes into mine as he reached deeply into my soul with a longing only I could understand. His voice rang out that he would know the moment he saw her that he had met his true love, and at that moment it seemed all he saw was—**me**.

His words pierced my soul and took away all the pain my heart had suffered. It was in that moment I realized I was falling in love with him, although according to Allison, I wasn't even supposed to know his name.

The class sat silently, awestruck by his impressive baritone. Even Ms. Carducci seemed to be at a loss for words. He just sat on the stool, guitar in hand, and kept his eyes focused on mine as if we were the only two people in the room.

Finally, Ms. Carducci spoke up. "That was fantastic, Chris!" she exclaimed and began clapping her hands.

The rest of the class joined in the applause. I could hear whistles and shouts of 'wow!' and 'awesome!' and 'that rocked!' from several students.

Chris thanked the class and made his way back to his seat. Several girls giggled and blushed as he walked by them. He never even noticed.

Class resumed and I felt sure that Chris felt as lost in thought as I did. I saw him jot something down on a small piece of paper. When the bell rang, he jumped up and tossed the folded paper in my direction and headed out the door. Carefully, I opened it up. It read:

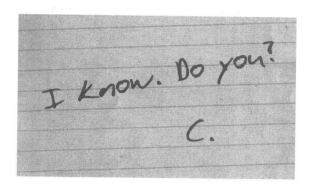

I thought I felt the earth shake around me as my heart violently broke in half. I wasn't sure I would be able to stand up. If I did stand up, I knew my legs would be more shaky than the ground beneath them. I highly doubted I could even make it through the rest of the day. Of course I *knew*! I had known from the moment our eyes met outside by the gym that day! Openly, my tears revealed the truth my heart already knew. Chris and I lived in two different worlds. Two worlds that would never—could never—join together. I folded the paper and stuffed it into the bottom of my shoe. Trevor would never see it hidden there. I was not letting go of the only thing that connected me to Chris King.

I regained my composure knowing that Trevor would be waiting for me after class. I hoped he wouldn't be able to read the pain in my eyes. I took a deep breath when I saw him leaning against my locker. He reached out for me as soon as I got close enough to him. Robotically, I gave him a cold, indifferent hug in return, praying he wouldn't take notice.

"So, are you excited about our hike this weekend?" he asked, oblivious.

"Sure," I deadpanned, refusing to make direct eye contact with him.

"Good! Wear a white T-shirt," he said, grinning from ear to ear.

Raising an eyebrow, I speculated, "Why?"

"Just in case it rains," he smirked. His wink left me repulsed.

Puh-lease. Someone shoot me and put me out of my misery. I just rolled my eyes at him.

"I gotta go to practice. I'll see you later," I grumbled, turning around and practically sprinting for the nearest exit.

Later that evening I got an instant message from Chris.

ChrisRocknrollKing: Y didnt u tell me u decided to take Trevor back?

Cheerchick88: U wouldnt understand

ChrisRocknrollKing: I couldnt help but feel like I was singing that song just 4 u 2day. U have been on my mind all afternoon. U r all I think about anymore.

Cheerchick88: I cant stop thinking about u either

ChrisRocknrollKing: Then why r u still with Trevor?

Cheerchick88: Pls dont be mad. I just cant explain it. If only u knew how I felt! I wish things could be different. I really do.

ChrisRocknrollKing: But they wont be, will they?

Cheerchick88: Wont be what?

ChrisRocknrollKing: Different

Cheerchick88: I guess not

ChrisRocknrollKing: I understand. ☹ So I guess I'll see u at school?

Cheerchick88: Yeah I'll see u in class

ChrisRocknrollKing: 1 more thing. No matter what, never let anyone tell u that u r anything less than AMAZING.

My heart fluttered in my chest after reading his last message. I knew I probably shouldn't even be talking to Chris behind Trevor's back. For some unexplainable reason, I couldn't feel guilty. Between Trevor and me, there was a large gaping hole in our relationship that seemed impossible to repair. All the pain he caused, that I allowed and enabled, drove the wedge deeper and deeper. I became devoid of any emotions. That moment on the retaining wall when I first met Chris with his guitar in hand, there was a magnetic draw so strong, it was difficult to deny or resist. That magnetism managed to dull the pain; it was a tug, more powerful than his music, that closed the gap and replaced that emotional void with sweet, sweet music to my heart. I couldn't explain it. Every moment we spent together, with every passing minute we spent talking, the empty space seemed to disappear. While I should have felt like I was betraying Trevor, I didn't—not after all he'd put me through. The pull Chris had on me was undeniable and a feeling I wasn't sure I could resist much longer.

I ambled around like a zombie the rest of that week. Somehow I made it through each day—each excruciatingly boring class. Seeing Chris during Theatre Arts felt like a new wound driven into my heart each day. We barely spoke, but I felt sure that he could sense my sadness. Our eyes met a few times and it seemed he was just as plagued about the situation as I was—living in two worlds, wanting nothing more than to hold each other and love each other. Mechanically, I made it through every conversation, and every argument with Trevor. Each night, I managed to complete my homework and pick through my food during dinners. Bedtime was always the hardest. Miserably, I tossed and

turned for hours before falling asleep. Sometimes I woke up well before sunrise and stared blankly at the ceiling, unable to fall back to sleep.

Chapter Fourteen

Saturday came more quickly than I had wanted. I dreaded the hike with Allison, Eric, and Trevor the same way I dreaded final exams. I lay in bed a little longer that morning praying for rain and trying to convince myself that I was too sick to go. Finally, with a little prodding from my mother, I dragged myself out of bed and headed for the shower.

"Today is a great day for a hike. The weather is perfect!" Trevor sounded excited as he opened the door of his truck for me. I hopped out and looked at the cloudless sky, the heat of the sun already warming my face.

"Good. I was hoping for good weather today," I lied.

We met Allison and Eric at the trail. Montford Falls was a three mile hike to the top. The waterfalls were gorgeous and worth the trek. From the top, you could see for miles. The mountains in the distance were picturesque against the cool, blue sky.

"You ready?" Allison asked excitedly.

"As ready as I'll ever be," I replied unenthusiastically.

"Awww, come on," she teased, "it'll be fun!"

Trevor grabbed his backpack out of the bed of the truck. "Don't worry," he said. "I'll keep you safe. We've got everything we need right here in this backpack."

The hike was fairly easy. The weather was cool enough that we didn't break a sweat while walking. We took our time and stopped every so often to snap a few pictures. About halfway into it, I actually started to enjoy myself. A little fresh air went a long way for me. We stopped for lunch at a little picnic area by the lower falls. The rushing water thundering down the cliffs was rhythmic…calming. Trevor was such a gentleman the entire time by holding my hand, helping me over rocks, roots and stumps. He kept his arm around me protectively. It was such a relief—comforting even.

We sat at the picnic area for a while, enjoying the scenery. Allison and Eric decided they wanted to branch off from us for a while for a little private time. I didn't mind, as it would have been nice to spend some quiet quality time with Trevor. Maybe that was just what I needed to snap out of it.

"Let's hike to the top," I suggested to Trevor.

"Sounds great!" he said, hopping to his feet.

"I think we'll stay here and enjoy the scenery a little while longer," Allison told us.

"Okay, we'll see you later." I waved as we headed up the trail.

Trevor and I hiked in silence. The silence was refreshing. Most of our conversations turned into arguments anyway. I watched him walk ahead of me. He looked stunningly handsome that day. I realized that I hadn't taken the time to really notice him lately. His muscles tensed under his shirt. His calves were stout and chiseled as he walked. The sun rays bouncing through the trees made his corn silk colored hair glisten in the light. No wonder everyone viewed him as a god. He looked like Adonis.

He stopped walking when we got to a clearing near the top of the waterfalls. "This is a good place to take a break," he said, taking my hand and pulling me to a shady spot off the trail.

"Good," I said. "I'm thirsty."

"Me too," he agreed.

We sat down on a blanket he spread out under a tree. Trevor handed me a water bottle he had pulled from his backpack. "Cheers," he said as he tapped his water bottle against mine and winked at me.

"Cheers," I replied and took several big gulps. The water felt smooth and refreshing as it cooled my throat on its way down. We sat silently for a little while sipping our drinks and listening to the river plunge down the rocks from the falls.

"Kaitlyn," Trevor said, piercing my eyes with his beautiful green irises.

"Yeah?" I asked.

"You are my whole world. I love you more than you know. I know we've had our share of arguments. I know I've not always been the boyfriend I should have been. I'm sorry for that. I just wanted you to know that I'm sorry, and I love you."

Stunned, I stared at him for a few seconds. After all I'd been through the last few weeks, I wasn't really sure how I felt, but I lost myself in that moment. Trevor's charm got the best of me, and I surrendered. "You're right, Trevor," I agreed. "Things have been rough lately. But, the more I try to push you away, the more I see that I can't let you go. I do love you. We've been together too long for me not to love you."

With that remark, Trevor kissed me. I succumbed to the soft and gentle touch of his lips on mine. My heart felt overwhelmed with love and confusion. The feelings I had nearly two years ago resurfaced and I couldn't stop myself from kissing him. I felt the urgency in Trevor's kiss. My desire to be close to him yielded as he pushed me back against the blanket.

I cupped his face in my hands, pulling him toward me while I longed for the intimacy we had lacked the past few months. The love I had for Trevor was unexplainable. After all we'd been through, I knew that love was the very *last* thing I should have felt for him. But, I just couldn't help myself.

Lying on top of me, his kisses intensified. I resigned myself to the warmth of his tongue in my mouth, relishing the delicious swirling heat that rippled its way down my body. He pressed his pelvis firmly against me, thrusting against me with his growing arousal. My body reacted naturally to his, tingling in places I had never given much thought before and aching for an exquisite release. I still knew how far I was willing to let Trevor get—it wasn't as far as I assumed he wanted to go. I felt him tugging at my pants, realizing exactly where he hoped his kisses would lead.

"Trevor," I murmured.

He tugged harder, trying to pry the button on my pants open. I felt the button snap off. He shimmied them down my hips, sliding them completely off and tossing them on the ground behind us. I could hear him unzipping his own khaki cargo shorts. In that moment, I became fully aware of Trevor's intentions, and the determined look in his eyes frightened me.

"Wait, Trevor—"

"Shhhhh," he whispered as he kissed me again, more urgently than before. He thrust his hips deep between my legs pressing himself against me. The only thing separating us was the thin cloth of my underwear.

I tried to wriggle myself away from him. "No. Please stop, Trevor," I begged, suddenly feeling foggy and disoriented.

Seizing my panties and with a single jerk of his hand, he ripped them off and tossed the tattered cloth to the side. I shoved his chest with all of my might, trying to push him off of me; he didn't budge.

"Stop, Trevor! Please, don't do this." I could hear the repulsive, panting sound of his putrid breath in my ear; it was a sound that would forever haunt me. I tried my best to pull away from him, squirming violently beneath him.

No, this can't be happening! Allison! Eric! Oh god, please help me! My mind screamed in agony as the event that was about to take place registered in my mind. *Please god, don't let this happen! Please!* Dizziness began taking over my brain while my body started feeling strange…heavy.

"Kaitlyn, don't," he said. "You know we both want this." He continued to thrust himself toward my most sacred place—the place where no one had gone before. I clenched my legs, trying to keep it away from me, but he forced my legs to open wider by grinding his hips into me, sending me into full panic mode.

"No, Trevor," I pleaded desperately. "I don't wanna…do this…" My mouth had a hard time forming the words, almost as if I had been….*drugged?!*

Pinning my hands above my head, he held himself firmly against me. His breath felt hot against my cheek. "Just relax," he whispered gruffly.

"Trev…please," I slurred, clawing hysterically at his wrists to free his hands from mine. I kicked my legs, trying to wiggle my way out from under him, but the more I kicked the harder he dug his pelvis into me.

My mind floated in and out of consciousness as the drugs that he must have slipped into my water took over my body. *No, no, no!* I thrashed my head from side to side trying to escape the sickening heat of his breath on my neck, which made me feel dizzy and nauseated. I didn't have much energy left in my body. The drugs that ran through my veins made me feel weak and tired.

With my last bit of strength, I desperately tried to free myself from under his weight. Trevor's repulsive kisses on the soft skin on my neck became frenzied and more forceful. *Oh god, please, no!* Frantically writhing beneath him, I tried to alleviate the pressure on my chest; his weight was too much to bear.

"Stop...please...don't..." I willed my mouth to speak one last time as I felt my mind spiraling down into a disoriented blackness. Feeling as though I was losing consciousness, I struggled to breathe. Just before my last breath ran out, I surged forcefully beneath him trying to escape him and to avoid the inevitable, but my efforts were unsuccessful. I felt Trevor's weight on my body as he forced his way into mine. My mind went blank as the drugs finally took over. No longer having any control, I blacked out.

It was cold and dark when I woke up. I bolted up; my eyes tried to adjust to the darkness. *Oh god, where am I?* A sharp, painful memory flashed through my mind. The fog in my brain and the soreness between my legs served as excruciating reminders of the event that had occurred just hours earlier. Shivering, I wrapped the blanket around myself as my eyes tried to adjust to the darkness. The moon was bright above the trees, which helped me see my jeans piled by a tree. Grabbing them, I attempted to get dressed. My legs felt like lead which made it difficult to go through the motions of putting them on. Zipping them up, I remembered the missing button

Trevor had snapped off, and again my mind flashed back to the painful moments prior to me blacking out.

Numbly, I sat back down and surveyed my surroundings while I tried to get my bearings. Tall shadowy trees loomed above me. Crickets chirped an eerie song around me. I could hear the rushing water of the falls through the trees. Alone and scared, I trembled beneath the blanket that I kept wrapped around my shoulders. Panic began to set in. Frozen by fear, I had trouble deciphering what to do next. I didn't think; I just stood up and ran. I ran as fast as I could toward the sound of rushing water. I'm not sure how long it took to run there, but before I knew it I was standing at the top of the waterfall looking down at the crashing water thundering down jagged, slippery rocks. My lungs frantically gasped for air.

Why had my life gotten so complicated? How could I have been so foolish? This was my fault. This was *all* my fault. I was stupid to trust Trevor. Yet again, I let myself believe his lies of apology and love; and, look where it got me! What an *idiot* I had been! How could I have been so stupid? Oh god, I *let* this happen. Heaving sobs stole my breath. My innocence…it's gone! It's gone and I'll never get it back. He ripped it from me, and now I'm just sloppy leftovers that no one will want. Why did I ever agree to come up here with him? What was I thinking? Why did I let myself fall victim to Trevor's lies *again*? He tore my soul in two, and it's partially my fault. I marched right up here to the top of this waterfall, spread out a blanket, and let him yank my innocence away from me like he was stealing candy from a baby.

Tears burned my eyes as I angrily wiped them away. I made it easy for him. I walked right into his arms like he was the Trojan horse, and he defeated me. Part of me died underneath him—a part of me that can never be restored. *I want it back, God. Please! I want it back!* The tears dripped down my cheeks to the dirt below me. What's the use in begging now? What's done is done. Now I'm just some dirty, used piece of someone else's garbage. I loathed the ugly part of me that Trevor left behind—the distraught and irrational part that stood at the edge of a cliff reliving the moments that took place right before I blacked out. Peering down at the crashing, swirling bottomless pit below me, I inched my toes closer to the edge.

Emotionless and empty, I imagined the fall into the dark abyss. It looked so easy. Just one tiny step and I could have made it all go away; the pain would end. No one cared about me. They left me all alone in the woods. Just a few more inches. All I had to do was take…that…last…step.

My phone suddenly began to ring in the pocket of my jeans. Startled, I stumbled backward and landed on a patch of wet moss. I immediately jumped up and fumbled for the phone, flipping it open on the last ring.

"Hello?" I gasped, out of breath.

"Kaitlyn?" The soothing voice on the other end snapped me back into reality.

I took a quick breath. "Chris! Thank God, it's you!"

"Why? What's wrong?" Concern suddenly filled his voice.

I looked around as if I were seeing my surroundings for the first time. "Oh my God, what am I doing? What was I thinking?"

"Jesus, Kaitlyn, what's going on? Where are you?" Chris sounded frantic.

"I'm…uh…I'm at the top of Montford Falls," I took another step back and leaned against a tree, trying desperately to catch my breath. I could feel my heart pounding fiercely in my chest.

"With who?" Chris asked suspiciously.

I hesitated, looking around the shadowy woods that surrounded me, encasing me like a crypt. "I'm by myself." I choked out the words.

"What the hell? It's after nine o'clock and dark as fuck out there. What are you doing up there so late by yourself? Never mind, I'm coming to get you. I can be there in two hours. Stay there. Don't try to walk down in the dark. I'll hike up to you with flashlights. Just promise me you won't move…you won't go anywhere. Please, Kaitlyn!" Chris's soothing voice pleaded with me.

All I could think of was being safe with him again. "Okay, Chris. I…I promise." I stammered.

While I waited, I sat by the tree listening to every sound. I wasn't sure if Trevor or some wild animal was lurking behind a bush waiting for me. The darkness suffocated me while I tried not to move. Two hours felt like an eternity. Crunching leaves caused by approaching footsteps startled me. I froze.

Chris's voice cut through darkness. "Kaitlyn?"

I heaved a sigh of relief. "I'm right here."

He pointed his flashlight toward the sound of my voice. The sudden bright light in my face stung my eyes.

"Oh god, Kaitlyn! I was so scared!"

"Chris—" I started but the sobs choked off the words that wanted to come next. By then Chris had lifted me up off the ground and surrounded me in the warmth of his hug.

"Shhh, baby, you're okay now. It's okay." I nuzzled deeper into his chest and breathed that crisp, clean, familiar scent. I was safe. When my sobs subsided, he pulled away to look at me. Tucking a strand of hair behind my ear, wiping a tear off my cheek, and gently lifting my chin to look me in the eyes, he whispered, "I'm here now. You're safe with me."

Silent tears continued to slide down my cheeks. I looked into his dark brown eyes, nearly black from the darkness that surrounded us. Only the light of the moon illuminated the outline of his face.

"You saved me," I managed to squeak out. "I was so close, and you saved me."

He glanced at the edge of the cliff, watching the water thunder down the rocks with powerful force. An awareness crossed his face as he registered exactly what I was trying to tell him. Staring at me in the darkness, his lip trembled, holding back emotions he dare not release.

He grasped the back of my head and pulled me toward him. Cradling my head against his chest, he whispered, "Oh god, baby, I don't know what I would do if something happened to you. Thank god you're all right." The desperation in his voice sent shivers down my spine as butterflies fluttered in my belly.

"I'm sorry." It's the only thing I could think to say before my eyes glossed over again.

Caressing my hair, he gently kissed the top of my head. "Come on, baby, let's get you out of here, away from this place," he said as he grabbed my hand, intertwining his fingers with mine and pulling me farther away from the dangerous cliff.

Chris held my hand all the way down the trail and back to his car, helping me over rocks, stumps, and exposed tree roots. His black CRX looked almost invisible in the dark parking lot. Empty beer cans lay in the spot where Trevor had parked his truck. I just couldn't understand why Eric and Allison would leave knowing I was still up there.

After I was buckled in and Chris was sitting in the driver's seat, he turned to me. With a look of concern he said, "I don't know exactly what happened, but I think I should take you to the hospital to see a doctor or talk to someone."

"No!" I yelled, a little louder than I had intended.

"But, Kaitlyn—"

"No, Chris! I can't!" I screeched with a terror-stricken voice.

"Kaitlyn, talk to me. What happened?"

"I just…can't. Please, just take me home." I begged. I could never tell anyone what happened with Trevor.

Never.

"Kaitlyn, please."

"No, Chris! Please! If you care for me at all, please just take me home. I just want to go home!" Tears fell down my cheeks and panic filled my mind.

Chris stared at me long enough to make me feel uncomfortable. I felt like anyone who looked at me long enough would be able to see the secret I kept hidden. He sighed. "Okay, Kaitlyn. For you, I will. But, I'm telling you now, it's against my better judgment."

"Thank you. I'll be fine. I swear."

We drove home in silence. I could tell Chris wanted to ask more questions, but didn't. Maybe he knew the truth and was trying to save me from having to explain myself and bring up the painful memories all over again. I appreciated the silence. However, even in the silence, I could feel Chris's comforting presence as his hand found mine in the darkness.

Just as Chris's car pulled into the driveway, my mom stormed out the front door of my house.

"Mom!" I said as I jumped out of the car.

"Just where have you been, young lady? Out gallivanting around with this…this…trouble maker?" She hissed.

"No, mom, I—"

"Get in the house, Kaitlyn! I've been worried about you for hours and all this time you've been with this convicted felon and drug dealer's son!"

"No, mom! It wasn't like that!"

"Mrs. Davenport, I can explain," Chris offered.

"And you," she seethed at Chris. "You get off my property before I call the police."

"Please Mrs. Davenport, if you'll just let me explain—"

"No!" she yelled. "Now get off my property before I have you arrested!"

"Mom, stop!"

"Get in the house, Kaitlyn," she growled.

I looked at Chris apologetically. Shrugging in defeat, he sunk back into the driver's seat of his car and drove away.

"Mother, how could you?"

"Kaitlyn, ever since that boy came into your life you have been a mess. You barely eat. You barely sleep. You have been disrespectful of me and your father. Your grades have been slipping. Everything has gone downhill ever since you met Chris!"

"Mom, if it weren't for Chris," I glared at her furiously, "I wouldn't be standing here right now!"

With that outburst, I turned, ran up to my room, slammed my door, and threw myself onto my bed, clutching my pillow to muffle my sobs.

Chapter Fifteen

I stood in the shower longer than usual the next morning, scrubbing my skin raw under the scalding hot water which did nothing to rinse away the painful memory from the day before, or hell, from the past *two years*. I felt ugly, dirty, and betrayed. No amount of soap and water would wash away the hurt or the pain. I crouched in the shower, letting the water run across my back. Hugging my legs and pressing my forehead onto my knees, I cried. I grieved the wasted two years I'd spent with Trevor. I grieved the loss I knew I could never get back; the hurt he caused would forever leave a blemish on my soul. I cried confused tears that couldn't understand why anyone would do what he did to me, or why my best friend would walk away knowing I was still out there somewhere. I cried aching tears that longed for someone to understand without me having to actually *speak* the truth. I begged to God for the courage to speak out and tell someone. I cried angry tears that wanted to claw the tiles off the wall and sling them across the bathroom to crack that sobbing mess of a reflection in the mirror into a trillion shards of broken glass. The hot water soothed my nerves, washing the tears off my face and down the drain. At that moment, every range of emotions was coursing through my body, and I felt myself collapsing against the fiberglass tub in an exhausted heap. *Let me die. Let me go to sleep and never wake up.* I sobbed until my energy was spent and the water ran cold. The cool blast from the shower head jolted me back to reality.

Climbing out of the shower, I wrapped myself in a towel and flopped down on my bed. I didn't have the energy to move. I didn't have the will to get up, to get dressed, or anything. I just lay there, wallowing in my sorrow long enough for my hair to dry.

A soft knock came at the door. "Kaitlyn, honey, is everything okay?" my mom's muffled voice asked me through the closed door.

"I'm fine, mom."

"I brought you some breakfast," she said sweetly, as if her peace offering would make up for the events that transpired the night before.

I groaned into my pillow. "I'm not hungry."

"You need to eat something."

Food was the last thing on my mind. But, I appreciated my mom for trying to smooth the waters between us. "Okay, I will. Thanks. Just leave it there. I'll get it in a minute when I get dressed."

"Okay, honey. Please try to eat something."

"I will," I promised.

I heard her set down the plate and skitter down the steps. Dragging myself off my bed, I got dressed in some pink pajama pants and a plain white tank top. I knew I didn't want to leave my room, much less the house, so my lounge clothes seemed like the best option. Opening the door, I found a steaming hot plate of scrambled eggs, grits, and bacon. The smell invaded my nostrils, and immediately my stomach growled. The last time I had eaten anything had been lunch the day before.

Closing my door again, I sat in my chair and balanced the plate on my knees. I grabbed a slice of bacon and took a bite. My ravenous stomach eagerly welcomed the morsel, and I quickly realized how starved I truly felt. After devouring the rest of it, I sat the empty plate on the floor. There was only enough room on my desk for my desktop computer. I logged into instant messenger, and the familiar sound of the creaking door alerted me that several of my friends were logging on as well.

Sk8erboi04: Hey Kaitlyn

FirstFlutegirl87: Girlfriend, what's up?

GoBulldogs42: Yo Katydid! How u doin girl?

Ugh. I don't know what I was thinking…mere habit I guess. Maybe it was a desperate attempt for some type of normalcy, but I just wasn't in the mood. The thought of trying to carry on a conversation with anyone churned my stomach. Just before I logged off, a familiar screen name popped up.

ChrisRocknRollKing: Hey, u there?

I stared at the blinking cursor in the reply box, debating my next move. I just wanted to crawl back into bed and forget the world. Finally, I let my fingers begin typing.

Cheerchick88: I'm here

ChrisRocknRollKing: u ok?

Cheerchick88: not really

ChrisRocknRollKing: I'm sorry

Cheerchick88: not your fault

ChrisRocknRollKing: I know. I just hate you're having a rough day

'Rough day' was the understatement of the decade, but I couldn't blame him. He had no idea.

Cheerchick88: Sorry about my mom last night.

ChrisRocknRollKing: I don't blame her. She just doesn't understand. She's trying to protect you. I get that. I wish she would give me a chance. But it's all good. I understand.

My eyes brimmed with tears. He was right. She didn't understand. No one understood.

Cheerchick88: I wish things were different

ChrisRocknRollKing: Me too

Cheerchick88: Thanks for being there for me when I needed you

ChrisRocknRollKing: I will always be here for you when you need me

I needed him more than I was willing to admit to myself or anyone else. I needed someone to erase my pain. I needed the hurt from the day before to be eliminated by his—or anyone's—reassuring hug. I wished I was younger again, when I was still small enough to climb into my mom's lap. I missed that comforting feeling of being safe in my mom's arms.

Cheerchick88: Thank you. I needed to hear that.

ChrisRocknRollKing: I mean every word

Cheerchick88: I appreciate it. I'm gonna go lay down. Not feeling well. Ttyl

ChrisRocknRollKing: Ok, hope u feel better soon.

Cheerchick88: me 2

I logged out and sat back in my chair. Covering my face with my hands, I sucked in a deep, staggering breath. I wasn't sure I could face the world at school the next day. I wasn't ready. The thought of coming face to face with Trevor nearly launched me into a full blown panic attack. I clambered for my bed—my safety net. Hiding beneath the blankets, I tried to make myself invisible. Curling up into a tiny ball, I cried myself to sleep, hoping I would wake up to a new reality instead of the horrific nightmare that had become my life.

My mom continued to check on me throughout the day, bringing me food and checking my head for fever. Lying to her, I told her I thought I might have a stomach virus. I guess it wasn't technically lying; my stomach really was tied in knots over the impending school day. I didn't log into instant messenger again the rest of the day. I just couldn't bear the thought of having to pretend I was fine, when really I just wanted to disappear.

After hours of praying for a new day, the sun finally set, and I welcomed the glow of the starry "night sky" stickers of my ceiling. Memories of my friendship with Renae and our time of innocence, when we used to sit up all night eating ice cream and talking about kissing boys, crept into my mind. For once that day, I felt a fleeting smile cross my face.

The next morning, my clock radio alarm woke me up with the song *My Immortal* by Evanescence. I threw a pillow at it to try to shut it off. It was the last song I needed the radio deejay to play that morning. Unfortunately my pillow just knocked the radio off my bedside table onto the carpet below, but the song kept playing. The lyrics infiltrated my mind; lyrics about unyielding pain and haunted dreams crept their way into my soul and bubbled the ache of my own affliction to the surface. I just couldn't face my demons that day. I curled myself up tighter under my blankets and prayed my mother wouldn't notice my absence from the breakfast table.

Within minutes, the soft knock at the door told me my prayers didn't work. "Kaitlyn, are you okay?"

"No, mom. I don't think I'll be able to make it to school today. Stomach bug kept me up all night," I lied.

I had never skipped school before, so my mother would never suspect my lies. She opened the door and poked her head in. "All right, honey. I've got some errands to run today. I'm taking Grandma to the doctor. I hope you feel better. I'll bring you some chicken soup for lunch."

"Thanks, mom."

My mother disappeared and I clutched my pillow to my chest. The pit of my stomach felt like it held a lead cannon ball that weighed me down, pressing me to the bed and suffocating me amongst the pillows and blankets. A few minutes later, mom reappeared with a package of plain white salted crackers and a glass of ginger ale. "I hope you can keep this down," she said, laying the items on my desk. "Take little bites and small sips."

"I will. Thank you," I whispered.

"I love you, Kaitlyn. You know that?" She looked at me as if she wanted to say more, but refrained.

"I know, Mom. I love you too." I cracked a tiny reassuring smile.

"Okay then. I'll see you later." She patted my head gently and walked out the door.

I nestled into my pillows. I knew I couldn't sleep all day. Eventually I had to face reality, but just not that day. I grabbed my diary and wrote furiously until my hand ached, spilling into it my innermost secrets.

Oddly enough, I didn't feel as sad as I thought I might. Instead, I was angry. I hated Trevor for what he did. I hated him more than I had hated anyone before. I was ashamed that I let him treat me like a prisoner until it was too late. He stole a sacred part of me, and instead of cowering like the willing victim I had let myself become over the last two years, it lit a burning rage in me I didn't even know existed. His gruesome act only fueled my fury, and I knew I would no longer succumb to him or any other guy who treated me less than what I deserved.

By the afternoon, my mom had brought me the chicken soup, which I devoured. She was happy to see me feeling well enough to eat. She checked on me once again that afternoon to refill my ginger ale and was glad to see I'd taken a shower, gotten dressed, and had even applied some make-up. I told her I was feeling better, and to be honest, I really was. I knew I would never fully recover from the unspeakable act Trevor put me through, but I also knew a part of me felt more empowered than I ever had before. I was no longer going to be his victim. I was no longer going to allow myself to be a pawn in Trevor's little game of manipulation. My hurt and anger spawned confidence that I wouldn't have felt otherwise.

My curiosity got the best of me, and I logged into my instant messenger. Three messages popped up immediately. One message was from Allison. It simply read, 'Where are you?' I didn't respond. I just couldn't. I didn't even know how I would face her the next day.

The second message was from Trevor. 'Why are you not at school?' *Are you kidding me?* What an asshole. I didn't know who he thought he was, but I had words for him that had been reeling in my mind for two days. *Fuck him!*

The third message was from Chris. 'I went to school today and searched for you but you weren't there, so I skipped out. Are you okay?'

I looked, and he was online.

ChrisRocknRollKing: Thank god you just logged in. I was about one second away from driving to your house!

Cheerchick88: I'm here. Thanks for checking on me

ChrisRocknRollKing: I was worried

Cheerchick88: I know. I'm sorry. I just couldn't go to school today

ChrisRocknRollKing: What happened?

Cheerchick88: Stomach bug

ChrisRocknRollKing: I'm calling bullshit, but I understand if u don't wanna tell me

Cheerchick88: I'll be back tomorrow

ChrisRocknRollKing: Good ☺ See you then

Cheerchick88: See ya later

I logged out of instant messenger and shut down my computer, realizing I needed to get out of the house. I needed to get out of my bedroom before I completely shut down or lost my mind. I told my mom that I felt much better and had totally recuperated. I insisted that I needed to get out of the house for some fresh air. She eyed me suspiciously, but granted me permission to leave.

I drove to Chris's house later that evening. I didn't know what he would think, or how he would react. Honestly, I didn't even know what I would say. But at that moment, he was the only person I felt safe enough with to talk to. I couldn't be sure that I would even tell him about what happened. I didn't even want to think about it, much less discuss it. But I just needed to hang out with someone for a little while. Maybe hanging out with him would help get the past weekend off my mind.

He was sitting on the front porch playing his guitar when I drove up. As soon as he saw my car pull into the driveway, he laid his guitar down and rushed over to open my car door. Gently, he pulled me out of the driver's seat and hugged me. His little brother, who looked to be about ten years old, watched us while he dribbled a basketball under the goal in his driveway.

"Hey," his brother said, throwing a hand up to wave at me. I waved back, smiling through my tears.

Chris pulled back to look me in the eyes. "I was worried I would never see you outside of school again," he whispered.

"I just needed to see you. I just wanted to talk," I admitted.

He hugged me tighter and wiped tears from my bloodshot eyes. "Wanna go inside and hang out?"

"Sure."

He held me by the hand, led me into his house, and up the stairs to his bedroom. "Sorry. This is about the only private room in the house."

I looked around his room. Posters of musicians and famous bands hung on the walls. In one corner, a keyboard stood on a stand. Clothes and magazines littered his bedroom floor. His bed was unmade and the blankets were hanging crooked off the bed. Sheet music lay cluttered on his desk. "It's okay. It's perfect," I said.

"Sorry," he apologized again as he tried to straighten his room a little.

"Really, it's okay…don't worry about it," I told him as I settled down on one corner of his bed.

"All right," he said as he plopped down on the bed beside me, "what did you want to talk to me about?"

"Nothing specific. I just wanted to chill here for a while. I just needed to get out of my house."

"Okay," he said, dragging out the word, suspicious of my cryptic explanation.

Tears immediately filled my eyes. Regret filled my chest. Maybe I'd already said too much.

Chris brushed a strand of hair from my face. "Go ahead. You can talk to me if you think it will help you."

"Well…" My voice trailed. *Shit.* I couldn't do it.

"Please, baby, talk to me," Chris urged. He wrapped his arm around my shoulders. I flinched. Being alone in his bedroom with him, especially after knowing what he and any other male was capable of, I had a fleeting terror-stricken moment of panic. The look on my face must have given me away because Chris's concerned look on his face said it all. "What's the matter? Did I do something wrong?"

"No." I tried to keep my cool, but inside I was freaking the hell out. I needed air, space away from a man's touch. I couldn't take the suffocating feeling. "I need to get out here. I'm sorry." I jumped up off the bed and reached for the doorknob.

"Wait, Kaitlyn. Please, talk to me. What's going on?"

"Nothing. I just need to go. I'm sorry." I jerked open the door. The weight on my chest felt so heavy I could barely breathe. Hyperventilating, I bounded down the stairs, two at a time. Chris was hot on my trail.

"Kaitlyn, stop. I'm sorry, okay? I won't make you talk. I won't even touch you. Just please, don't go..." His voice trailed off to nearly a whisper, "I won't hurt you."

I stopped dead in my tracks. Why was I running? Who was I running from? It shouldn't have been Chris. Chris wasn't Trevor. He was nothing like Trevor at all. He was right. He wouldn't hurt me. *Right?* Chris was not the enemy. If anything, he rescued me. He was there for me on more than one occasion. He saved me from myself. He showed me what love could be, *should* be. Slowly, I turned around to face him.

"Baby, please." He looked solemnly at me. His glassy eyes held emotions I couldn't decipher as he quietly whispered, "I'm not *him.*"

A large lump settled in my throat. I could feel two years' worth of pent up hurt and anger launching their way up from the dark pit that I had stuffed them down into. A sound escaped my throat, a guttural growl so deep I didn't even recognize my own voice.

I ran at him, pounding my fists so hard into his chest it should have knocked the wind out of him, but he wrapped his arms around me. He held me close to him, consoling me while I sobbed and pounded my hurt and anger into his solid chest like a punching bag.

The whole time I walloped him, he hugged me and repeated, "Let it out, baby. Let it all out," while he cradled the back of my head against his chest. He held me until my sobs subsided. "It's okay," he reassured me once my wailing cries turned into muffled snubs against his soaking wet shirt. Snubs were the kind of heaving breaths you take after a hard cry; those uncontrollable gasps of air that come like hiccups when you're all cried out.

Kissing me gently on top of my head, he whispered under his breath, "God, Kaitlyn, what did he do to you?" He wasn't searching for an answer; he was just bewildered by my outburst.

I didn't look up. I couldn't look into his eyes. I just clung to him, surprising even myself with my response. "Trevor stole from me the one thing I held most sacred; something I can never get back. He took my virginity. He…he raped me." Chris didn't flinch. He didn't move as the last part came out in a quiet whisper—but it clicked. I heard him suck in a breath and hold it. With my ear against his chest, I could hear his heart pounding, fast and furious. Cautiously, I peeked up at him. His eyes were wide with shock.

"Oh no! Oh god, baby, I'm so sorry," Chris encapsulated me in his arms, holding me, rocking me back and forth, clutching the back of my head to his body. "That bastard," he growled through his teeth.

"I'm okay, Chris. I'll be okay…really," I tried to lie.

"Kaitlyn, please, you need to tell someone. You can't keep this a secret. What if he hurts you again? What if he hurts someone else?"

I hadn't thought of that…but, no, I wasn't ready to tell anyone else yet. I just shook my head. Chris hugged me with understanding. My secret was safe with him for the moment.

Chris held my hand as he walked me to my car later that evening. "Promise me you'll call me if you need me, for anything. Even if it's just to talk," Chris looked at me with pleading eyes.

"I promise," I told him.

He hugged me one last time as he opened the door for me. His longing eyes held mine for a few seconds before he pushed the door shut.

I drove away feeling a pressure on my chest that I couldn't explain. I hoped my parents were in bed when I got home, and thankfully they were. Tiptoeing upstairs to my bedroom, I crashed on my bed where my nightmares were filled with waterfalls and sinister green eyes.

I awoke the next morning still wearing the clothes I had worn the day before. I dreaded having to face everyone at school that day, especially Allison. I just couldn't understand why she left me in the woods that day.

My eyes were glued to the floor in front of me as I made my way to my locker that morning. Having worn my hoodie that morning, I hid my face as deep into the hood as possible. Breathing a sigh of relief when I finally made it to my locker, I heard an angry voice from a few lockers down.

"Where were you?" The high-pitched voice asked accusingly.

I turned to look at Allison. "Where was I?" I asked, shocked. "The real question is, where were *you*?"

"Trevor told me what happened. He said you guys got into an argument and you took off down through the woods. We spent an hour or more searching for you! What did you do? Run off and hitch a ride with that loser, Chris?" Allison rolled her eyes in disgust. "And, by the way," she added, "thanks for ruining my afternoon." Allison glared at me angrily.

I just stared back at her, appalled, unsure of what to say. Moments later, Eva came up to Allison and threw her arm around Allison.

"Come on, bestie." Eva smirked at me as she turned to lead Allison down the hallway.

"Unbelievable," I mumbled under my breath as tears pooled in my eyes. Angrily, I wiped them away and stormed off to my first class, praying for a miracle to make me invisible.

When the lunch bell rang, I reluctantly made my way toward the cafeteria. I had been able to avoid Trevor all day, ducking into classrooms and sneaking into the bathroom when I would see him coming down the hallway. Lunch was a different story though. I knew, without a doubt, that I would have to face him. *Oh god, help me through this.* I scanned the crowd. His face didn't jump out at me, thank god. Hopefully, I could just get through the line and hide in a far corner of the cafeteria until lunch was over. I ambled my way toward the cafeteria, hoping to avoid the rush of the crowd. Just as I rounded the corner, a set of hands grabbed my shoulders, spun me around, and slammed me into the brick wall. Menacing hazel eyes glared at me from above. *Shit!* Sheer terror shot through my body like a bolt a lightning.

"Trevor." My breath caught in my throat.

"I've been looking for you," he snarled.

"I...I—" Fear hijacked my voice.

Trevor loosened his grip. I glanced left and right, praying someone would walk by and see us. However, with my dawdling, the tardy bell had rung and all the students were either in their classrooms or in the cafeteria. No one lingered in the hallway.

Trevor leaned his head down to whisper in my ear. The sickening heat of his breath caused my mind to flash back to the last time I had felt it against my cheek. My stomach lurched with the thought of it. "Kaitlyn, don't try to avoid me. You can't escape me."

I closed my eyes and swallowed back the bile that threatened the back of my throat. Suddenly, without warning, I felt Trevor's hands being ripped from my shoulders and the sound of the wind being knocked out of him. Trevor grunted as his body was slammed into the wall next to me.

"Get your hands off her, asshole," Chris glowered, staring him down like a bull ready to charge.

"Fuck you," Trevor growled, spitting his words in Chris's face.

"Don't move, motherfucker. Don't you fucking move one inch or I'll slice your jugular faster than you can take your last breath."

Something flashed out of the corner of my eye. Chris held the sharp blade of his knife taut against Trevor's throat. *Oh shit!*

Glancing at me, Chris hissed, "Get out of here, Kaitlyn."

I struggled to breathe, let alone move.

"Go. Now." he urged.

I didn't think. I just panicked and ran. My legs felt like jelly as I clambered to escape the moment. Just as I rounded the corner, a small group of students walked by me. Their chatter echoed past me, completely unaware of the event taking place just a mere few feet away. I tried to command my voice to speak, to warn them, or to beg for help, but it refused. Panic and fear held me captive within myself.

I ran into the cafeteria and sank into a chair, breathing a sigh of relief. I should have said something. I should have done more. I laid my head on the table, trying to collect myself when I heard a loud ruckus just beyond the doors of the cafeteria.

"Fight! FIGHT!" I heard some students yell. Several people jumped up from their table to see the commotion.

Allison yelled at me from the doorway. "Kaitlyn! It's Trevor and Chris!"

Automatically, I jumped up and ran out the door. Sure enough, Chris had tackled Trevor and was punching him repeatedly. I saw the knife lying beside them, just out of Chris's reach. "Chris!" I screamed frantically.

"C'mon, punk! Whatcha gonna do about it? You think you can lay your hands on a girl? Well, let me teach you a little something, asshole." Venomous words spewed from Chris's clenched teeth as he continued to thrash wildly.

Coach Harrison ran through the door and broke through the crowd. With the help of Mr. Abernathy, the history teacher, they pulled Chris off of Trevor who had blood dripping from his nose and lips.

A long string of profanities erupted from both boys' mouths as the two teachers dragged Chris down the hallway to the principal's office. Mrs. Lowman grabbed Chris's knife, and Mrs. Yount helped Trevor up off the floor, guiding him down the hall toward the nurse's office.

Panic overwhelmed me as I realized what was happening. It would only be a matter of time before

Chris would be sent back to juvie. The principal had already threatened Chris that one infraction would land him right back at Fairbanks. Possession of a knife on school property, along with the fight with Trevor, would probably mean he'd finish up the year there. I loathed Trevor for being the center of the whole mess.

"Great," one of the football players said sarcastically. "There goes the game Friday night."

A few others grumbled around him. The crowd dissolved, and I stood there motionless.

"Kaitlyn, you okay?" a familiar voice asked.

I turned to see Arnold standing behind me. "Yeah," I whispered.

"Well personally, I'm glad Trevor got his butt kicked. He deserved it." Arnold winked at me before he turned to walk away.

"Yeah," I repeated, still in shock.

Chapter Sixteen

Later that night I got an instant message from Chris.

ChrisRocknrollKing: They're sending me back

Cheerchick88: I figured they would :(

ChrisRocknrollKing: U are worth it. That punk needed 2 b brought down a notch or 2. He thinks he owns this world and every1 in it but Ive got news 4 him

Cheerchick88: Thanks 4 standing up 4 me. I just wish it didnt mean that u have to leave

ChrisRocknrollKing: I know and I'm sorry

Cheerchick88: When do u leave?

ChrisRocknrollKing: In the morning :(

Sighing, I fought back the rush of tears.

Cheerchick88: Ok :(

ChrisRocknrollKing: I have to see u 2night

Cheerchick88: idk

ChrisRocknrollKing: Pls sneak out and come see me. I just want to see u…2 spend time with u before I have 2 leave. Im begging…pls Kaitlyn

I debated the idea. The thought of being alone with him, while the rest of the world slept, made me a little apprehensive. Part of me wasn't ready to be alone with any guy, but Chris was leaving. I didn't know if or when I'd get to see him again. I couldn't let him be shipped off without saying goodbye. After all, he did save my life. I felt strong feelings for him that left me exhilarated and heartbroken at the same time. I needed to say goodbye. I knew I had to see him.

Cheerchick88: Ok. I will find a way

ChrisRocknrollKing: Thank you. Call my cell when u get here. And be careful!

Cheerchick88: Ok. It will be @11:30pm

ChrisRocknrollKing: I'll b waiting ;)

Everything got quiet downstairs as I waited nervously for my parents to go to bed. I had left a note on my pillow just in case my mom came in to check on me and found me missing.

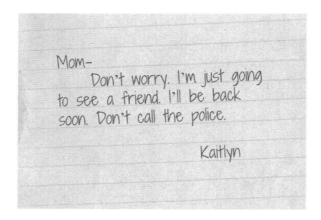

Mom—
Don't worry. I'm just going to see a friend. I'll be back soon. Don't call the police.

Kaitlyn

The last thing I needed was for the police to track me down at Chris's house.

When I felt certain my parents were asleep, I crept downstairs, through the kitchen, and out the back door. Quietly, I got in my car, but I didn't shut the door for fear it would be too loud. I shifted my car into neutral and let it roll backwards down the driveway. A car in neutral was much harder to steer, but I steered it enough that I could coast down the hill a little ways from my house before starting the engine and slamming the door shut. My plan had worked out perfectly. I was on my way to see Chris! Waves of adrenaline and excitement pulsed through my arteries, and my heart slammed in my chest.

When I had gotten close to Chris's driveway I called his cell. He picked up on the first ring. "I'm already outside waiting," he admitted. He was at my car door almost as soon as I pulled into his driveway. With an eager grin, he opened the car door and pulled me to my feet. "Thank you for coming," he whispered. He held me in his arms for several seconds.

Waves of passion tore through my body as he pulled me closer; a frightening feeling welled up inside me. A panic attack threatened me, similar to that same moment of terror I felt when he had wrapped his arm around me the day before. I took a deep breath to try to control my pounding heart and inhaled his familiar spine-tingling musky scent that immediately calmed my nerves. I remembered the conversation we'd had—the meltdown where I pounded the shit out of his chest and he just held onto me, comforting me and allowing me my moment of rage. *He won't hurt me,* I reminded myself.

"Come on," he whispered, as he pulled me away from my car. "I've got somewhere to take you."

He shuffled me through the darkness and into an open field behind his house. The moon shone brilliantly across the grass. The gentle breeze swayed the tall grass back and forth while the wind whistled through the trees lining the field. Twinkling stars flickered like tiny lightning bugs in the night sky. Crickets chirped and frogs croaked in the darkness. The gray-blue mountains in the distance served as a picturesque backdrop.

"I come out here at night sometimes when I can't sleep," he explained, "or when I need to think."

"Wow," I whispered. "It's beautiful."

"Will you dance with me?" he asked me quietly.

"But, there's no music," I said.

"Don't worry. We don't need any." He turned and held his hands out to me.

I surrendered easily and let him surround me in his arms. We swayed in silence. He held me close to his body and gently placed his hand on the small of my back. My breath caught in my throat as the intense feeling of wanting to kiss him surged through my body. Somewhere deep inside me, the capsule of fear threatened to burst again. It forewarned me that it would detonate a nuclear bomb of panic, leaving a mushroom cloud of regretted words and broken spirits. I tried my best to release the valve on the expanding balloon of anxiety, while at the same time, I melted from the passion that smoldered in his dark, penetrating eyes.

"Look, Chris, I'll go to the principal. I'll tell him everything. I'll tell him you were just trying to protect me. I'll—"

"No," he interrupted me. "I can't let you do that. I won't. You've been through enough already. Like you said, Trevor and his family have this whole damn town in their back pockets. In case you haven't noticed, me and the good ole boy network just don't mix. You do *not* need to get wrapped up in these shady small town politics. It would only end up hurting you more in the long run. Besides, I would have done the same thing a thousand times over if it meant I was protecting you. You are worth it…" his voice trailed off as he pulled me closer and gently kissed the top of my head.

I felt the wind gently blowing around us. Softly, he began to sing. I recognized Garth Brooks' *The Dance* immediately. The words he sang made me realize how thankful I was to have met him. Even though the thought of being ripped apart was absolutely devastating, having the chance to fall in love with him was worth it in the end. Staring at his face, I memorized every feature, every crease, and every dimple. I listened to the sweet timbre of his voice as he sang to me from what I could only imagine as the deepest depths of his soul. Tears glistened in his eyes and threatened to fall, conveying unspeakable emotions. I was losing him. He was leaving, and I was *losing* him. I squeezed him tighter as if I would never let go, and he wrapped his arms more firmly around my body. I could have stayed there in his arms all night. I breathed in the wonderful aroma of him—fresh, woodsy, and masculine. He sighed with a deep, staggering exhale as he pressed himself even closer to me.

His breath was hot on my lips. I could almost feel the electric pulses of sexual tension that radiated between our bodies. Confusion permeated my heart. I had feelings for Chris I couldn't explain, yet at the same time I felt ugly inside. My natural reaction to the feelings I had for Chris didn't feel natural at all; thanks to Trevor, they felt dirty. I tried to console myself. *This isn't wrong. This isn't bad. He's not going to hurt me.* Tenderly, he brought his lips to mine. The supple, yet intense passion of his kiss spread a blanket of warmth throughout my body. I gently kissed him back. The desperate yearning between us gave way as we held tighter to each other and moved our lips in rhythm. The soft sensation of his velvet tongue on mine sent shivers down my spine. I held onto the feeling of his body against mine and the taste of his gentle kiss as long as he would let me. He pulled away, leaving me breathless.

"Kaitlyn, I've never felt this way before. I've tried to put you out of my mind from the minute I first saw you. I knew you were so far out of my league. I knew there was no chance that a guy like me would ever have a chance to be with a girl like you. The more I spend time with you the more I realize that I can't help falling for you. I know we could never be together—not the way we want to be. I'm not dumb. I know what people say about me…and about you. I know that there is never going to be a chance for 'us.' I just want you to know that you are the most amazing girl I have ever met. I have fallen hard for you despite my efforts not to. Even if I never have the chance to be with you like I want to, at least I can say that I gave it my best shot. Just know that you will always hold a special place in my heart. Always."

My tears slid silently down my cheeks. They fell because I knew he was right, but I didn't want him to be right. I wanted to curl up into his arms and never let go. I wanted to have the freedom to fall in love with the guy standing right in front of me without the fear of judgment. I was tired of pretending that I didn't have feelings for him—that I couldn't love him. I just wished that everyone would give him the chance that he deserved and would stop being so judgmental. Chris was everything I wanted—*needed*. The thought of walking away from him at the end of the night knowing that we could never be "we" was enough to cause me to hyperventilate under the implosion of my heart. My sobs heaved as I buried myself in his chest.

"Shhhhh, baby," Chris said, pulling me tighter against him. "Please don't cry. I didn't say all that to make you cry. I just needed you to know how I felt."

"Chris, when I am with you, I can be myself. You have made me realize how love could be—*should* be. You saved me in more ways than one. I can't thank you enough for that."

He stared deeply into my tear-filled eyes. "I love you, Kaitlyn." He didn't wait for a response. I don't think he expected one. Instead, he gently kissed me again. That time his kiss felt sorrowful. I could taste the tears that fell from my eyes and felt the emotion that heaved from his chest as he swallowed the lump that must have been forming in his throat. We stood there in the moonlight holding each other, wishing things could be different between us. "I have had the most amazing night," Chris said as he walked me to my car and held my car door open for me.

"Me too," I smiled.

"Just know that no matter what happens, I will always love you. I mean that with every fiber of my being. You will always hold my heart. *Always*," his voice cracked as a single tear escaped his eye and slid down his cheek.

I knew that feeling he was describing—that overwhelming feeling of emotion you could feel in every atom of your body; I felt it, too. *Why can't I say it?* Instead, I whispered, "Chris, no matter what happens, I will never forget you." My heart shattered as I said those words because I knew, without a shadow of a doubt, I meant them…and *more*.

I slunk down into the seat of my car. He shut my car door, watching me through the window as I buckled my seatbelt and started the engine. His eyes were glassy, and his lip trembled. He touched my window, holding his palm firmly against it. I placed my hand against his. The thin sheet of glass that separated us felt like a metaphor for our lives. 'I love you,' he mouthed the words. *Oh god I can't do this! I can't leave him. I just found him. I can't let him go!* But, I had to. I blew him a kiss through the window just as another tear slid down my cheek. *Goodbye, Chris.* Reluctantly, he turned around and trudged back toward his front porch. Sadly, I watched him walk up the steps and out of my life.

Driving away in tears, I felt as though I had left the key to my *soul* sitting in Chris's driveway.

Chapter Seventeen

Three months later

The days passed slowly; it had been nearly three months. I still desperately yearned for Chris, but I hadn't heard from him. I began to give up hope that I would ever see him or speak to him again. I barely managed to make it through each day. So many things had changed since Chris left for juvie again. I avoided Trevor at all costs. He had set his sights on Eva, so he barely even looked at me anymore. The other cheerleaders managed to alienate me. Thankfully, the season had ended so we didn't have to see each other every day at practice. They avoided me like the plague and glared at me like I was the enemy. Everyone believed Trevor's lies. Either that, or they were too afraid that not believing him would send them straight to the bottom of social hierarchy. I rarely got phone calls on the weekends, so I spent most of my time working on homework and studying. My parents were happy that my grades were going up. At home, I could feel the division between my mother and me. She and I had barely spoken to each other since our last argument about Chris. I had never felt so alone in my life. My depression overcame me. I numbly went through the motions of my life.

The school was buzzing with excitement about our annual Winter Formal. Flyers lined the hallway. Girls chatted about their new dresses. Guys bragged about the car their dad, uncle, or grandfather was going to let them drive. I could really care less. All I knew was that Trevor was going to the dance with Eva and I would try, at all costs, to avoid them both. I wasn't sure I even wanted to go at all, especially since I would be going alone.

One Saturday afternoon, my mom begged to take me dress shopping. Since I had hoped to iron out the wrinkles in our relationship, I agreed to go. She seemed excited. I was just happy to not have to spend another Saturday alone. We spent nearly two hours looking at dresses until I finally found the perfect one. Not too flashy, it was a strapless, T-length red dress with a simple red silk ribbon just below the bust line. A single diamond-like stone sparkled in the center of the ribbon—perfect. I felt like Audrey Hepburn in that dress. The Winter Formal seemed to get a little more exciting that day.

I sat quietly on my bed the night of the formal. I debated with myself on whether or not to go. I dreaded going alone. While I knew I would not be the only single person there, it still didn't make it any easier. Just then, my dad softly knocked at my door.

"Come in," I squeaked, sounding like a hopeless cause.

"Sweetheart, you look stunning!" my dad beamed as he opened my door.

"Thanks, Dad," I glanced down, embarrassed, and nervously smoothed out invisible wrinkles on my dress. "I'm not even sure I plan to go." I continued looking shamefully at the floor, feeling defeated.

"Listen, Kaitlyn," my dad began as he sat down on the bed beside me, "I know these last few months have been hard on you. But, it's like I've always told you, sometimes you gotta pick yourself up by your boot straps and keep going. Now, you get out there, hold your head high, and enjoy your senior formal. You only get this opportunity once in your life."

I glanced up at him glaring down at me like a young child being scolded for sneaking cookies from the cookie jar. "I know, Dad, but—"

"But nothing, young lady," he interrupted. "Here are the keys to the Mercedes," he said as he handed me the silver keychain with a smile. "Take care of her. Now, get out there and have a great time."

"Okay," I nodded meekly, but tried to sound enthusiastic as he pulled me to my feet. "Thanks, Dad," I said as I gave him a quick peck on the cheek and headed down the stairs. My dad never let anyone ever drive his pride and joy, so having the keys to his Mercedes in my hand was a real treat.

Parked outside the building, I took a few deep breaths. The Formal was almost over. I had timed it perfectly. "Okay, Kaitlyn, you can do this," I told myself. Hesitantly, I stepped out of the car and watched as a group of couples whirled past me in a rainbow of colors. "Just a few minutes…you can handle just a few minutes," I tried to convince myself. I fumbled with the keys and slipped them into my handbag while I walked anxiously toward the door.

The music was thumping and voices were buzzing as I stepped into the room. A sea of colors bounced and flashed in the center of the room on the dance floor. I took a minute to survey the room. A few students mingled near the buffet table, munching on finger foods; they seemed lost in conversations. I spotted Allison and Eric in the middle of the dance floor. I made a beeline toward the food table in an effort to avoid them. Pouring myself some punch, I tried to blend into the crowd. Just then, the music slowed and more couples started gathering on the dance floor. I thought I was successfully camouflaging myself among the tacky decorations and streamers when someone tapped me on the shoulder.

"Would you like to dance?"

I turned around to see a tall and lanky, blue eyed, blond haired guy staring at me.

"Hi," he said shyly. "I'm Michael."

"I'm Kaitlyn."

"Nice to meet you." He stuck his hand out awkwardly. *Really? Teenagers don't shake hands, do they? Kinda dorky, but I'll go with it.* I reached out to shake it.

"Nice to meet you, too," I said with a chuckle.

"About that dance, would you do me the honor?"

Apathetically shrugging my shoulders, I responded with, "Sure. Why not?"

Michael led me out onto the dance floor. The disco ball cast millions of twinkling lights across the faces of the students dancing in the middle of the room.

"So," Michael asked as he wrapped his arms around my waist, "what's a beautiful girl like you doing here at the Formal all alone?"

"It's a long story," I sighed. I looked up into his deep, blue eyes. Something about them seemed honest—safe. I let myself relax a little. "I almost didn't show up tonight."

"Well, I'm glad you did," he smiled down at me with a crooked grin, "or I would still be standing alone by the punch bowl."

I glanced over at the group of socially awkward students hovering by the buffet tables. "Yeah, me too," I agreed.

He laughed. I laughed. We danced through three more songs, talking and laughing.

The rest of the night seemed pretty okay after all.

"So," Michael asked nervously as he walked me to my car at the end of the evening, "I'd love to take you out sometime. Like maybe on a real date?"

"Yeah, I'd like that."

"Great! Can I call you sometime?"

"Sure," I said a little more passionately than I had when he had first asked me to dance.

I found a pen in my dad's console and wrote my screen name and phone number on Michael's hand.

"Cool. Thanks," he said, looking down at his hand and smiling.

"Thank you for helping to make the Winter Formal not suck so bad."

"You're welcome...I think."

I just grinned at him and hopped into the Mercedes. I drove away that night with the smile still plastered on my face. It was the first time in three months I had felt genuinely happy.

Who knew that Chris would pop up eight years later and throw a kink in the life I had built for myself since he left?

Chapter Eighteen
Eight years later
April 20, 2013

Bumping into Chris during Girls' Weekend at the Beach, after I hadn't seen him in eight long years, had completely thrown me for a loop.

My mind had been reeling all night. I finally climbed out of bed around sunrise to go for a walk on the beach. Hopefully the therapeutic sound of the crashing waves would help soothe my battered heart. Rehashing every detail of my past with my friends the night before had pushed my emotional stamina to its limits. I felt like I was teetering on the edge of a complete breakdown. I pulled on my swimsuit and grabbed my cover-up on my way out of the bedroom. The rest of the girls stayed asleep while I tiptoed through the condo. I carefully opened the front door, hoping not to wake anyone. The warm blast of salty air against my face immediately assuaged my frazzled nerves. Squinting my eyes, the sun seemed to pierce my pupils while they tried to adjust to the sudden brightness after having been cooped up in the condo with the curtains drawn. I quickly made my way to the stairwell and nearly skipped down them to get to my morning 'therapy session.'

The sparkling sand squished between my toes while I walked; it was a comforting feeling, like my favorite pair of slippers back home. The warm heat of the sand radiated across my skin on the pads of my feet. It sure beat stepping on the occasional tiny building brick that Eli had left laying out on the hardwood floor. I walked toward the pier in the distance, searching for take home worthy shells along the way. The tide was on its way out, exposing plenty of shells that had washed up overnight. Most of them were broken fragments, but I had gathered a few whole shells in my pockets. I was reaching down for another handful when suddenly, out of nowhere, a giant orange blur ran up to me and tackled me. I tumbled to the ground, along with my collection of shells.

"Hey!" I yelled, just as a wet slimy tongue licked the side of my face.

"Whoa, Jasper!" a bellowing voice called in the distance.

I laughed. The golden retriever only wanted a few sloppy kisses before he bounced off me and pounced around in front of me, begging for attention. "Hey, boy," I chuckled as I petted his sandy, wet fur. He sat down on his haunches; his tail propelled globs of pasty sand across my face. I tried to stand up, just as another hand reached down to help me.

"So sorry about my dog." I immediately recognized Chris's voice as he grabbed my hand to rescue me from the catapulting sand bullets.

I looked up; dark eyes stared down at me. His windblown hair spiked all over the place in a sexy hot mess. His muscles were taut while grasping my hand and pulling me up. "Oh my god, Kaitlyn. I didn't realize it was you. I'm so sorry," he apologized, reaching his hand to my cheek to try to wipe away the sticky sand. "But, I'm really glad I ran into you this morning."

I shivered at the touch of his skin on my cheek. Closing my eyes, I relished the tingle of his fingers on my jaw line. The proximity of his body to mine sent heat waves pulsing through my body, as I took a deep breath of his rough, masculine scent. "Me too," I concurred. Jasper continued to lick my hand and wag his entire rear end as fast as he could to get more attention. Attempting to change the subject, I said, "I guess this is *your* dog."

"Yeah, I was just taking him out for a jog before the sun gets too hot. I imagine all that fur is like living in a furnace. My roommates ask me all the time why I keep a long haired dog at the beach."

"Oh, you live around here?"

He pointed farther down the shore. "Yeah, just a few blocks north of here. Jasper just likes to keep me company on my morning runs. Apparently, he likes to tackle beautiful women, too," Chris winked.

A nervous giggle escaped my mouth. I leaned down to scratch Jasper behind his ears, "You were just being friendly, weren't you buddy?" Jasper barked in response and ran toward the water, splashing in the surf.

Chris chuckled while he watched Jasper nip at the tiny schools of fish swimming in the shallow waves. "Where are you guys staying?" he asked.

"Sand Dunes Village," I replied.

"Oh okay. After I give Jasper a bath, maybe I can swing by and pick you up. We can go have lunch or something."

"I don't know…" I hesitated. My mind refused to allow me to think of having a date with Chris.

"Well, if you're not comfortable with that, maybe I could just drop by and say hi."

I nodded. "Sure, that sounds great."

Dropping by to say hi was innocent enough, right?

Jasper ran up to Chris and shook his soaked fur all over us. I didn't mind the cool spray of water. It seemed to extinguish the spark that had momentarily ignited between us.

Chris laughed. "I'd better get this drowned rat home and get him cleaned up. My roommates are going to kill me." His deep voice reverberated in his chest, more hearty and masculine than in high school, but a gentle reminder of the same laugh that coated my soul with happiness years ago.

"Okay," I nodded again as I pushed a strand of my matted wet hair behind my ear.

Chris ran his hand through his own windblown hair. Eyeing me from head to toe, he slowly shook his head at me.

"What?" I asked innocently, suddenly aware of every imperfection in his line of sight. Glancing at my toes that dug nervously in the sand as if they were trying to find a place for me to hide, I twisted the knotted strand of hair around my index finger.

"God, you're beautiful…just like I remember you." With that remark, he smiled, turned around, and jogged off with Jasper eagerly racing ahead of him.

I stood there watching him run away while my heart fluttered in my chest.

Get a grip, Kaitlyn. This can't happen, whatever this is…

I nearly floated back to our condo replaying Chris's words over and over in my mind. Being told I was beautiful seemed to fill a void I never even realized existed until he said it. The adoration I felt from Chris seemed foreign to me, but I liked it. Most of the time when I stepped out of the bathroom and asked Michael if I looked okay, he usually responded with, "You look fine. Now come on, we're almost late."

Hearing, 'God, you're beautiful' swelled my heart, especially coming from a man with whom I was once hopelessly in love. I guess I just never realized how amazing it felt to be told I looked beautiful. I practically skipped down the boardwalk when I reached our resort. Cloud Nine was a wonderful place from which to view the world.

I quietly opened the front door of the condo and tiptoed inside.

"Good morning," Shannon whispered.

"Are you the only one awake?" I asked.

"For now. Want some coffee?"

"Sure."

"Early morning jog on the beach?"

"Yeah, something like that. Just took a walk to clear my head."

"I don't blame you. After last night, I'd need a breather too."

"Thanks." I smiled as Shannon passed me a steaming hot mug of coffee.

"You really loved him, didn't you?" Shannon asked, as she sat down beside of me at the bar.

I sighed, before I took a sip of my coffee. "Yeah, I really did."

"I can tell."

We sat in silence, lost in our thoughts, drinking our coffee while we waited for the rest of the girls to wake up. Slowly, they trickled into the kitchen, filling their mugs and sitting quietly on the sofa until the caffeine kicked them into gear.

"Are you guys ready to hit the pool?" Tori asked. "I might hit the gym downstairs first, and then meet you guys after. Is that okay?"

"Sure," Lisa piped up. "Let's go get our tan on." She smiled, tossed her hair into a messy bun, and grabbed her swimsuit from the balcony where she'd laid it out to dry.

The pool chairs were already getting filled up by the time we made it downstairs. Thankfully, there were four chairs left side by side in the far corner of the pool area. We draped our towels across them and sat down to apply our sunscreen, preparing for a day of tanning and relaxing.

We enjoyed the pool for a couple hours, watching the planes fly low over the shoreline dragging their advertisement banners behind them. The hot sun baked our skin, and we relished the feeling of lifted spirits that our newly bronzed skin seemed to bring us. The gentle breeze off of the ocean kept us cool enough to enjoy the rising heat of the sun. Shannon spent most of her morning floating on a long pink pool noodle, relaxing in the water, while Lisa looked at the latest celebrity magazines. I read my newest downloaded novel, It All Started With a Lima Bean by Kimi Flores, on my e-reader. Tori finished her workout and then joined us at the pool area, but spent time in the hot tub before crashing on the lounge chair next to me.

"There's just nothing like a day spent at the beach," Tori announced. "Anyone want to take a dip in the ocean? The salt water is good for your skin," she coerced.

All the girls agreed to go with her, except me. I was completely immersed in the book and wanted to get to the end of the chapter. They headed off to the ocean while I continued to stretch out on my chair, soaking in the sun rays and drowning myself in the story. I could hear my friends laughing in the distance. I welcomed the sound. It was a sound of happiness and freedom—a sound I had longed to hear for quite a while. Sometimes laughter and time spent with girlfriends could be the best kinds of therapy. I knew we all needed a good dose of it.

After an hour or so, the girls made their way back to the pool area. I had long since finished my chapter and had gotten sucked into the next few when I heard the gate open and slam shut. Loud, masculine chatter echoed across the pool.

"Dude, I totally had you."

"Nah, bro. You didn't. I smoked your ass."

"Whatever, man. I'll challenge you again later. We'll see who wins."

"I will. Like a boss."

The guys laughed as they rounded the corner and saw us all stretched out, lounging on our chairs.

"Whoa," I heard one guy say under his breath.

"Yeah," another one agreed.

"Kaitlyn, there you are," Chris playfully punched his friend on the arm and gave him a 'back off, dude' look.

I bolted up, grabbing the bikini straps that I had untied to avoid tan lines across my neck and chest. The girls all stirred and sat up too, admiring the eye candy that had just stepped around the corner.

Quickly tying the strings around my neck, I stammered, "Chris, I...sorry, I didn't know for sure when or if you were coming."

"We brought lunch," he said proudly, grabbing the giant aluminum rectangular pan from one of his buddies. "Fresh steamed shrimp and oysters from Captain Joe's."

"Wow, thank you," I said.

Shannon smiled. "Smells delicious."

The scent of Old Bay seasoned seafood wafted toward me, and my stomach growled. "Are these your roommates?" I asked.

"Unfortunately." Chris grinned and gave a sidelong glance to the guys beside him.

"Don't listen to him. He's lucky to have us," the tall blond said as he tossed a football in the air and caught it.

"That's Jeremy," Chris nodded in the blond's direction. "He's my drummer, and God's ultimate gift to women."

From the corner of my eye, I saw Lisa smile and give a slight nod of agreement that went unnoticed by anyone else.

"Don't hate the player, hate the game," Jeremy chuckled with obvious sarcasm.

Chris nodded toward the other guy. "And that's Preacher, but you can call him Tommy. He plays bass."

Tommy was a bit shorter, but had brown hair and brown eyes just like Chris. Well, maybe they were hazel; it was hard to tell with that swoop of hair he had drooping over them. Tommy flicked his head to get the hair off his face. He reached out his hand to shake mine and introduce himself, "Name's Tommy *Bishop*, hence the 'never gets old, ever-so-funny' joke." He rolled his eyes toward Chris, then glanced back at me. "It's a pleasure to meet you, Kaitlyn." Tommy's sweet disposition seemed completely opposite of the persona standing in front of me. He was covered in tattoos and piercings that screamed self-absorbed rock god. But, when he spoke, he sounded like he stepped right off a page in Emily Post's book of etiquette.

"It's nice to meet you, too. These are my friends: Shannon, Tori, and Lisa."

Tommy took a moment to shake each of my friends' hands. Like a gentleman, he lifted each hand to his lips to gently kiss the top of it.

"Awww, look at you...all sweet on the ladies," Jeremy teased.

"Better take notes," Tommy winked at him, then grinned at me.

Chris interrupted, "Who's hungry? Let's eat!"

Jeremy opened the lid of the aluminum pan that held about ten pounds of steamed shrimp and oysters. We all dug in, peeling shrimp and shucking oysters until the juice dripped down our chins and ran down our arms. It didn't take long before the aluminum pan was empty, and we were feeling fat and happy.

"You guys are awesome. Thank you for bringing us lunch," Shannon said as she wiped her sticky fingers on a napkin.

"Yeah, that was delicious," Lisa agreed.

Tori nodded. "There's nothing like local seafood. That was fantastic."

Chris grinned, knowing he'd won the hearts of my friends with his kind gesture.

"Who's ready for a little football on the beach?" Jeremy asked tossing the ball at Lisa.

"I'm down," she grinned. "It's a good thing my husband taught me how to throw a ball."

"Damn, you're married?" Jeremy whined.

Lisa nodded. "Almost seven years."

"Well, there's no harm in tossing the ball around," he shrugged. "Let's go."

"Ladies," Tommy held his elbows out for Tori and Shannon, "may I?"

The girls giggled and interlocked their arms with his.

"Tommy, you're such a gentleman," Shannon flirted.

"I try my best." He winked at her. I could almost see her swooning from where I sat. I couldn't blame her. Tommy was definitely a player, and he knew the game well. Shannon just played along for the fun of it, knowing nothing would come of it.

I stuffed my e-reader into my bag to head down to the beach with the rest of them.

"Do you want to take a walk instead?" Chris asked as he held his hand out to me to help me up from my lounge chair. As many hours as I'd spent sitting there, my backside felt numb. A walk sounded nice to get my blood circulating again.

"Sure," I nodded. "Let's go."

"Great." We walked, arm in arm, down the boardwalk toward the sand.

Once we were a good distance away from our group, Chris piped up. "Kaitlyn Davenport, I honestly thought after high school, I'd never see you again."

"Thomas," I corrected him.

"Thomas?"

"Kaitlyn Thomas."

"Oh."

The word hung in the air like a dense fog.

"Happily married, huh?" Chris finally asked.

"Yeah..." my voice trailed off. *Married, yes. Happily, not so much.* It was the first time in six years I had even an ounce of regret about my marriage. I mean, I knew our marriage needed work, but I never regretted it—not until that moment. The thought terrified me.

"Wow, how long have you been married?" Chris finally asked.

"Almost six years. We have a son. He's five. His name is Eli."

"That's great. He's a lucky little boy to have you for a mom."

"Thanks. He keeps me busy."

Chris chuckled. "I bet he does. That's why there's no way I'm ready to have children right now. I'm sure they're a blessing and all, but they take a lot of time and sacrifice that I'm just not prepared to give right now."

I laughed. He was right about the time and sacrifice part, hence my desperate need for a vacation at the beach in the first place. "So," I asked, "what have you been up to all these years?"

"Just working and writing music," he said. "I moved to the beach after I got out of juvie. I used to do maintenance work on the piers down here. But, once I signed with my first agent, I started writing music full time. You've probably heard a few of the songs I've written for other singers on the radio, like *In Love with a Memory*."

The title struck me, and a few of the lyrics filtered into my mind.

> *Who knew we'd have to say goodbye?*
> *I can't get you off my mind.*
> *I'm in love with a memory.*
> *So in love with a memory.*

"Really? Wow! That was yours? That's fantastic. I love that song."

Could that song be about me? Nah. There's no way.

Chris nodded as if he could read my mind. "Thanks," he said humbly. "It's nothing much really. I keep my bills paid doing gigs around town. My band and I are almost finished with our first album. Then hopefully you'll be able to actually hear *me* singing my songs on the radio."

"That would be awesome!"

"Yeah…" his voice trailed off. "So, how about you?" Chris asked, changing the subject. "What have you been up to all these years? That is, besides being a wife and mother."

"I went to college, but got married right after I found out I was pregnant. I was able to finish my psychology degree, but decided to stay home with Eli instead of going to work."

"What ever happened to that asshole?"

"Oh, Trevor? Well, it's a long story."

My mind flashed back to that day in the bathroom.

I heard the door slam as someone stomped into the restroom. The sound of someone jerking paper towels from the dispenser and running water splashing from the faucet, echoed off the tile walls.

"Stupid jerk," a voice muttered.

I flushed the toilet, grabbed the travel size hand sanitizer from my purse, and slipped out of the stall hoping to make a quick escape, but I instantly recognized the reflection in the mirror.

"Eva?"

"Go away, Kaitlyn," she grumbled, dabbing the wet paper towel under her eyes to erase the runny mascara lines.

"What's wrong, Eva?"

She stopped and scowled at me in the mirror. "What do you care?" She tossed the paper towel into a nearby trashcan.

The proof of her pain was immediately evident to me. "I care because I know."

"You don't know shit," she barked, the tears brimming her eyes.

"I dated Trevor long enough to know those bruises on your wrists didn't come from practicing cheer stunts in your backyard during sleepovers with the girls."

Eva stared at me, her eyes wide with fear, confusion, and relief. As if we shared some secret club password, she slowly nodded her head. Covering her face with her hands, her knees buckled as she sank to the floor and sobbed uncontrollably.

"Well, what happened? Did Trevor win Prom King and live happily ever after?" Chris joked.

"Actually, no." I smiled, thinking back to the day they took Trevor away in handcuffs. "A few days after the Winter Formal I found Eva crying in the bathroom. With a little coaxing, she admitted to me that Trevor had been abusive to her. He raped her too, Chris. I felt terrible. I wish I would've listened to you and told someone before he did it to someone else."

"You can't blame yourself."

"I know. I try not to, but it's hard sometimes. Anyway, Eva and I ended up going to the authorities with the truth. It was a big mess for a while, but he ended up taking a plea bargain that made him serve five years in prison."

"Good. That asshole deserved every day he spent behind bars, and then some."

"I absolutely agree. So tell me, what happened to you after juvie? Did you go back to high school? Did you graduate?" I had finally narrowed the million questions I had in my head down to three.

Chris looked at me; an undeterminable emotion crossed his face. He seemed to be having an internal debate, maybe deciding how much to divulge to me.

"Well, I didn't go back to high school. I got my GED while I was in juvie. I didn't want to have to go back to that hell hole."

"I don't blame you."

"When I got out of juvie, I lived at home for a while. But that just wasn't working out. It's hard to come back home, living under your mom's wing, when you've been so used to living without her for so long. I worked a few odd jobs and worked as a cashier at a convenience store for a while. That was probably the longest running job I had before moving to the beach."

"What made you decide to move down here?"

A sidelong glance told me he didn't really want to hash out details, but he sighed and answered anyway, "A girl."

"Oh," I said, embarrassed.

"No, it's okay. I mean, it was a few years ago. I met this girl at a party back home. We hung out a few times, then she left town to come down here to college. I thought to myself, what the hell? The following weekend, I packed my stuff and moved here to be closer to her."

"What happened? Are you still with her?"

Chris's sad and distant stare indicated his answer before he even spoke. For a moment, he seemed to leave the here and now, lost in thought, reminiscing about a time gone by. "No, we're not together anymore," he said absently.

I didn't pry. I didn't want to upset him. He already seemed on the verge of tears. I watched him, staring off into the distance and seemingly unaware of my gaze.

Reaching up, he caressed a small scar in his eyebrow; a pained looked flashed in his eyes. "She died."

"I'm sorry." I was so shocked, it was all I could think to say.

He pinched the bridge of his nose and creased his eyebrows.

"I didn't mean to bring it up. I'm sorry."

"No, it's okay. It helps to talk about it sometimes. I had been living here about six months when it happened. She was supposed to be going back home that weekend to visit her parents. But, I talked her into staying that Friday night to go to a party my boss was throwing, and heading out on Saturday morning instead." Clenching his fists by his side, he gritted his teeth and flexed his jaw muscle. He fought hard to keep his tears at bay by squeezing his eyes shut. I could see a look of painful regret spreading across his face. Only the redness around his eyes gave away any hint of sadness. The rest of his body exuded anger. "I was driving that night. We were on our way to the party, arguing about something. I don't even remember what we were arguing about now. I just remember that she punched my shoulder, not even hard enough to hurt me, but just hard enough to cause me to cross the center line. I over-corrected, ran off the road in a sharp curve, and lost control. The last thing I remember is screaming while we flipped down an embankment, and then silence, except for the hissing steam coming from the radiator. I woke up two days later in the hospital, but Noelle was…gone." He choked out a single sob, but restrained the rest.

I leaned into him, pressing my head against his shoulder, gently rubbing my hand across his shoulders in an effort to console him.

"I should have just let her go—let her go home on Friday night like she had planned."

"It's not your fault," I whispered. My heart broke for him. I couldn't imagine the guilt he had been harboring for so many years, carrying the burden like Atlas carried the world on his shoulders.

He continued, "I couldn't even look at her parents at her funeral. They knew I had talked her into staying down here with me that night to go to a party. They knew I was the one driving. The only thing that redeemed me was the fact that I hadn't been drinking...*yet*. I should have let her go home that night. I shouldn't have been arguing with her, and I shouldn't have been driving so fast." Tears brimmed in his eyes.

"None of this is your fault, Chris. It was just a terrible, horrific tragedy. Accidents happen. You have to stop blaming yourself."

Chris slumped his shoulders and sighed. "That's what the grief counselors at the hospital told me. You can see how well that worked out." He looked down at his feet, heedlessly digging his toes in the sand. "You know what I think the hardest thing about all of this is?"

"What?" I asked.

"Knowing that Noelle sacrificed her life for someone who wasn't in love with her."

I stared at him, astounded, unsure of what to say. He stared back at me; regret and sadness manifested across his face.

In a moment of sudden clarity, he said, "Oh my god! I remember what we were arguing about now!"

"What?"

"You."

Horrified by his answer, I screeched, "Me? Why me?"

"Well, not *you* per se, but Noelle knew I wasn't completely into her. We had been on dates, and I had hung out with her and her roommates a lot, but she knew I wasn't in love with her. The accident happened around the same time I wrote that song, *In Love with a Memory.* That song meant everything to me. Writing it, at that time, was my lifeline and a desperate attempt to ease my heartache. She knew it, and she was jealous. I guess I don't really blame her. But, I remember now. It was the first time I had heard the song being played on the radio. She wanted to change the station, and the argument began. She flipped to another station, and I switched it back. That happened several times before she finally hauled off and punched me on the shoulder." He looked sadly at the ground. "I should have just let her change the station," he whispered.

We walked the rest of the way in silence. The quiet between us would have seemed awkward to anyone else, but to us it was pleasant. The chemistry between us felt so natural. It didn't matter if we were talking, silent, happy, or sad. It all just fell into place so naturally. Our souls felt connected like two pieces of a puzzle. I missed that feeling. I missed the feeling of *just being* with someone, without any expectations. What a refreshing feeling!

"Looks like the girls are winning," Chris said as we got closer to the group.

I laughed. The girls were sitting on the sand, watching Jeremy and Tommy toss the ball back and forth between them, strutting around and showing off like roosters in a hen house.

"I guess so," I agreed.

"Well, I guess we better get going," Chris announced to the guys as he intercepted the ball.

"Yeah, we need to practice our set for tonight," Tommy said, winking at Tori.

"You girls gonna be there?" Jeremy flashed his smile at Lisa who grinned back.

"Definitely," Shannon confirmed, glancing at Chris and me as she said it. "We wouldn't miss it."

"Too bad you girls aren't gonna be here next weekend. We're opening for The Rifters." Tommy strummed his air guitar for effect.

"Wow, I wish we could see that. I hear that Seth Jordan is a sexy beast," Shannon teased him. "I guess you give him a real run for his money, huh?"

"You got that right, babe," Tommy pursed his lips and nodded his head with confidence, jutting his chin out as if to proudly proclaim his player status.

Chris searched my eyes. I recognized the sadness in them because it was the same feeling welling up inside of me. While I was as happy as I could be that I had bumped into him after all these years, I knew the inevitable was coming—*goodbye*. I wanted this weekend to last forever.

"See you tonight," Chris whispered.

I just nodded as my eyes glossed over.

Chapter Nineteen

I sat nervously in the booth with my fingers fidgeting in my lap. I had unbuttoned and re-buttoned my sweater at least twenty times. I tried not to concern myself with the inevitability of seeing Chris again, but even the ring on my finger could not stop my heart from beating out of my chest. As much as I didn't want to admit it to anyone, there was still a tiny corner of my heart that Chris occupied, even after all these years.

"So, girls, what are we drinking tonight?" Lisa piped up as we waited for our appetizers. "It's Amaretto Sours for me. Those are definitely my favorite."

"I love the Cotton Candy Cosmos!" Shannon shouted over the loud music.

"Me too," My voice cracked anxiously.

"Well, I love me some Mango Margaritas. You girls don't know what you're missing!" Tori cried.

"Oh don't worry. I'll have one of each!" Lisa squealed excitedly.

Geez, we really don't get out much, I laughed inwardly.

Casually, I glanced toward the bar to see if *he* had arrived yet. *Bummer...*

Lisa playfully bumped her shoulder into mine. "Who are you looking for, Kaitlyn?" she teased.

"No one, just looking for our waiter," I fibbed.

"Well, honey, if you were looking for Chris, we'd *all* understand! He's a major hottie!" Shannon giggled like a giddy teenager. The others nodded in agreement.

"Speak of the devil…" Tori's voice trailed off as she looked toward the door.

My heart immediately started racing in my chest. I ducked down, trying to avoid being seen.

"Kaitlyn, I've never seen you this way. That guy really has an effect on you," Shannon declared.

Lisa announced, "He's looking around the room. I think he's looking for you!"

"Geez, Lisa, don't make it so obvious!" I hissed.

"Okay, okay. Uh oh, too late. He just saw me." She ducked down. "Here he comes," she whispered loudly.

I caught my breath. My cheeks burned and I broke out in a nervous sweat. Quickly, I ripped off my sweater. I figured damp armpit stains wouldn't look very attractive.

"Ladies," Chris turned on the charm as he approached our table. "Welcome back to Captain Joe's."

"Hi, Chris,"…"Hey,"…"Hello." All the girls spoke in unison.

"Kaitlyn." Chris grinned as he gave a gentleman's bow.

"Hey, Chris." My voice wavered as I gave a bashful smile.

"I was hoping you ladies would be here. We're performing tonight at ten. I hope y'all can stay for our show."

"Absolutely," Shannon affirmed readily.

"Great!" He gave his award-winning smile. "Kaitlyn, if you get a few minutes, I'd love to catch up with you again. Maybe we could go for a walk on the beach later."

"Uh..." I hesitated.

Shannon piped up. "She'd love to."

"Shannon…" Tori hissed in a reprimanding tone, shaking her head with disapproval.

Chris just winked at me. "Okay, great. I'm looking forward to it."

I just smiled at him like a buffoon as he turned around and walked away in search of his band mates.

Tori spoke up. "So, what do you girls wanna sing tonight? I vote for *Girls Just Wanna Have Fun.*"

"I vote for *Pour Some Sugar on Me,*" Lisa countered.

"Girls, girls, girls..." Shannon laughed, shaking her head. "I say we bring the house down with *Love Shack.*"

I just sat there, aloof and bewildered. *Was I seriously about to take a walk on the beach, in the dark, alone with the man of my dreams from eight years ago? What would Michael say?*

Later, when Tori and Lisa had gone to the bar for some more drinks, I interrogated Shannon. "What are you doing?"

"What?" she responded innocently. "I'm just finishing up these mozzarella sticks," she said as she popped the last bite into her mouth.

"No. I'm talking about when you agreed that I would go for a walk with Chris. What were you thinking? I'm married, Shannon. *Married.* I can't just be *alone in the dark,* on a beach with a guy anymore."

"Come on," Shannon replied. "You're just going for a walk. To talk. To catch up. To reminisce."

"Yeah, but you don't understand the history we had or the connection between us."

"I know enough to know that you won't do anything you'd regret," she said with a smile.

I looked down at my hands, not knowing how to respond.

Chris caught my attention from the stage as he was helping the stage crew set up his band's equipment. He looked absolutely amazing in his black Affliction Henley. I couldn't believe that I was staring at the same guy I fell in love with eight years ago. For a moment, the image of Michael reading a bedtime story cuddled up with Eli in his bed seemed like a cloudy, distant memory. Instantly, a flood of guilt washed over me. *Michael.* I shook the feeling away, and tried to focus on this moment with Chris. *Who gets this chance? The chance to revisit the past? The chance to make amends? The chance to reconnect with someone who once had your heart?* No, tonight I would enjoy the moment, and tomorrow I would have no regrets.

"Hey Kaitlyn, are you ready to take that walk?" Chris smiled as he walked up to me.

I grinned sheepishly. "Sure!" I replied.

The girls congregated on the dance floor with the rest of Chris's band mates. I had been sitting by the bar, secretly hoping that Chris would take that moment to steal me away. We walked side by side out the door. I caught a glimpse of Shannon as I passed by her. Her smile spread from ear to ear. At that moment, I felt certain she was living vicariously through me.

The moon was bright against the dark sky. The waves kissed the shoreline in a constant rhythm. We began our walk in silence, lost in our own thoughts. Our shoulders brushed each other, and the spark between us sent a shiver down my spine.

Chris finally broke the silence. "Kaitlyn?"

"Yeah?" I asked.

"Have you ever thought about me—about *us*—over the years?" he whispered, looking at the ocean where the moon's reflection illuminated across the water. Stuffing his hands into his pockets, he sloshed his feet in the lapping waves as he walked.

Sighing, I slumped my shoulders and scuffed my toes against the gritty, wet sand. "More than you know," I finally admitted. I felt defeated, knowing that it didn't matter. No matter how much I had thought about him over the years, it still didn't change the fact I had exchanged vows with someone else.

Chris stopped in his tracks. I took a step or two before I realized that he had stopped behind me. "What's wrong?" I asked, turning around to see why he had stopped.

"I just can't believe we are here…together. I just can't believe I'm having the opportunity to see you, talk to you, and be with you again, even if you are married." Absently, he picked up a flat shell and skipped it across the water. He continued, "You have no idea how many times you crossed my mind—how many nights I dreamt of you after I left. You don't know how many times I picked up the phone to call you, but couldn't do it. When I saw you last night, my heart did somersaults in my chest."

"Mine too." Tears had already begun to sting my eyes. "Why didn't you?" I asked him.

"Why didn't I what?" he asked, seeking clarification as he skipped another shell across the lapping waves.

"Call me," I answered.

Chris turned to stare at me. Even in the darkness I could see his jaw twitching with an emotion I couldn't quite put my finger on. "Kaitlyn, it wasn't that easy. Juvie was harder on me the second time around. They enforced stricter rules on me. I wasn't allowed to use the phone for the first three months. I guess the judge had it out for me so I would never grace their doors again, but I wrote you letters."

I froze. "Wait, what?" My eyes narrowed. "You…wrote…*letters?*" I paused after every word, spitting them individually as if each of them were poison in my mouth.

"Yeah, why?" Chris sounded confused as he tossed the last shell across the water and crammed his hands into his back pockets, rocking back on his heels.

"Because I never got any of your letters! Not one!" I cried. "My mother must have intercepted them and hidden them from me." My anger flared in the pit of my stomach. I vowed at that moment that I would get to the bottom of this little secret my mother had kept from me. How dare she interfere with my life, regardless if she thought she was protecting me.

"Yeah, I started out writing letters every single day for the first few weeks, but I never heard back from you. After the first month, I just wrote letters once a week. Then, once every two weeks. But, I never gave up, not until I finally had the chance to use the phone. When I finally got a chance to call home, my little brother told me he saw you in town and it looked like you had already moved on with someone else. I just wanted you to be happy. I didn't want to interfere. I mean, it had already been three months, you know? For all I knew, you were done with me and had forgotten all about me."

"Chris, I never stopped thinking about you. I was sinking deeper and deeper into my depression after you left. Not hearing from you only made it harder. I figured I would never hear from you or see you again. Then I met Michael, and he helped pull me out of the deepest depths of depression. I didn't know what else to do. I wanted more than anything to be with you!"

Why? Why couldn't I have seen him six years ago? Why did I have to be married before I had the chance to see him again? Now the vows I took six years ago were preventing me from grabbing him and kissing him on the spot!

I couldn't help but curse fate. I nearly shook my fists toward heaven.

"Kaitlyn, I'm sorry." Chris gently wiped the single tear that had escaped my eye. "I didn't want to make you cry tonight."

"It's not you," I said, taking a ragged breath. "It's just that I never imagined I would see you again. I've been happy these last eight years, but seeing you last night brought back a flood of emotions that I wasn't prepared to handle. I'm sorry. I'm really happy to see you. You just have no idea how happy..." my voice trailed off as Chris took a step toward me.

"I do have an idea. That is, if you are even a tenth as happy as I am. Kaitlyn, I've missed you. I've missed you something fierce these last eight years. I never thought I'd see you again, and yet, here I am with you, the most beautiful woman in the world. I don't want this weekend to end. I don't want you to leave, and reality to set in—the reality that I will probably never see you again. I am so happy you're here. But part of me wishes I hadn't seen you at all. I thought I had healed from the pain of losing you the first time. Seeing you again just ripped that scar wide open. Knowing that you're *married* with a kid...I don't think I'll ever be able to recover from that. My heart has always belonged to you, but you belong to someone else. I just can't take it." He reached out to hug me, swallowing me up into the warmth of his arms.

My body went rigid; it was the first time I had felt intimacy like that, with someone besides Michael, in a long time.

"I'm sorry." Chris pulled away from me.

"No. Don't be." I leaned in toward him, silently begging him to reach out again.

He slipped his hands around my shoulders and ever so gently pulled me closer to him. I breathed the scent of his cologne. It was a similar musky scent I remembered from high school. I wrapped my arms around him and laid my head on his chest. Silently he swayed me back and forth and we danced to the rhythm of the lapping waves. Our breaths fell into a synchronized rhythm. I heard his heart pounding in his chest and felt mine doing the same. Our bodies seemed to fit perfectly together like the opposite poles of two magnets. I felt melded to him.

And the two shall become one.

The phrase resonated in my mind. Quickly, I pulled away. "I'm sorry!" I said, suddenly feeling very panicky.

"What's the matter?" Chris asked alarmed.

"I'm sorry. It's just...I'm married. I can't let myself feel this way with you. I just can't. I'm sorry."

"Kaitlyn, it's okay," Chris reassured me. "I understand. I'm sorry, too. I never should have brought you out here. It's my fault."

"I'm so sorry!" I cried as I turned to walk back toward the bar. The tears freely fell from my eyes.

I just wanted to turn the clock back a few years! I really needed this moment! What a dirty rotten trick for fate to play on me!

"Kaitlyn, wait. Let's start over. I'm sorry. I won't put you in that position again. Just walk with me. Please."

I slowed my pace and considered his offer. *What would it hurt?* "Just a walk?" I asked.

"Just a walk," he confirmed.

So, side by side we were strolling again on the sand down by the water.

"I haven't walked out here at night in ages," Chris stated, trying to avoid the obvious tension between us.

"Really?" I feigned interest. "Wow, if I lived here I'd be walking on the beach every night."

He shrugged. "I guess I've just been too busy."

"It's so beautiful out here," I said.

"I guess when you live here you take the beauty for granted."

"Yeah..."

The awkward conversation served as a pitiful mask for the emotions stirring in our hearts.

"Kaitlyn, I'm sorry." Chris stopped walking and looked earnestly at me. "I can't do this. Being with you like this is harder than I thought it would be."

"Yeah, I get that feeling too."

"Maybe we should go back," he sighed.

"Yeah, maybe we should."

The walk back to the bar was the longest, most painful walk I have ever had to endure. The intense throbbing pain deep in my soul reminded me of the time I fell out of the tree and broke my collar bone when I was eleven years old. Back then, I had sprawled out on the ground moaning from the ache that pulsated across my chest and radiated down my arm. I had prayed I would never feel a hurt like that again.

What happened to seizing the moment? What happened to no regrets?

Either way, it didn't matter. We had made our way back to the bar, and Chris had opened the door for me to step inside. Chris's band was setting up on stage.

"Looks like you're up," I said, hiding my anguish.

"I guess so," Chris said. "Thanks for the walk...and the chat."

"It was my pleasure," I grinned at him playfully. My pathetic attempt at flirting did nothing to disguise my heartache.

"So? How was it?" Shannon squealed when I plopped down into the booth with the rest of the girls.

"It was good," I replied, shrugging my shoulders.

"Good? Just good?" Tori asked inquisitively, eyeing me suspiciously.

"Yeah," I said, glancing down at the trembling hands in my lap.

"Aw, come on!" Lisa whined. "You've gotta give us more than that."

"Sorry, guys, there's not much to tell," I lied, averting my eyes to an invisible spot on the wall.

"Well, did he try to kiss you?" Shannon inquired.

I jerked my head back to the staring eyes around my table. "No!" I said emphatically. "He was a perfect gentleman."

"Awww!" they all sang in unison.

Chris the rest of the members of *Fifth Wheel* stood on stage preparing to perform. Chris perched on a bar stool at the front of the stage. The spotlight shone down on him as the dark figures behind him disappeared into the blackness. He had his acoustic guitar poised on his lap for the first song.

"Ladies and gentleman, I have a special song for you," he began. "It's a song that's near and dear to my heart. I've not had a chance to play it yet, but tonight is the perfect opportunity. It means a lot to me to get to sing it for you tonight. I think you will like it, too."

His eyes scanned the crowd and landed on me.

Shannon squeezed my arm. "I think he's playing this song for you," she whispered excitedly.

He held my gaze with the same eyes that I remember staring at me that very first day I saw them by the gymnasium—those dark, penetrating eyes that searched my heart and unlocked my soul. He picked up his guitar and started to strum. I immediately recognized the first few chords of *You and Me* by Lifehouse. His heartfelt sincerity echoed through the microphone as he sang about never feeling more bewildered, nor more energized than he did at that moment. He crooned about not being able to speak the right words because his mind was completely addled. He sang about standing with me

231

in the throngs of people and not being able to tear his eyes away from me. Every word, every verse, every note...all of it was meant for me.

"Oh Shannon, what am I going to do?" I pleaded.

Shannon responded with the ongoing joke we made during our car ride down there. "What happens at the beach stays at the beach."

"You don't really mean that, do you?" I asked.

"Not really," she admitted, "but, I know you will walk away this weekend without any regrets."

"I sure hope so," was all I could say.

The rest of the evening I sat listening to the thumping music and the droning voices around me, while I nursed a beer and peeled its label. It seemed the girls understood my emotional dilemma and had left me alone to collect my thoughts while they made spectacles of themselves on the dance floor.

A neatly folded napkin flew over my shoulder and onto the table. Curiously, I opened it and found a note written on it:

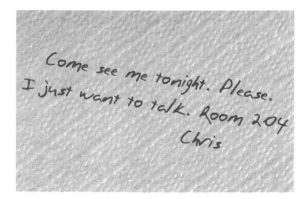

I couldn't help but smile. That jittery feeling returned. My heart started racing and I felt the adrenaline pumping through my body. The giddy grin stayed glued to my face the rest of the evening.

Chapter Twenty

"Hello?" I said as I brought the phone to my ear.

Michael had called to check in again. "Hey, honey." he said.

"Oh, hey," I said. The guilt churned my stomach.

"How's it going?" he asked.

"Great. We're having a lot of fun."

"That's wonderful."

"How are things going at home?" I asked.

"Well, don't freak out, but Eli spilled cherry Kool-Aid on the quilt your great-grandmother made," Michael admitted sheepishly.

"What?" I cried. "Oh no. Michael! Why did you let him have Kool-Aid in the living room? You know how much that quilt means to me! I'll probably never be able to get that stain out!"

"Kaitlyn, I'm sorry. I had something I had to do for work. I was on the computer. I had no idea he had poured himself a cup."

"You weren't watching him? You're telling me you couldn't go just one weekend without having to work? Honestly, Michael, just one weekend! That's all I asked for! You can't handle just one weekend?"

"Of course I can handle one weekend. It's just that something important came up and I had to get it done. Look, I'm doing the best I can. I'm sorry."

"Okay," I huffed. "Just spray it with stain remover and I'll see what I can do when I get home."

"One more thing," he said hesitantly.

"What?"

"The electricity bill came. You must have forgotten to mail last month's bill. We owe double this month."

I breathed a deep and audible sigh. "Good grief. I wish I had realized that last month. I don't think I have enough budgeted to pay double this month."

"Don't worry about it, we'll figure it out when you get home. Try to enjoy the rest of your weekend. We'll be fine."

"Okay, I'll call you tomorrow before we head home."

"Goodnight, babe."

"Goodnight," I said flatly.

I hung up the phone feeling exasperated. On any other night, a stain on a quilt would not have sent me over the edge. But, my emotions were already running rampant, and I just couldn't control them. No one tells you how difficult "playing house" is as an adult. You don't comprehend the commitment you are making when you take your vows and bring a child into the world. One of the hardest parts of growing up is realizing that making changes in your life is not as easy as it once was when you could just say, *I don't want to play this anymore,'* and walk away to do something else.

As much as I had the urge to walk away at times, I could never do anything to hurt my family. I would never walk away from little Eli who is too young to understand what was happening. Michael was good to me. He worked hard to provide for us. He really was a good man, a great husband, and a wonderful father.

However, if all of those things about Michael were true, then why did I have such an urge to visit Chris? Something in the back of my mind nagged, begged, and pleaded with me to go see him.

I pulled the napkin out of my pocket and read Chris's words one more time. I felt like I was standing at a crossroad, watching my head and my heart go to war with each other over what path to take.

Which choice would incur the most regret: Doing something I'm not proud of or walking away, wishing I had done it anyway?

"It's okay if you do it," Lisa spoke from behind me.

"Do what?" I asked, startled.

"Go see him. You will always regret it if you don't."

"I'm afraid I'll never forgive myself if I do."

"Kaitlyn, life only happens once. Maybe you need to see him for closure."

"You're right," I agreed as I stuffed the napkin back into my pocket. "Closure. Maybe that's all I need."

"Then go," Lisa urged quietly. "Just *go*."

Chapter Twenty-One

My hand trembled as I knocked on the door. Chris opened it immediately as if he had been standing on the other side, waiting for me.

"Kaitlyn," he said. "I'm so glad you came."

"Do you live here?" I asked as I looked around the plain, cookie-cutter hotel room.

"No," he said sheepishly. "I just took a chance that you would come see me and I talked the manager into letting me have a condo overnight. I just wanted a place we could talk. Alone."

I stood uncomfortably in the doorway.

"Come in. Sit down," he said leading me toward the sofa. "Do you want anything to drink? I bought some sodas from the machine down the hall."

"No, thanks. Not yet."

"Okay." He plopped down beside me on the couch.

"So…" His voice trailed off.

"So…" I repeated.

The awkward silence was deafening.

"Kaitlyn," Chris said finally, "I've waited eight long years for this. Ring or no ring, I just had to see you tonight."

"Me too," I agreed shyly.

Chris turned to look at me. His knees brushed mine and it sent a shiver down my spine. Gently, he brushed a strand of hair away from my face and his thumb slid down my cheek sending fluttering sensations down the length of my chin. I took a staggering breath.

"Wow, you're as beautiful as ever," he whispered.

A nervous giggle escaped my mouth.

"It's true. I remember watching you from a distance. You were one of the most beautiful girls in that school, but you never let it get to your head. You were always so sweet to everyone, which made you even more beautiful in my eyes. Nothing has changed. You are just as amazing as I remember. I've had dreams about this moment."

"Me too." They seemed to be the only two words my brain could remember.

"I never felt as strongly about anyone as I felt with you. I dated a few girls here and there. But, no one came close to the feelings I had for you. I can't explain it. You just completely overwhelmed me. You overwhelmed my thoughts—my dreams. It was like you were a magnet to my soul, and seeing you here tonight…it's a dream come true."

Slowly, Chris leaned toward me. Sucking in my breath and holding it, this time I was certain not to flinch or push him away. *No regrets,* I reminded myself the moment his lips touched mine.

Waves of excitement immediately pulsated through my body. His lips were as soft and supple as I had remembered. A gentle peck quickly turned into deep probing kisses. His thumbs softly caressed my cheeks as he gently cupped my face. My hands slowly made their way to the back of his head as I pulled him closer to me. Gingerly, Chris's hands stroked down my back where he clutched me as though he never wanted to let go. Our lips moved in rhythm as our tongues delved for a deeper connection. My gut quivered with anticipation. With strong, capable hands, he carefully pulled me down on top of him as he leaned back against a pillow on the sofa. Straddling him, I continued to kiss him with a longing I had not felt in a long time. Chris quietly moaned with yearning while he pulled away from my kiss.

"Kaitlyn," he whispered breathlessly, with a deep and sultry voice.

"Hmmm," I responded with my eyes still closed, then opened them to see him staring intently at me.

"The feeling I get when I am with you comes back to me again so easily after all this time."

"I know what you mean. I never imagined myself in this situation. Ever. I mean, when we walked away from each other that day I thought I'd never see you again. I have never had my heart broken, obliterated even, like I did that day. It took a long time to let you go, but even then you always seemed to creep up in my mind from time to time. It's unbelievable how quickly the heart can remember. The chemistry we have is downright mind-blowing."

"We may never get this chance again. I'm not a fool to think this night will last forever. As much as I want to, I could never ask you to forsake your family and stay here with me. So, after tonight you will go back to your own life and I will go back to writing music, and our lives will once again take separate paths. Let's make this night count. No regrets."

The fire of lust burned on my lips, craving more from him. I felt vulnerable as the warmth of his kiss, once again, radiated throughout my body. Slowly, I lifted my hands and cupped the back of his neck while my fingers gently tousled his soft black hair. He nibbled his way down to my neck. My body trembled at the touch of his lips on my delicate skin.

Chris stopped kissing me and looked solemnly into my eyes. He spoke with pure honesty in his voice, "You are amazing. You never saw that quality about yourself, but I did. Besides my dad, you were the only person who made me *want* to make better choices in my life. Honestly, when I looked at you, I saw my future."

My breath caught in my throat as I felt the tiny fissure of my heart crack wide open at his admission. The intimacy of the moment stirred tears in me, and I couldn't stop them from spilling out.

Through my tears I managed to respond. "I wanted so badly for you to be a part of it, but life moved on after you left. Life shuffled me through each day. I eventually got married, and I have one of the most wonderful, beautiful children I could ever ask for. I'm so grateful for him. I really am happy with my life. I love my family with all my heart. I guess life comes with its share of heartaches, and you were just one of those for me. Over the years I have learned to accept that fact. But, *not once*, did I ever stop loving you—not for one second."

Utter confusion crossed Chris's face; his eyes were wide with shock. "You loved me?"

I nodded. "I couldn't say it back then. I don't know why, but I just couldn't. I did love you, though. I fell for you so fast, it scared me. Also, knowing my situation with *him*, I was afraid. I was scared to admit just how much I loved you, but I did know. I knew when I drove away that night that I would *never stop* loving you."

He blinked back the tears threatening to overflow his eyes. Pulling me toward him, he kissed me gently on the forehead. His voice thick with overwhelming emotion, he whispered, "You don't know how long I've waited to hear those words from you."

He softly caressed my skin with his thumbs as he held my face in his hands, wiping the tears as they slid down my cheeks. With a tenderness I had not felt in quite some time, he gently touched his lips to mine. The salty taste of tears slid down my throat. My body ignited with a sweet passion that reminded me of the innocent love we had for each other nearly eight and a half years ago. Softly, yet with lustful intensity, his lips pressed against mine and kissed me with wanton hunger. A delicious slip of his tongue into my mouth tantalized my taste buds with a hint of his minty flavor. The rhythmic movement of his tongue in my mouth triggered a flittering response that rippled its way down my body. My heart fluttered in my chest, and my stomach quaked with burning desire.

Swiftly, he stood up from the couch and lifted me into his arms. Carrying me into the bedroom, he gently laid me on the bed. He pulled a lighter from his pocket and quickly lit the candles on the nightstand. I watched lustfully as he pulled his shirt over his head and tossed it to the floor. Strong muscles deeply defined their shape on his rippled stomach. His tanned skin glistened in the candlelight. His biceps flexed as he reached out to slowly unbutton my shirt. I trembled nervously. *Is this really happening? Should I let this be happening?*

Tossing my shirt to the floor, he whispered breathlessly, "I want you, Kaitlyn. I want you like my lungs *need* air."

Crawling onto the bed and lying beside me, he gently ran his lips across my shoulders. His hands caressed the skin on my back and I shivered with excitement. Holding me close, his bare, perfectly formed chest touched mine. The heat of his skin stirred my senses and exhilarated me. He pulled my pants off me and tossed them carelessly to the floor with the rest of his clothes. "Are you okay?" he asked, concerned, trailing his fingers over the delicate skin around my navel.

"Yes," I purred, searching his dark irises that swirled with longing and passion for me.

"Good," he winked. "Now get over here." He pulled my body closer to him. Propping himself up beside me on one elbow, his fingers lightly traced my skin from my stomach all the way up the length of my body to my face. Gently brushing my hair away from my forehead and caressing the skin on my cheek with the edge of his thumb, he said, "I can't tell you how amazing this weekend has been. Seeing you here has messed with my head. God, what I would give for you to stay here with me. You're the only woman I've ever truly loved. I can't explain it, Kaitlyn. I don't even understand it myself. All I know is that I loved you then, and seeing you here this weekend has fucked me up inside." He teased my skin with the tantalizing circular motions of his fingers, which drove me crazy with desire. "And now, you're here with me in this bed, and I'm touching you like this. You have no idea what it's doing to me."

He was wrong. I knew exactly what it was doing to him. I knew because I felt it pulsing against my thigh. "Mmmhmm." I closed my eyes with a mischievous grin spreading across my face. If only he knew what it was doing to *me*; only I think he knew. The closer his hand got to the lower half of my body, the more I bucked my hips toward the gentle pressure of his fingers as they danced their way across my sensitive skin, causing seismic shock waves of sexual tension rippling their way down my core, screaming for a euphoric release. "I do know, and I like it." I opened my eyes to find him staring at me. His stormy eyes were filled with heady appetite.

"You're so fucking beautiful. I just can't take it." He leaned down and kissed me again, pressing me hard against the pillow behind my head. I welcomed the feel of his deliciously soft lips on mine as we sucked and nipped at each other with sensual passion. I felt him thrust himself against me; the enticing sensation of his aching desire continued to throb against my hip.

Pulling back, I panted, "I've waited so long for this. I need you, Chris." With a faint smile on my lips, I closed my eyes, anticipating the moment—a moment for which I knew my body had yearned for every bit of eight years and five months, almost to the day.

He rolled on top of me and kissed me again, breathing me in as if he were trying to connect our souls. I welcomed the taste of him, savoring the moment before our bodies united. His eyes were wide open, watching me kiss him back. We stared at each other, cherishing the beautiful moment our hearts had longed for all these years.

He positioned himself, and I gasped as I felt him slide himself into me. I exhaled a sigh of both relief and pleasure while he released a low tantalizing moan that started deep within his chest. I welcomed the feeling of him as he gently thrust himself into me. *Oh god, this feels so different.* Everything about him felt so different. A brief moment of guilt zipped through my conscience. I didn't know if I should panic and run, or clutch him tighter and appreciate the sensation of our linked bodies.

I guess the look on my face gave it away, because Chris asked, "Are you okay, baby? Do you wanna stop?"

I shook my head. My heart ached with intense passion for him as I focused on him watching me, acutely aware of every transient emotion that crossed my face. "I'm okay." I smiled and wrapped my legs around him to prove it.

He kissed me with a deep probing kiss that caused my stomach to quiver and ripple its way down my body, awakening the most sensitive areas. Never closing his eyes, he held my gaze as we continued to make love by the flickering candlelight. We enjoyed exploring each other's bodies, appreciating every passing minute of our experience together. We took turns taking control, finding new and exciting positions neither of us had experienced before. Neither of us in a hurry, we savored every moment and welcomed every second of intensifying ecstasy that built up within us. I never wanted the feeling to end—the feeling of our connected souls through our linked bodies. After a while, the moment of pure intensity was upon us, and Chris pumped harder and faster in response to the tightening he felt from my body. Every nerve ending inside me ignited as he rocked his hips into me. I bucked against him and relished the sensitive tingling my body felt from each exhilarating thrust.

"Oh Chris," I moaned, in response to the quickening of my swollen bundle of nerves that threatened to burst with shuddering delight. I closed my eyes, anticipating the moment that was swiftly building inside me.

"Look at me, baby," Chris whispered. "I wanna watch you."

I opened my eyes as his final thrust caused the wave of euphoria to crest and topple inside me—a blissful quaking that took my breath away. Chris moaned, lost in his own mounting release. A moment later, he grunted and surged inside me, enjoying his own sublime undulation.

Our bodies trembled with lingering aftershocks as we cuddled beneath the blankets, clinging to our delirium as long as possible. Chris cradled me in the crook of his arm while I rested my head on his chest. He gently stroked my arm, and our breaths synchronized.

The silence spoke words neither of us was willing to say out loud. *This was it. Goodbye. Again.*

Letting our bodies relax in each other's arms, we both slowly drifted off to sleep.

Before long, rays of sunshine peeked through the curtains and splashed onto my face.

No! It can't be morning already!

I was alone in the bed. I opened my eyes and looked around the room, trying to get my bearings.

"Good morning, sunshine."

I glanced toward the sound of his voice. Chris was sitting in a chair in the corner of the room, dressed only in a pair of faded jeans, exposing his bare chest in the soft sunbeam that poured through the curtains.

I bolted up and wrapped the sheets around me, feeling embarrassed in broad daylight and realizing that my clothes had been tossed somewhere on the floor the night before. "What are you doing?" I asked, suddenly aware of the inevitable rat's nest that occurred overnight in my hair. I ran my fingers through it trying to smooth the crazy bed head.

"Watching you sleep," he admitted with a sexy grin. He propped his feet up on the edge of the bed and lifted the steaming hot mug of coffee to his lips, winking at me before taking a sip.

"Why didn't you wake me up?" I asked, rubbing my sleepy eyes with the palms of my hands.

"You looked so peaceful. Besides, you're beautiful when you sleep." He tilted the corner of his mouth up in a half-smile, then took another sip of coffee.

I squinted my eyes at the piercing sliver of daylight that shone through the crack in the curtains. "It's morning already," I pouted. "I'm not ready to leave yet."

Setting the coffee down on the floor, he strode over to my side of the bed. "I'm not ready for you to leave either." He reached his hand out to me. Gently pulling me out of bed, he wrapped me up in his arms and hugged me tight. "I want you to stay. I really, really want you to stay."

"I can't—"

"I know."

"I can't do that to Eli. He is my life."

"I know. That's why I'm not asking you to stay. You have a family."

Tears had already pooled in my eyes and threatened to fall.

"Promise me this," he said. "When we're old and gray and widowed, promise me you'll look me up in the nursing home so we can finally be together." He grinned at me.

I couldn't help but smile back, blinking back my tears.

"I promise," I affirmed, boldly trying to hold it together. "But, for now, I gotta find some mouthwash."

He laughed and kissed my forehead. "I'd take you, morning breath and all."

"Hush," I teased and playfully pushed him away, making a quick getaway to the bathroom.

Chris was sitting on the sofa flipping through the channels on the television when I stepped out of the bathroom. I quickly managed to swish my mouth with the complimentary mouthwash I'd found on the bathroom counter, run a comb through my hair, and apply a little lip gloss in record time. "Wow," he said when I stepped into the living room. "Are you sure you have to leave now?" he asked with a wink.

"Unfortunately," I sighed.

He stood up and walked over to me, reaching out for me. I let him encompass me with his warm embrace. "Kaitlyn, I will never forget you. I will never forget this moment, your beautiful face, or the love we made last night. Thank you for coming to see me. In some ways it's the best thing that has ever happened to me, but saying goodbye to you—*again*—is the hardest thing I have ever done." His voice cracked on his final word, just as the first tear fell.

"Oh, Chris, I thought I'd never forgive myself if I came to see you last night. But honestly, I think if I had walked away without seeing you, I would have regretted it the rest of my life. I'm not sure how I will process all of this, especially since I'm going back home to my husband and my son. I can tell you this…I will never, ever forget you or the way I feel this very moment."

Chris kissed me gently on the lips, then softly kissed the tears away that slid down my cheeks. Holding me tightly, he rested his chin on top of my head. I buried my face into his chest while I clung desperately to him, breathing in the memory of his scent, singeing it into my brain. Both of our shoulders shook from the sobs that reverberated in our chests. We stood together, wallowing in our sorrow, for several minutes.

That moment felt all too familiar to me. The memory of the night we stood in his driveway before he left for juvie again flashed through my mind. I was losing him—*again*! It was another goodbye that would send my depression into a tailspin. I felt so alive in his arms; I couldn't let him go. I wanted so desperately to cling to him forever. A love I had tucked away so deeply into my soul was reignited eight years later by a single glance. I didn't want to say goodbye again! *Why, God? Why?!* Finally, one of us had to pull away.

"I gotta go," I whispered.

"I know," he sighed, his eyes bloodshot from crying.

He slowly walked me to the door, the sadness nearly palpable between us. Kissing one last time, our lips lingered a little longer than a peck as we both relished that very last moment.

"Never forget me?" His lower lip quivered with repressed sorrow.

"Never," I promised. A final tear escaped my eye and slid down my cheek just as I turned to leave. I walked away feeling as though I had left my heart at the door of room 204. *Oh, God, what have I done?*

When I stepped into my condo, the girls were busy packing up to head home. Tori saw me first. "Kaitlyn's home," she announced flatly, rolling her eyes. I didn't think she would let my decision affect our friendship, but I could definitely sense her reproach to the matter.

"Kaitlyn!" The other girls shouted simultaneously and came running at once.

"Tell. Us. Everything!" Lisa cried.

"Girls," Shannon chided, "can't a girl have a few private moments in her life?" Then she turned to look at me. "Let me ask you this, do you have any regrets?"

"No," I tried to say with a straight face.

"Then that's all we need to know," she said with a smile. I could not have been more thankful for her friendship at that moment.

Chapter Twenty-Two

Calling my mother was the first thing on my agenda the minute I dropped Shannon off at her house.

"Mom," I said anxiously when she picked up the phone. "Can I come over for a minute? I've been looking for something and can't find it anywhere. Do you mind if I stop by and search the attic. I might have left it there when I moved out."

"Sure, sweetheart," she replied. "What is it you're looking for? I may be able to help you."

"It's nothing you'd recognize. Just an old box of mementos I kept from high school."

She laughed. "Oh, okay. I pretty much just boxed everything up and carried it to the attic when you moved out. You should be able to find what you're looking for up there."

"Thanks, mom," I said quickly, trying to disguise my seething anger, and hung up the phone.

I pulled into the driveway of my old house. Just sitting there in my car brought back so many memories...setting up my first lemonade stand, helping my dad wash the car, building snowmen in the front yard with mom that year it snowed almost a foot, my first kiss with Trevor, and the night I sneaked out to see Chris the last night before he left for juvie.

My memory of that night reminded me of my mission, which was to find those letters–that is, if she even kept them. Knowing my mom, the hoarder, she had them boxed up somewhere in that attic. I was determined to find them.

"Hi, honey," my mom said when I walked into the kitchen.

"Hi, mom. I'm in a hurry. I just need to check the attic, then I'll be out of your hair. Michael and Eli are expecting me."

"Okay, just go ahead. I'm going to stay down here. That old attic messes with my allergies…all that dust."

I headed up to the attic, fearful and excited to find out the truth. The musty smell of the dark attic overwhelmed me as I stepped across wooden beams lining the floor. Boxes upon boxes were stacked against the walls. While my mother was a hoarder, she was also a very organized one. Every box was labeled. *Kaitlyn's baby clothes. Kaitlyn's stuffed animals. Kaitlyn's wedding dress. Photo albums. Vacation souvenirs. Christmas decorations.* It didn't take me long to figure out the box that didn't have a label was the very one for which I had been searching. An old, round hat box sat in one corner of the attic, beckoning me to open it. I rushed to it, grabbing it up as if I were a child on Christmas morning reaching for that first big gift. Before opening it, I closed my eyes. Part of me prayed the box would contain exactly what I needed, but the other half of me prayed it wouldn't, for fear I wouldn't be able to handle the truth that my mother had kept from me all these years. My nerves quaked my stomach while my trembling hands lifted the lid. A thick manila envelope stuffed to its max was crammed inside. Carefully, I pulled the envelope out.

About twenty white, letter sized envelopes dumped out into the box with each and every one of them addressed to me. Tears stung my eyes. Anger gripped me as I desperately tried to contain the roar in the back of my throat, threatening to escape.

"Mother, how could you?" I growled under my breath, bitter thoughts and resentment built a fortress around my heart. "Un-fucking-believable," I groaned, as I opened the first letter.

> Dear Kaitlyn,
>   It's been two weeks since the last time I saw your face. I can't get you off my mind. This place sucks. I hate it here. But, god, you were worth it. You are worth a thousand years spent in this place. If I had the choice, I would do it all over again. I'd give the shirt off my back for you. If you were my girl, I'd treat you like the princess you deserve to be treated like. I love you. I love you like I've never loved anyone before, nor ever will. The only way I make it

through the day is knowing I'll
see you in my dreams at night. You
are the only reason I have to make
it through each day. I miss you.
I don't even miss home as much as
I miss you. God, I miss you...
your beautiful face, your perfect
body, your sweet personality. I
just miss everything about you. I
wish you would write me back. I
need to hear that you miss me too.
I need to know that you think
about me as much as I think about
you! At mail call each day, I pray
that I'll get a letter from you. I
love you more than even I can
comprehend. My heart aches for
you. Please write me back,
Kaitlyn. Please!

Forever and always,
Chris

Letter after letter with the same declarations of love, Chris pleaded for me to write him back, to no avail. In that moment, I was livid at my mother for what she had done, interfering in a way she had no right to interfere. It wasn't until I opened the last letter that my heart had even an ounce of understanding. The last letter wasn't from Chris. Instead, it was written by my mother's hand.

Dearest Kaitlyn,

If you're reading this, you have found the box of letters I have kept from you all this time. Before you make any rash decisions, please hear me out. I love you. I love you more than you will ever understand until you have children of your own. My job as a mother is to protect you. I felt I was doing the right thing by keeping these letters from you.

I know you loved him. I could see it in your eyes that night he brought you home and I threatened to call the police on him. I remember that look—that feeling. I had it myself once, before your father. It's not something I ever talked to you about, or anyone for that matter. But, please understand, I had my reasons for protecting you from Chris. Three years before I met your father, I fell in love. Young and dumb, I made decisions I would regret for the rest of

255

my life. Like Chris, this man swept me off my feet. I ran away from home at the young age of seventeen to marry him. He was a loner, a trouble maker, but for reasons I couldn't understand, I was drawn to him. So, we ran away together. I thought I would be living my dream. He couldn't hold down a job. I worked off and on as a waitress, but my meager salary wasn't enough to pay rent and put food on the table. I tried to make it work. Before long, he got caught up in dealing drugs and it took him getting arrested before I was able to accept the fact that this was not the environment in which I wanted to raise a family.

So, two years, three different cities, and eight jobs later, I was packing my bags to move back home, as painful as it was. Chris reminded me so much of him... a charming, handsome, bad boy. I didn't want to see you making the same mistake

I did. I didn't want to see you get hurt. I just wanted you to be happy. Please understand why I did what I did. I just wanted to protect my only daughter from getting hurt. You mean the world to me. I love you with all of my heart. And if given the choice, I would do it all over again. Please understand I would do anything to protect you from the same heartache I felt. I love you, my precious daughter. ~Mom

Tearfully, I folded the letters up and stuffed them all back into the hat box. A million thoughts ran through my mind at once. Was I angry? Yes. Was I hurt? Yes. Did I understand why my mom felt the need to protect me? Maybe. Would I do the same for Eli if it came down to it? Probably. Was I planning to say anything to her about it? Nope, not single a word.

I'd made my mind up not to mention it to her. I stuffed the box back into the corner, and once again closed that chapter of my life. Wiping my tears on my sleeves, I stood back up and made my way across the wooden plank floor toward the attic door.

"Did you find what you were looking for?" My mom asked me over her newest Better Homes magazine. She eyed me suspiciously. Assuming my cheeks were streaked with tears, and my eyes were red and puffy, I didn't really feel like stopping to chat.

"Nah," I said as I briskly walked toward the front door. "It's no big deal, though. I've probably overlooked it in our garage at home. Thanks anyway, mom."

"Okay. I'll talk to you later, then," she said as I stepped out the front door and practically ran to the safety of my car before the waterworks started again.

"Mommy!" Eli cried when I walked in the door. He ran up to me and hugged my legs. "I missed you!" he shouted.

"Awww, sweetie, I missed you too," I said as I knelt down to return a hug.

"Hey, honey," Michael kissed me quickly as he grabbed for my suitcase. "We both missed you," he added.

Michael carried my suitcase to our bedroom while Eli ran around the room, stringing sentences together as quickly as he could, giving me the rundown of his weekend.

"Son," Michael called from down the hall, "why don't we let Mommy get fully into the house and give her a minute to breathe first."

"Okay, Daddy," Eli said happily and bounded down the hall toward his room. He stopped when he reached his door. "Mommy!" he called to me.

"What, baby?"

"I'm really glad you're home," he grinned and then bounced into his room.

My sweet little boy. My reason for breathing.

"So, how was your trip?" Michael asked as he heaved the suitcase onto the bed to be sorted through later.

"It was good," I said, trying my best to disguise my guilt.

"What did you do?"

"Oh, we just hung out by the pool and the ocean all day, and headed to the bar at night."

"Do you feel refreshed?" he asked.

"I guess."

But, I was too late in trying to gulp back the audible sigh that escaped my mouth because Michael asked, "Is something wrong?"

"No, why?"

"I don't know. You're just not usually such a woman of few words."

"I guess I'm just tired. Sorry."

"It's okay. Are you sure you're all right?" He seemed genuinely concerned.

"Yeah, I'm fine," I lied. "Really. I'll be fine." Tears threatened me, but I choked them back and dared them to fall. *Not now! There are too many questions he could ask that I'm not prepared to answer!*

I had to let Chris go—move on. My life was here now with Michael and Eli. My chance with Chris had come and gone, and there was nothing I could do to change that. I just had to pick up the pieces of my broken heart and try to live the life I had created with my family. I knew, with a little time and separation, my moments spent with Chris would be another faded memory.

Later that evening while I was unpacking, I found a plastic bag buried deep inside my purse. Curiously, I pulled the bag out to inspect it more closely.

Affliction.

I opened the bag and the black Henley fell out into my hands. Immediately, I held the shirt up to my face and took a deep staggering breath of that familiar musky cologne. Chris must have hidden it there while I was sleeping. I looked down at a CD and the note attached to it that had fallen out of the bag along with the shirt.

> K, Hope you enjoy the CD. It's a few songs I recorded a while back. Take care of yourself, and remember, I'll never forget you. You always have been, and always will be on mind and in my heart.
>
> Love always,
>
> C.

Tears streamed down my face as I held the shirt up to my cheek. I inhaled the wonderfully cool and refreshing scent that still lingered on the soft cotton. Swaying back and forth, I remembered the feeling of my cheek as it pressed against the shirt while he wore it, with his warm arms wrapped around me as he hummed softly and gently ran his fingers through my hair. I desperately clung to the loose shirt, refusing to let the sound of his beating heart fade from my memory. Instinctively, I dug through my pockets, searching for a scrap of paper with his phone number written on it. That scrap of paper that had always been there when I needed it in high school. The scrap of paper that always kept me linked to Chris. My hands grappled with my vacant pockets and emerged empty. There was no scrap of paper—no phone number, and no link to Chris. That deep, sinking feeling felt heavy in the pit of my stomach. The knot tightened in my chest. *So, I guess that's it. He's gone. I don't think I can do this!*

Michael's footsteps creaked the hardwood floor as he walked down the hall toward our bedroom and immediately snapped me back to reality. Quickly, I stuffed the shirt, CD, and note back into the bag and hid it at the bottom of my purse again.

Michael poked his head into the doorway. "Honey, I got Eli ready for bed, but he wants you to read him a story."

Wiping tears and trying to look busy, I said, "Okay, I'll be there in just a minute."

"What's the matter?"

"Nothing," I lied. "I'm just tired. You know how emotional I get when I'm tired."

"Okay," he said hesitantly. "I'll go tell Eli you'll read to him in a minute."

When Michael was out of the room and down the hall, I rummaged through my purse and pulled the CD out of the bag. The shiny disk reflected two distorted red, tearful eyes. Written on it with a permanent marker were the words:

These songs are dedicated to someone special

She knows who she is

Carefully, I placed it into the CD player and pressed *play*. The first few chords of the same song he had played for me at the bar began, and immediately the tears spilled out again. Chris's smooth and hypnotic voice poured softly through the speakers. Hearing his voice again sent shivers down my spine. Oh, how my heart ached for him!

"Mommy!" Eli's voice jolted me back to reality. "I'm ready for stories and kisses."

I stopped the music and dried my tears with the back of my sleeve. "Okay, sweetheart!" I answered, my voice wavering with suppressed sobs.

Stuffing the CD along with the note, and his shirt back into the plastic bag, I hid them deep in my closet behind a stack of clothes I hadn't worn in more than three years. I flipped the light switch and shut the door. *Talk about skeletons in my closet.*

"Guess what, Mommy? I picked your favorite book tonight."

"Yay!" I said, trying to sound enthusiastic as I stepped into Eli's room. Snuggling up next to him in his bed and reading to him was the best medicine I needed to clear my head.

I knew I needed to shake my weekend with Chris off and get back to reality; my family needed me. A quote from Eli's favorite movie resonated in my mind about the past being called history and the gift of today being named the *present.*

I looked down at my precious gift lying beside me in his bed. His sweet little face smiled at me, anticipating my hugs and kisses. His adorable blue eyes peeked out beneath the blond curls I had been reluctant to cut. No matter the cost, nothing was worth losing my little family. I wrapped my arm around Eli as he looked at the pictures and told his own make-believe story.

"What's wrong, Mommy? Why are you crying?"

I smiled at him through my tears. "I just love you so much it hurts."

"I love you too, Mommy. You're the bestest mommy ever!"

I looked at him earnestly and spoke with conviction. "You're the best *present* I could ask for."

Chapter Twenty-Three

A month and a half had passed since my weekend at the beach with Chris. The more numb my heart became to the raw emotions I had felt the day I said goodbye to him, the more angry I became with myself and what I had done.

I applied my mascara and slammed the tube back down on the counter.

"You slut," I seethed at my reflection in the mirror. "You're no better than a two-bit whore. You harlot. You may as well tattoo 'adulterer' across your forehead."

Every day I cooked and cleaned and managed to live with the guilt as if nothing happened, but inside my conscience churned itself into an angry, depressed, guilt-ridden pulp.

"Mommy," Eli knocked on the bathroom door. "Are you almost done? I need to go potty!"

"I'll be right out, sweetheart," I called to him as I turned off my flat iron and put away my make-up bag. "You don't deserve this family," I growled at myself in the mirror. The taste of bile burned the back of my throat. I gagged at the thought of it. Turning around just at the nick of time, I retched the contents of my stomach into the toilet.

Three days later I stood in the same bathroom in front of a tiny plastic bathroom cup I had placed in front of me on the counter.

"Oh no. Oh god, no!" I focused on the two lines blazing up at me from the stick I held in my hand. "This can't be happening." Pulling another one out of the box, I tried again. "No, no, no, no," I repeated over and over as if the more I said it would help change the outcome. "This can't be happening."

Four sticks later, eight bright pink lines aligned themselves like an army battalion on the back of my toilet. Tears pooled in my eyes, my stomach twisted in knots. "Oh god, this is really happening." The contents of my stomach once again found their way to the porcelain bowl below.

"Hey, Shannon." Thank god she picked up on the first ring. Otherwise, I might have lost my nerve.

"Hi, Kaitlyn. What's up?"

I knew I just had to spill it; no hem hawing around. "I'm pregnant," I announced.

"Wow!" Shannon cried, "That's wonderful. Congratulations!"

"No, Shannon, I'm *pregnant*."

"Right. I heard you. That's fantastic!"

"No, you don't understand. I think I'm six weeks pregnant."

"Six weeks? I don't understand. This is a good thing, right?"

"Six weeks ago we were at the beach."

Silence.

"Shannon?"

"Oh my god, Kaitlyn," she whispered. "What are you going to do?"

Immediately my sobs echoed through the phone. "I don't know, Shannon. I'm terrified to tell Michael."

Shannon breathed a deep sigh into the phone—one of those long, drawn out, 'need time to think' kind of sighs. "Well, you don't have to tell him *everything*, Kaitlyn," she insinuated.

"I don't know. I'm not so sure I could keep it a secret. I mean, we've only had sex once in the last eight weeks, and that was the night after we got back from the beach…guilt sex, I guess. Just once. In eight weeks."

"Well, it only takes one time…obviously. Seriously though, about you and Michael—only once in the past two months?"

"Yeah. I mean, by the time he comes to bed at night I'm usually asleep. And half the time we end up with Eli in our bed at some point during the night. And the more that time passes, the more awkward it feels to initiate something. We never talk about it or anything. We just haven't really *done it*, except that one time." My words spilled out of my mouth almost faster than I could speak them.

"Well, you'll have to tell Michael something. You can't hide it forever."

I sighed. She was right; I had to tell Michael. I just didn't know how. "I know. I will. Oh, and please don't breathe a word of this to anyone yet, okay?"

"You know I would never do that. I'm here for you no matter what. I love you, my friend."

"Thanks, Shannon. I love you, too."

I waited until Eli had gone to bed before I talked to Michael about it. I also waited until Michael was sitting down before I broke the news. He was sitting on the sofa with his iPad on his lap, checking the stock market.

I wrung my hands and paced back and forth in the kitchen, trying to get the nerve to talk to him. I practiced under my breath while I paced. "*Michael*, I'm pregnant. Michael, I'm *pregnant*. *Michael*, by a miracle of God, I'm *pregnant*." I wondered how Mary from the Bible felt when she had to tell her fiancé, Joseph, about her immaculate conception, unsure of how he would react to the news.

Finally, I decided the only way to tell him was to just come out and say it. I had no other choice. He would either accept the fact that I was pregnant without hesitation, or he would berate me with questions until I broke and confessed my guilt. Without a moment's delay, I walked into the living room where he was sitting. "Michael."

"Mmmhmm," he barely acknowledged me, staring at his iPad.

"I need to tell you something."

"Okay." He still didn't look up.

"It's very important." I broke out in a cold sweat. Adrenaline pumped its way throughout my body. *God, this stress can't be good for the baby.*

He finally put the iPad on the coffee table and looked up at me. "What is it, Kaitlyn?"

I can't do this! "I'm pregnant," I barely squeaked out the words and closed my eyes, waiting for a response.

Silence.

I peeked at Michael who was still sitting there. "Really?"

"Yes. Really," I affirmed.

Michael just continued to stare at me, dumbfounded. "How far along?" he finally asked, looking skeptically at my flat stomach.

"Six weeks, I think."

"Hmmm, that's interesting," he mumbled under his breath, taking a moment to mull the idea over in his mind.

Idiot, I chided myself. *You're never going to get away with this.*

Then suddenly, without warning, he laughed and stood up to hug me. "Well, I guess what they say is true. It only takes once." Wrapping me in his arms, he swung me around in a full circle. "Looks like we're going to have another baby!"

I heard a nervous chuckle escape my mouth.

Yes. Yes, we are. I mean, **we** *are, right?* I smiled weakly. The uncertainty chipped away at my conscience like a pickaxe against stone.

Chapter Twenty-Four

It had been nearly three weeks since I'd broken the news to Michael. I barely placed the eggs onto the table before my face had time to meet with the trashcan by the sink. The smell of eggs alone turned my stomach, but to have to whip them up for Eli and serve them for breakfast was more than my will to suppress my gag reflex could handle.

Eli looked up from the table at his dad who had just stepped into the kitchen. "Mommy threw up again," he announced as he scraped the plate with his fork and shoveled a forkful of eggs into his mouth. My gag reflex threatened me again and I had to turn away.

"I take it your morning sickness is in full swing today, huh?" Michael asked as he swiped his to-go mug of coffee off the counter and took a sip.

"You noticed?" I said smugly, wiping my mouth on a paper towel and tossing it in the trashcan.

Michael smiled. "I don't remember you being sick like this with Eli."

"That's because I wasn't," I said flatly.

Chalk up another difference between this pregnancy and my last pregnancy.

I found myself scrutinizing every detail of this pregnancy, searching for any minute detail that would give me the answers I needed about the father of the baby. Guilt still found a way to rob me of the joy I should have felt in carrying another child. My pregnancy dreams had been so vivid lately; I hoped my conscience didn't decide to rear its ugly head, causing me to spill the truth to Michael while I slept. I had been known to talk in my sleep a time or two. It wasn't a pleasant feeling to have your dreams retold to you over the breakfast table.

"Well, I hope it ends soon. There's nothing like trying to enjoy your morning coffee mixed with the aroma of vomit." He tilted his mug up as if he were indicating me, and then took a sip.

"Thanks," I deadpanned.

Michael laughed. "I'm kidding. Seriously, I hope you feel better."

I tossed him the leftovers I'd packed up for his lunch. "So do I. Have a great day."

"You too." He bent down to kiss Eli's cheek, then tossed his hand up and waved to me before swiftly opening the door and stepping out into the garage.

"Love you too," I mumbled under my breath, staring at the closed door Michael had so swiftly dashed out of on his way to work.

Remind me again why I chose to come home.

"Mommy, I'm finished."

Oh, yeah. He's why.

I grabbed Eli's plate off the table and stood over the trashcan, gagging while I scraped his leftovers into the garbage.

I spent the morning on the sofa trying to keep my sickness at bay. Eli was home for summer break, so he spent the morning watching cartoons and playing with his wooden building logs. It wasn't until mid-morning that I felt like getting up and doing something. I decided to start my day with a shower.

The hot water spraying across my back felt like heaven. Guilt and nausea twisted my stomach into a million tiny knots. That night I would tell Michael the truth. I couldn't live like this any longer. Terror gripped me like a vice, but I knew I couldn't live with myself, giving birth to a child that may or may not be Michael's baby. He had to know the truth, regardless of the consequences.

I managed to make it through the rest of the day in one piece. Eli was a big help in bringing me cold washcloths and sips of water. I'd never had morning sickness that lasted all day. Of course, my festering guilt didn't help either.

Dinner went off without a hitch. I cooked and cleaned without a single gag. Hopefully the rest of the night would be a breeze, too. Well, except for the moment I spilled the truth to Michael. I had no idea what to expect, but I knew it wouldn't be good. I wondered if I should start packing after I finished washing the dishes.

Eli skipped into the living room where Michael had just sat down on the sofa, flipping through the list of his recorded stock market news and sports highlights television shows.

"Daddy, will you play a game with me?"

"Sure," Michael chuckled. "As long as we can watch my show at the same time."

"Okay, Daddy. I'll go get the game." Eli bounded up the stairs, but was back in a flash.

I heard them setting up the candy themed game board with the colorful playing cards, preparing for a father/son game night marathon. Eli usually liked to play three or four games in a row.

I took that time to make a short phone call.

"Hey, Shannon," I said when she answered her phone.

"Oh hey, Kaitlyn. How are you feeling?"

"I'm okay. It's been a rough day."

"I hate to hear that. Morning sickness is the pits."

"You're telling me," I laughed.

We made small talk for a few minutes about our day and the weather. We chatted about her son's upcoming birthday party. We even discussed her dreaded mother-in-law's impending visit.

After several minutes of superficial conversation, Shannon piped up. "So, what's *really* up?"

I breathed a sigh of relief. I didn't really want to have to bring it up. I was so thankful she knew me well enough to know I needed her to broach the topic. "I'm going to tell him tonight."

"I thought you already did."

"No, not yet. I told him I was pregnant, but I haven't told him the truth."

"You're going to tell him about Chris?"

"Yes."

Silence.

"Shannon?"

"Yeah, I'm still here...just wondering if that's a good idea."

"I can't live like this, Shannon. The guilt is killing me. What if this is Chris's baby? This baby will come out with dark brown hair and dark brown eyes, looking nothing like Eli. Michael will know then. I would rather tell him now and deal with it now than wait until the baby is born."

"Okay," she agreed. "I'm here if you need me, or if you need a place to come to when this is over."

"Thanks, Shannon," I said graciously. "Say a prayer he doesn't go off the deep end. I'm really freaking out here."

"It will be okay. I'll say a prayer, but Michael is a good man. Everything is going to be fine," she assured me.

"I sure hope so. Talk to you later."

"Bye, Kaitlyn."

I hung up the phone just as I heard Eli racing up the stairs toward his room. I timed that phone call just right.

"Eli, it's time for a bath and bed," I called up the stairs. "I'll come run your bath water."

"Awww," Eli whined. "I wanted to play the other game too."

"Not tonight sweetheart. Maybe tomorrow."

"Okay," Eli replied and sulked to the bathroom.

After I ran the water, helped him rinse his hair, and assisted him in getting his pajamas on, it was finally time to say goodnight. The day had been one of those days I couldn't wait for bedtime. It was hard to focus on being a good mother when I vomited all day while my guilt suffocated me.

"Goodnight, Mommy."

"Goodnight, honey. I love you."

"So much it hurts?"

He remembered.

"Yes, baby. So much it hurts." I shut his bedroom door just in time to wipe the first tear on my sleeve.

I avoided Michael until I knew for sure that Eli was asleep. I folded laundry in our bedroom while I watched my favorite recorded show about rich teenagers who party too much. It felt nice to lose myself in those mind numbing episodes. Before I knew it, I had finished folding and putting everything away. I had avoided the inevitable long enough. It was one of those 'now or never' moments. Quietly, I walked into the living room where Michael sat with his laptop, a bowl of Neapolitan ice cream, and his favorite sports show on television.

I wrung my hands anxiously, unsure of how to even start the conversation. "Michael, I need to tell you something." My voice sounded jittery.

"What?" he asked, stuffing a glob of ice cream into his mouth.

"No." I shook my head, grabbing the remote and turning off the television. "I *really* need to tell you something."

"Wow, you're serious," he said, as he set his laptop down on the end table, and laid his bowl of ice cream on the coffee table. "What's wrong? Is something wrong with the baby?"

"No. I mean, it's about the baby, but nothing's wrong with it."

"Then what is it, Kaitlyn? You're starting to freak me out a little bit."

"Michael, I messed up. I messed up big time."

"What do you mean?" Michael's wide eyes filled with worry.

I didn't know how else to put it, so I just came right out and said it. "This baby..." I said, pointing to my abdomen. "This baby might not be yours."

Michael stared at me, taking time to process the words I had spoken. A range of emotions presented themselves across his face, and I took a step back.

Suddenly, fury darkened his eyes. Glaring at me, he practically growled, "How?"

I said the first thing that popped into my head. "What do you mean, how?" *Idiot*, I chided myself.

"Don't give me that shit, Kaitlyn." His anger started to make its way to the surface. "Tell me, *how?*" he seethed.

"I screwed up, okay. I'm sorry. I don't have an excuse. I just totally screwed everything up!" I wailed, my tears bursting out of my eyes and flowing down my cheeks.

"You're damn right you screwed up!" Michael yelled and punched his fist into the arm of the sofa. He jumped up from the couch and stomped behind it to create a barrier between us. "When did this happen? Who did you fuck? How long have you been fucking him?" He paced angrily back and forth like a caged tiger.

"I...I..." The words just wouldn't come out.

"Tell me, Kaitlyn! I deserve to know! I'm your *husband*!"

"It only happened once, Michael! I'm not having an affair. It happened once and I haven't seen him since!"

"Who? Answer me that."

"Michael, please. I—"

"Tell me! Who?" he demanded.

"It was Chris, okay."

Michael stopped pacing back and forth behind the sofa and glared at me. "Chris?" he asked with a look of disgust. "Chris, my stock broker?"

"No, Chris King."

He stared at me incredulously. "Chris King? As in *high school* Chris King? The convicted felon?" His jaw muscle pulsed as he gritted his teeth.

"Yeah." Ashamed of myself, I lowered my eyes to avoid his menacing glare.

"When? How?" His breaths came hard and fast between words. He seemed on the verge of hyperventilation while he tried his best to contain his rage.

"While I was at the beach," I squeaked.

"Jesus Christ, Kaitlyn! What the hell? Please tell me you are fucking kidding me!"

"I wish I could." I trembled with fear. I knew I was safe because Michael would *never* do anything to hurt me no matter how angry he was, especially with Eli asleep just upstairs, but my nerves were still on edge.

"I can't fucking believe this." Michael's eyes welled up with tears. "Oh god, I just can't believe you did this to me." He stared at me in disbelief, with tears dripping down his cheeks and his lip quivering. The pain in his eyes was almost too much to bear.

"I'm sorry, Michael. Please forgive me. I'm so, so sorry." Reaching out to him, I continued, "I wish I could take it back, but I—"

"No!" Michael threw his hands up in the air, and took a step back. "Don't touch me. Just don't fucking touch me."

He whirled around and stomped into the kitchen, grabbing his truck keys off the hook by the door.

I followed him into the foyer where he stood in the open doorway leading out to the front porch. "Please don't leave! Stay here. Please, let's talk about this."

He turned his head to glare at me. "I have nothing to say to you." With that statement, he slammed the door in my face.

His truck roared to life, and the tires squealed their way out of the driveway.

I fell into my bed a blubbery mess. If it weren't for the sweet little boy sleeping three doors down and the tiny life growing inside me, I would have considered tossing a whole bottle of Valium down my throat. *"Get over yourself,"* I chided. *"Put your big girl panties on and deal with this!"*

It was three in the morning when Michael finally came home. I was still lying in bed, my eyes swollen from crying for hours. I heard him rummaging around in the kitchen and pacing around in the living room. Eventually, he made it to our bedroom. He plopped down on the edge of the bed and sighed. I didn't ask him where he had been. I didn't say a word. I just lay there, hoping he would speak first.

"Kaitlyn?"

"Hmmm," I answered.

"Just wanted to see if you were still awake."

"I am. I—"

"Shhhh," he interrupted. "Just let me speak. Just let me get this out. I'm not here for you right now. I came back because we have a son who needs us to be *us*. I'm not angry, I'm hurt," he whispered in the darkness. "I can't believe that the woman I love more than anything would betray me like this. I'm back, but I'm not back because of you. This isn't about you at all right now.

This is about Eli. I'm so hurt and shattered beyond words. Just please, don't speak to me right now."

I didn't say anything. Fear gripped my throat, threatening me not to make a sound. He wasn't back for me. But he was back. That was one step in the right direction. *Right?*

Silent tears bid me goodnight as I finally drifted off into oblivion.

It felt like only minutes had passed before I was awakened by the sound of dishes clanking in the kitchen. Apparently, Michael had already gotten up to cook eggs for Eli. I ambled into the kitchen with swollen and puffy eyes.

"Good morning, Mommy," Eli said happily as he shoveled scrambled eggs into his mouth.

I tried not to gag. "Good morning, honey," I said as I kissed the top of his head.

Michael threw a sidelong glance, but didn't speak.

I looked at Michael who was standing near the stove. "Thanks for cooking for him. It helped keep my morning sickness at bay a little while longer."

"Humph," Michael grunted at me. I didn't blame him. I guess if I were in his shoes I wouldn't want to speak to me either. He chucked the frying pan into the sink and stomped off to the living room.

Completely oblivious, Eli blew bubbles into his orange juice through his straw. "Look, Mommy," he laughed.

"You're so silly." I didn't have the energy to correct him or tell him it was rude to do that at the table. I sighed, poured my coffee, and plopped down in the chair beside him while he finished cramming eggs into his mouth like he was trying to win an egg eating contest.

"Slow down, Eli. You're going to make yourself sick—or me."

"I'm just trying to finish so you don't have to look at them or smell them anymore, and maybe you won't throw up today."

My precious little angel…the only reason I have to be here right now.

"You're so sweet. Thank you."

"You're welcome. I'm all done," he said proudly. He chucked his plate into the sink just like his daddy and ran upstairs to play his video game system.

I sat in peace, sipping my coffee and wondering how to act around Michael.

I was washing the dishes when Michael walked into the kitchen. "I'm leaving," he announced.

"For work?"

"No. I'm leaving for a few days. I need to get my head straight."

"Please don't leave," I begged. "Let's work through this. It was a mistake, Michael. A stupid, stupid mistake. I don't want my mistake to break up Eli's happy family."

Michael stared at me for a few seconds, as if to consider my offer. He finally piped up. "Tell Eli I'm going on a business trip for a while."

"No, Michael. Please don't go."

He scowled at me angrily, but the pain in his eyes projected a different emotion. "I'm not sure when I'll be back."

Tears rolled down my cheeks. "I'm sorry," I whispered.

"Don't." Michael snapped. He grabbed his suitcase and walked toward the stairs. "Eli," he shouted, "I'm leaving for work!"

"Okay, Daddy!" Eli replied. I heard him bouncing down the stairs. Giving Michael a big hug and seeing his suitcase beside them on the floor, he asked, "Where are you going?"

Michael's eyes welled up with tears, but he didn't let them fall. "I'm going on a business trip."

Eli's face fell. "When will you be back?"

"I don't know," Michael shook his head, "but I'll call you every day."

Eli nodded. "Okay, Daddy."

"I love you very much, son."

"I love you too, Daddy."

Michael gave him one last squeeze before grabbing his suitcase and heading for the door. Just before stepping out into the garage, he gave me a final look—a morose and dejected look—that held my gaze a few seconds before he gently shook his head in disbelief and closed the door behind him.

Tears exploded from my eyes and sobs heaved in my chest.

"Don't cry, Mommy. He'll be back," Eli tried to console me.

Get a grip, Kaitlyn.

"I know, baby. Mommy's okay," I said, wiping tears on my sleeve and taking deep, controlled breaths to contain my sobs.

I called Shannon that afternoon to tell her the news. "He's gone, Shannon. He packed his bags and left."

"Where did he go?"

"He didn't say. I don't think he'd go to his parents' house because he wouldn't want them to know anything was going on. He just left and said he didn't know when he'd be back."

"Maybe he just needs time to process everything. It's a lot to have to soak in."

"I know. I deserve it. He's been nothing but good to me, and I had to go and ruin everything. I mean, I know our marriage isn't perfect, but I didn't have to go and screw things up like I did. I don't know what I was thinking."

"People make mistakes, Kaitlyn. No one is perfect. At least you owned up to your mistakes. Just give him time. Let him think things over."

"Okay, I will. Thanks, Shannon. Thank you for not judging me. I know what I did was stupid. I just got caught up in the moment. My heart and my head were having a screaming match with each other, and I let my stupid heart win."

"I think your marriage was crumbling, and you were vulnerable. You let someone creep into your life at your weakest point. This kind of thing happens every day—that's part of the reason why they say fifty percent of marriages end in divorce. Give yourself some time to heal. Maybe when Michael comes back, you can focus on giving your heart back to him. Fight through this. It will be worth it, I promise." I didn't pry, but she spoke as if she had some experience in the matter.

"Okay, I will," I promised, my lip quivering with suppressed tears.

Chapter Twenty-Five

Three long, grueling weeks passed. As promised, Michael called Eli every day, and every day Eli begged him to come home. "Not yet," was always his answer.

Alone. It was a word I had learned to accept in the weeks since Michael left for his 'business trip.' Alone wasn't something I had ever considered until the first night I spent in our bed after he left. The house seemed eerily quiet, even with Eli just down the hall. Eli must have thought so too because he ended up in my bed most nights. My morning sickness had finally subsided, but my depression seeped its way into my everyday life. Daily activities were such a drain on my energy; I barely functioned most days. However, I knew I had to be strong for my son. My attitude affected his little life. I never knew how strong I was until my husband left me. I never realized how *good* I had it until the day my life, as I knew it, had been ripped away from me.

I tossed and turned in bed one night, trying to get some sleep, with no success.

Suddenly, my phone buzzed beside me on the bed stand. Eagerly, I grabbed it, praying it would be a text from Michael:

Michael:

I'm coming home. Didn't want to scare you since it's late.

Thank God!

I anxiously awaited his arrival. Around midnight I heard his key turn the lock, and he tiptoed into the kitchen. He made his way up the stairs and stood at our bedroom door.

"I'm awake," I whispered in the darkness.

"Okay," he whispered back.

"I'm glad you're home. I've missed you."

I heard an audible sigh.

From the sound of it, I assumed the worst and asked, "Or, did you just come home to get more of your stuff?" I sat up, hugged my knees, and wrapped the blankets under my chin.

Michael plopped down on the bed. "I'm not here to get more stuff."

I released a grateful sigh of relief and lay back down on the bed. Michael kicked off his shoes and laid down beside me.

"Michael—"

"Please, Kaitlyn. Just hear me out." He sounded tired, destitute even.

"Okay."

"In some ways, I can't blame you. I know I haven't been the kind of husband you've needed me to be."

"Don't blame yourself, Michael. It's not your fault."

"I'm not blaming myself. I'm just trying to comprehend and justify *why* you would do this. I know you loved him. I knew the night I met you at the dance who held the key to your heart. I just thought I could love you enough to forget him. Now I see that I was wrong. I'm hurt beyond belief that the only woman I have ever loved has broken our vows, given her heart to someone else, and shattered mine."

My eyes were brimming, but I didn't speak. What could I have possibly said in that moment? No words, no apology, and no act of valor could erase the damage I had done.

"I forgive you," Michael whispered.

What? I stared at him incredulously, although in the darkness I knew he couldn't see my face.

"I took my vows seriously when I promised 'for better, for worse, until death do us part.' It's taken me a while to get my head straight, but I have forgiven you. Now, I just have to try my best to forget."

I sat in silence, unsure how to process what he had just told me. *He's not kicking me out? He's not sending me packing? He's not threatening to divorce me? I don't deserve this man—this good, faithful, loyal, and amazing man.*

Ever so slowly, I reached across the bed and found his hand in the darkness. The warmth of his hand that enveloped mine felt like a sonic boom to my heart, reigniting a passion between us that had long since burned out.

"We'll get through this," I spoke softly.

Michael pulled me close and wrapped me in his arms. "I love you," he whispered, "more than you will ever know. You cut me deeper than you will ever realize, but I am willing to fight for us. I don't want to lose you. I don't want to lose the family bond we have created with Eli. This family means everything to me. I am willing to fight to save it. The tiny life growing inside of you, it didn't ask for this—to be born into a broken home. If need be, when we're ready, we can take a DNA test. If it proves I'm not the biological father, then we can determine the right time to discuss the truth with the child. But, I will love this baby, no matter what."

Michael was my best friend. He was the one I'd stood at the altar with and vowed to love, honor, and cherish for life. He was the father of my child. I trusted him and depended on him. He was safe—my shelter from the storm. He was everything I needed, and nothing I deserved.

"Michael, there's nothing I can say to fix this. There's nothing I can do to make up for what I've done. I never wanted to hurt you. I was selfish. I'm sorry. Those words seem so empty right now, but please understand that I mean them from the deepest part of my soul. I'm so, so sorry."

Silent tears slid down both our faces as we held each other close, and fell asleep in each other's arms.

My overly sensitive gag reflex jarred me from my semi-lucid state. I sat up quickly, clamping my hand across my mouth. *Oh no! I thought this morning sickness stuff was over!* I barely made it to the bathroom in time. Hugging the toilet as if it were my life raft in an angry sea, my traitorous stomach heaved violently into the cold porcelain bowl. I wasn't sure if it was a virus, morning sickness, or my body purging itself of the torturous guilt I'd harbored for four months, but I prayed hard it would end soon. In my weakest moment, just when I thought all my energy had been spent and my rebellious stomach had won the battle, I felt my hair being lifted from around my face.

Michael stood behind me, holding my hair, "It's okay," he consoled me. "It's okay."

I collapsed onto the cool tile floor, draping myself across the rim of the toilet seat, overcome with defeat, crying tears of utter exhaustion. Michael continued to hold my hair back and began rubbing his hand across my back in an effort to soothe me.

"You're going to get through this. *We're* going to get through this, together," he reassured me.

"I don't deserve this," I cried into the crook of my arm. "I don't deserve you being this nice to me."

Michael ran his fingers through my hair. "We're in this together, Kaitlyn. I'm not giving up. We all make mistakes. I'm not perfect. You're not perfect. I don't know what happened between us to make you run into the arms of another man, but I'm going to make damn sure you're never tempted again. Things are going to change, starting right now."

With that, he pulled me up from the floor and held me against his chest. Surrendering myself to his embrace, I nuzzled into the softness of his shirt, breathing his familiar scent that translated to *home* in my mind.

"I love you, Kaitlyn."

"I love you, too, Michael…more than I ever realized."

He tensed his jaw in an effort to control his quivering lip. His voice cracked as he spoke, "We're a family. Families stick together no matter what, through thick and thin. We are going to come out stronger after this—just you wait."

We heard a soft knock at the door. "Daddy? Is that you?"

"You bet, buddy," Michael opened to the door to a sleepy-eyed little boy who stood in the hallway holding his stuffed T-Rex by one clawed foot.

Immediately, Eli's eyes perked up. "Daddy!" he squealed with delight. Eli dropped his T-Rex, ran toward us, and grabbed our legs, joining us in a group hug.

Chapter Twenty-Six

Michael had been amazing throughout the entire pregnancy. From late night runs to the 24-hour drive thru to pick up my never ending craving for fast food French fries, to holding my hand through every ultrasound and medical test, he had been nothing short of wonderful. Every day I beat myself up internally for doubting our marriage and breaking our vows. But, Michael never brought it up again, never let me wallow in self-guilt, and never threw it in my face. With a lot of marriage counseling and many late night talks, we were able to put the past behind us. Our marriage had become stronger than ever, just like he promised.

Michael even sent me flowers the day after we found out we were having another boy. I was in the closet, sorting through a box of maternity clothes, when I heard the doorbell ring. I wasn't expecting anyone. I rushed to the door. Opening it, I saw a beautiful bouquet of roses hiding the face of the man delivering them.

"Mrs. Kaitlyn Thomas?" the delivery guy asked.

"That's me."

"These are for you."

"Wow," I said, taking the flowers from his hands. "They're beautiful."

"Enjoy." The flower delivery guy chuckled and bounded down the steps toward his white van parked in the driveway.

"Who was it?" Eli asked at the top of the stairs.

"Flowers for me."

Eli shrugged. "Oh, okay," he said and traipsed back to his room. I guess flowers don't really impress a five year old.

I placed the flowers on the kitchen table and opened the envelope that had been pinned to one of the leaves. The card simply read,

Something I should have been doing all along.

Love, Michael

Hours were spent trying to come up with boy names since we had used our favorite boy name on Eli. Late one night we overheard Eli talking to his stuffed animals in his bedroom. He was explaining to them that he would have to share them with his baby brother, Ethan. Michael and I immediately looked at each other and said, "That's it!" So, Eli's brother finally had a name, and it couldn't have been more perfect.

"You're beautiful, you know that?" Michael said one night as we were getting ready for bed.

"Stop. You're just saying that to make me feel better," I said as I examined my stretch marks in the full length mirror.

"There is nothing that would make you any less beautiful in my eyes." He stared at me, enamored by my protruding belly. "This baby will be gorgeous, just like his mama. I can't believe in less than two weeks we will have another new baby in our house."

"I can't believe it either," I agreed, rubbing my hand across my stomach to see if baby Ethan would kick me. "I don't think I'm ready."

"You have been a wonderful mother so far to Eli. This baby just gives you, *us,* a chance to do it all over again." He smiled at me and reached for my hand.

"You will be a wonderful daddy to him too, even if he ends up not being your flesh and blood."

"He's part of you, and you're everything to me. He's no less. I love you, Kaitlyn," he said as he pulled me close to him, hugging me and my enormous belly against him.

"I love you too," I nuzzled into his chest.

Just then, little Ethan kicked me hard, and Michael jumped.

"Hey, little man." Michael bent down and put his cheek against my stomach. "Don't be jealous. I love you too!" Ethan gave Michael another kick on the cheek, and we both laughed.

Neither of us realized that night as we went to bed that I would wake up, waddle my way to the bathroom, and barely make it in time before my water would break all over the freshly mopped tile floor.

The nurse turned around and gently placed my little bundle of joy into my arms. I stared at the miniature picture of perfection as he blinked his eyes and rooted for me against the fuzzy blue blanket.

"He's perfect," I whispered.

"What are you going to name him?" the nurse asked as she checked my vitals.

I looked at Michael. He nodded at me, knowingly.

"Ethan Levi." I smiled at precious little Ethan who was making his first sweet sounds in my arms.

"Ethan Levi," the nurse repeated. "Are those family names?"

Michael reached out and scooped little Ethan into his arms. "You could say that, I guess," he said as he nuzzled the newborn and kissed him on the forehead.

I smiled lovingly at Michael while he cuddled Ethan in his arms. "Both names have Hebrew origins. Ethan means 'strength,' and Levi means 'unity.' I'd like to think this sweet boy has joined us together, stronger than ever," I told the nurse.

"I see," the nurse said as she jotted something on her clipboard. "Well, the name suits him well, then." She grinned, erased something on the whiteboard above my bed, and walked briskly out the door.

"I think it's time to feed this little guy," Michael said as he placed a grunting Ethan back into my arms.

Unwrapping Ethan's blankets and adjusting my hospital gown, I got myself ready to nurse him. "He's just so perfect," I cooed. Dark fluffy hair poked out from under his tiny hospital cap. Ethan's dark gray-blue eyes blinked through the greasy ointment the doctor had put in them shortly after birth.

"He has your nose," Michael chuckled.

I giggled, "I think so too."

"Kaitlyn," Michael's deep, gravelly voice sent shivers down my spine, an indication this conversation was about to get serious. "I love you. You know that?" I looked up at him from my hospital bed. Tears glossed his eyes. His hand reached for mine.

"I know. I love you too," I said as I clasped his strong, capable hand against the stark white hospital blanket.

"I have always loved you. From the moment I met you by the punch bowl, I knew you were the woman of my dreams. I know we've had our share of ups and downs. I'm sorry if I wasn't always the husband you needed me to be."

"Don't say that, Michael. You are a wonderful husband. I'm the one who messed up. It was my fault. I should have been a better wife. I never should have—"

"Shhhh." He looked down with adoration at Ethan eagerly nursing like a champ. Then, he caught my gaze, his ice blue eyes piercing mine. "All is forgiven. *All*," he repeated, "is forgiven." Tears spilled down my cheeks. "You know I love you," he continued, "and I want you to be happy. You deserve to be happy, Kaitlyn. That's all I've ever wanted for you."

"You do make me happy, Michael. You have made me happy during times I wanted to give up. You have given me a life I could never dream for myself. You loved me when I was unlovable. You forgave me when I was unforgivable. Thank you so much for fighting to save our family."

A wide grin spread across his lips. "I'll always love you, sweetheart," he whispered and bent down to kiss my forehead.

I had Ethan on my shoulder, gently patting him on the back when Eli burst through the door with his Nana, his happy little voice barreling into the room.

"Mommy!" Eli shouted. "I got the highest score of the day on Race City!"

"That's wonderful, baby," I whispered excitedly, hoping not to wake Ethan who was sleeping soundly.

"Yeah," Eli smiled, "and, I got two hundred tickets!" He proudly handed me a handful of wadded up tickets.

"Why didn't you cash these in?"

"I was going to pay them to the doctor so we can take my baby brother home now."

I grinned and looked up at my mom walking toward me. "Thanks for taking him to the arcade for a little while. I got to take a little nap while you were gone."

"I'm glad, hon'," she smiled. "You need all the rest you can get now that you have two little ones."

"Oh, and I colored baby Ethan a picture!" Eli proudly held out a picture of a big lollipop and a little lollipop that looked like they were tied together.

"What a beautiful picture, Eli! Your lollipops are perfect," I told him.

"They're not lollipops. The big one is me and the little one is my baby brother; I am holding his hand," he said emphatically.

"Aww, how sweet. I will hang it up in his nursery when we get home."

"Can I see him?" Eli asked curiously.

"Of course."

I laid Ethan across my legs and let Eli climb up on my hospital bed to get a better look.

"Hey baby Ethan," Eli patted his blanket gently. "I'm your big brother."

Eli waited, expectantly. "He's not saying anything, Mommy."

Everyone in the room giggled.

"He will, in time. He's just too little to talk right now."

"Okay," Eli nodded. "I will just give him kisses then."

"Good idea," I agreed.

"Don't worry, Ethan. I'm going to be the best big brother ever," he said proudly. With that, Eli leaned down and left a wet, sloppy kiss on his baby brother's tiny cheek.

Three weeks later, I was sitting on the recliner, rocking Ethan. It was late at night and Michael was stretched out on the sofa, surfing the internet on his iPad. Eli had long since been in bed. I was trying to hold Ethan off, hoping he'd let me sneak in a few extra hours of sleep by skipping his usual 2am snack.

"Do you think we should just go ahead and do it?"

Michael looked at me, mischievously waggling his eyebrows, "Hubba, hubba," he teased.

I threw a pillow at him, laughing. "Hush. I was talking about the DNA test, silly."

Michael placed his iPad on the sofa beside him and clasped his hands in front of him. "Oh," he said with a more serious tone. "No. I don't think so."

"Does that mean, no, you don't want to do it *right now*, or no, *not ever*?"

"It means, no, *not ever.*"

"Why not?"

"Well, think about it Kaitlyn. What's that DNA test really going to prove? I already love Ethan enough for any father. He doesn't have to have my DNA to prove that. What if we take the test, and it turns out he *is* Chris's baby? What then? Are we just going to invite Chris into our lives? Is Chris gonna drop what he's doing and move here to be the kind of father Ethan needs? If not, are you willing to ship Ethan off, as often as a judge determines in a custody agreement, so he can spend time with a man you barely know? It's ludicrous, Kaitlyn. The possibilities are endless. *I* am Ethan's daddy. A DNA test doesn't prove anything. Taking that test will just complicate things."

I considered what Michael was telling me. It's true; taking the test could surely complicate our lives. And yet, at the same time, knowing the truth would put our *(my)* mind at ease. Ethan had my nose, for sure. Michael said he had my mother's dark brown eyes. Everyone said he had my father's dimpled chin. I looked at my sweet, sleepy boy and considered the possibility of shipping him off to visit Chris. While I may have been in love with Chris at some point, Michael was right; I didn't really know Chris well enough to ship my son off to live with him for indefinite periods of time. *Why did the decision have to be so difficult? Why did there have to be so much gray area in this black and white equation?*

I looked at Michael, the picture perfect dad. And for all we knew, Michael could truly be Ethan's biological father. If not, I knew he would love Ethan just as much as any father would love a son. One of Chris's comments at the beach echoed in my mind—the comment about not wanting a child anytime soon because he wasn't ready to sacrifice his time and energy to have one. Michael was right; we didn't need a DNA test to prove anything. All that we needed was each other—our little family. I hugged my precious angel closer and knew, in my heart, that not taking the test was the best thing for all of us.

Chapter Twenty-Seven
Five years later

As they say, the days were long, but the years were short. Eli had grown like a weed the last five years and was nearly as tall, if not taller, than me. And Ethan...well, I cried all the way home the day he started Kindergarten. By that point, I had been a stay-at-home mom for eleven years. I hardly knew what to do that first full day by myself. After a few days, I learned to appreciate the peace and quiet. But after several boring weeks, I decided to fill the void by returning to college to work on a Master's degree in Social Work. Still in the application process, I hoped I would be accepted so I could start classes the following semester.

I'd like to say our lives were perfect from the moment Michael told me he forgave me. They weren't—not by a long shot—but we made it. We were *still* making it. After that summer, we resumed our normal everyday lives. Michael focused on his accounting work, while I stayed home to raise our children. However, I guess I could say we lived our lives with a whole new perspective. We loved more, forgave more, and talked more in general. Michael started making a conscious effort to spend more time with us and less time in his home office. However, he still managed to eat the occasional dinner in front of his computer, coming to bed well after midnight. He even missed the boys' ball games from time to time due to working late on a project, but for the most part, he made every effort to be there for them—for us.

I learned to tolerate Michael's personal assistant, Bridget, and eventually grew to love her. A recent college graduate, she was in the process of dropping that stereotypical sorority girl image, and trying to make her way in the business world. Bridget became Michael's biggest asset in his workplace, helping him earn a promotion and a three percent raise that first year. I met Bridget, in person, at a company picnic that same summer five years ago. Surprisingly, we hit it off immediately. Turns out, she was just one of those sweet southern girls you wanted to hate, and couldn't help but like. She has since moved on to a corporate accounting job in another city, and Michael has had countless other interns as assistants. However, our argument over Bridget and his newfound respect for our marriage has kept Michael from blurring the personal and professional lines again with anyone at his workplace.

Our marriage was a constant work in progress—something I wish we had figured out years ago. But, the last five years had been the best years of our marriage, and we were about two months away from celebrating our twelfth wedding anniversary. So I guess, all in all, we had made a pretty good run of it.

"We'll need milk, too," I said absently as we stood in front of the cereal aisle at the grocery store one day.

Turning to Michael, I asked, "Would you mind going to grab some milk and eggs? Oh yeah, you might as well grab butter and cheese while you're over there, too."

"At your service, ma'am," he laughed, while giving me his best military salute.

"Very funny," I said with a straight face. Hoping to get this trip to the store over with as quickly as possible, I ordered, "Milk, eggs, butter, and cheese. Got that?"

"Got it, Sarge," he teased as he clicked his heels, maintaining his salute. The boys giggled beside me.

"Daddy's silly!" Ethan exclaimed.

I rolled my eyes and despite my efforts not to, I grinned at Michael. His sense of humor reminded me of why I fell in love with him in the first place. Michael took off toward the dairy section in the back corner of the grocery store, while I turned my attention back to the boys.

"Can I get that box?" Ethan asked as he pointed to a colorful box of sugar laden corn cereal.

I sighed. "Sure, why not?"

I looked at Eli, who at the age of eleven was a half inch taller than me now, which isn't saying much considering I'm only five feet tall on a good day. I asked him to reach the fiber concentrated cereal on the top shelf—the cereal that resembled miniscule bales of hay—while Ethan happily selected the bright and colorful box with the cartoon rabbit on the front that was strategically placed at his eye level.

"Thanks, sweetie," I said as Eli handed the box to me. I placed it into my cart and continued to push my way toward the next aisle.

Eli grabbed one of the tabloid magazines near the register as we passed by the rack. "Look, mom." He held the cover of the magazine in front of my face so I could read the words in the headline.

A collage of several photos of him with a different girl every night glared up at me from the cover.

"Isn't that the guy from our hometown?" Eli asked as he pointed to a picture of Chris with some large breasted, blonde bombshell sitting on his lap at a party.

"Humph," I grunted. "Yeah, put that back. We've got to finish getting what's on my list," I said, trying to downplay Chris's fame and hide my anguish.

I usually tried to avoid any press coverage of Chris King. Just seeing his picture on the cover of the tabloids messed with my head. Mr. ChrisRocknRollKing became a sensation overnight, and by the looks of those photos, he seemingly forgot just as quickly his father's advice to stay on the right track. Chris King was no longer a priority in my heart. He had his life, and I had mine. My boys were my life.

"Mommy?"

I looked down at Ethan as he tugged on my pants leg.

"What sweetheart?"

Only Ethan didn't answer. He just stood there, staring.

"What is it?" I asked again.

Ethan still only stood there, staring straight ahead. I shook my head and glanced back down to see the next item written on my grocery list. Dragging two children around at the grocery store, my patience wore very thin. I was just trying to concentrate on getting in, getting my groceries, and getting out, with very few distractions.

"Mom," Eli said in a hushed tone.

"What now?" In that moment, I looked up to see someone walking toward us, smiling.

Although he was still twenty feet away, I knew it was *him*. It had been six long years, but you don't forget a face that easily.

Eli looked down at the tabloid, and looked back up again. He did that several times before he finally whispered, "Mom, is that—?"

"Yes," I interrupted.

With stars in his eyes, Eli finally accepted the fact that the lead singer of *Fifth Wheel* was walking straight toward us.

Chris smiled. My heart immediately jump started in my chest. *Omigod, omigod, omigod.* In my mind, I sounded like a silly fan girl, although I could barely hear myself think over the pounding of my heart. I almost looked around for a place to hide. Instead, I pinched myself. *Yep. I'm awake.*

Chris strolled up to us without a care in the world, as if he weren't the same rock star celebrity that was plastered all over the cover of every magazine on the shelf.

He stopped in front of my cart, slipped his hands into his pockets, and said, "Hi, Kaitlyn." He pulled the corner of his mouth up into that dreamy grin he had become so accustomed to giving to the paparazzi that followed him everywhere he went. I wondered where the paparazzi were hiding and why they weren't clicking the camera in our faces yet.

"Hi," I said, dropping my chin and grinning bashfully while my cheeks flared. *Get a hold of yourself, Kaitlyn.*

"It's been a while," he acknowledged, with a quick nod of his head. His beautiful eyes stared deeply into mine. *Stop staring.*

"It has." My mind seemed to have forgotten how to function as I tried in vain to form sentences that were more than just one or two words long.

I tried to ignore his ~~sexy, seductive~~ *(ugh)* charming grin.

"How have you been?" he asked.

Brain, work! Speak. "Pretty good. What are you doing back in town? Don't you have a concert soon?" I asked when my brain finally shook itself from the dizzying fog.

"We do, but I figured while we were passing through town on the way to Charlotte that I'd stop in and see my mom. So like a typical mother, she sent me to the grocery store for some food and to the pharmacy for her meds. Leave it to my mom to keep me grounded."

I laughed. Chris smiled warmly. My heart did somersaults in my chest. *Mayday, Mayday, Mayday!*

"Are these your children?" He glanced at Eli and Ethan, but quickly caught my gaze again.

"Yes," I said, putting my hand on Eli's shoulder. "This is Eli. He's eleven now." Finally, I was managing sentences longer than two words. I breathed a sigh of relief as Chris held his hand out to Eli.

"Pleasure to meet you." Chris gripped Eli's hand and gave it a firm shake.

"You too, Mr. King," Eli said, smiling with a star-struck glimmer in his eyes.

Chris laughed a deep hearty laugh that tingled its way up my spine. "Please, call me Chris."

"Yes sir, Mr. Chris." Eli continued shaking his hand, completely enamored by this famous musician whose songs he had downloaded on his iPod and could recite every word.

Chris just continued to chuckle, then patted him on the shoulder. "Just Chris is fine, young man. Your manners are impeccable." Chris looked back at me. "You must be so proud of him."

I nodded. "Couldn't be more proud."

Just then, Chris looked down at Ethan and tousled his brown hair on top of his head. "And who's this little fella?"

Ethan looked up at him and grinned. "Hi," he said happily.

I put my arm around my sweet, brown eyed boy. "This is Ethan. He's five years old."

Ethan glared at me as if I had committed a cardinal sin. "I'm five and a half!" he demanded.

I chuckled. "Excuse me, he's five and half."

"Well," Chris bent down to look at Ethan on his level, "you're a handsome little five and a half year old."

Now that Chris was standing right in front of Ethan, the similarities were astounding. Michael had always said Ethan looked just like my side of the family, but seeing Chris and Ethan together made me question our decision *not* to administer a DNA test. Both of them stared at each other with dark brown hair that flipped out on the ends; both had dark brown eyes and thick black eyelashes. With their tan skin, they never had to worry about getting sunburned. Their similarities were so unlike Eli, whose fair features took after Michael's side of the family. I soaked in the image. Could it be that father and son were meeting each other for the first time, with neither of them knowing their possible relationship to each other? My stomach churned. *Maybe Michael and I should revisit the idea of a DNA test.*

Chris looked at me. I wondered if he could read my mind. He stood back up and placed his hand on my grocery cart. After several glances at both boys, his gaze shifted back to me, piercing me with those chocolate brown eyes that always kept me swooning what seemed like a lifetime ago. As if a light bulb switched on in his mind, a sudden awareness crossed his face; the cloud of confusion immediately lifted. The look in Chris's eyes was unexplainable. Was it hurt? Anger? Fear? Happiness? A combination of many emotions swirled themselves around in his beautiful brown irises. He pursed his lips, attempting to hide a pained smile that was tugging at the corners of his mouth, but it still didn't detract from the other emotions flooding his eyes.

Click, click, click, click...

Suddenly, from around the corner, a camera was in our faces and a member of the tabloid media was spouting questions to Chris faster than he could answer them. Ignoring them, he grabbed a pen from the inside pocket of his leather jacket, jerked my grocery list from my hand, jotted something down on it, and thrust it back at me. With the cameraman chasing after him, he darted around a magazine rack and around the cash register, disappearing out the electronic doors.

Peering down at the paper he had shoved into my hand, I saw a phone number scrawled below the last item written on the list—ten numbers that reminded me of a scrap of paper he had handed to me nearly fifteen years ago outside Club Millennium. Those were numbers I had kept hidden in my jacket pocket that saved me on more than one occasion. These were *new* numbers that would continue to keep me linked to the man with whom I was once hopelessly in love.

"Where did he go?" Eli asked, disappointed.

I stared longingly in the direction of Chris's disappearance. "He just had to leave, honey."

"Can we see him again?"

I looked down at the ring on my finger, imagining Michael at work every day, crunching number after boring number in order to provide for us—his family. He and I had worked too hard in the last five years to fix our marriage and maintain a stable home for our children. Then, I remembered the heartfelt letter I'd found written to me from my mother in the hat box in her attic. Those thoughts, along with one sidelong glance at the photos plastered on every magazine stacked on the rack of Chris partying it up and getting intimate with numerous women, provided me with my answer: "No, sweetheart. No, we can't."

My heart felt as if I were tearing a piece of it off and stomping it into the ground while my head begrudgingly encouraged me to rip my list, along with Chris's phone number, into a million tiny shreds. Determined and focused, showing no mercy, I tore the paper into as many pieces as possible. The ache from watching Chris walk away welled up inside me like a balloon ready to burst. I'd done it twice before, and I could do it again. This would be the last time. *Oh God, please let this be the last time.* My heart can't handle this kind of torture. I clutched the shredded handful of paper to my chest, my heart clinging to my past until the last possible second. *Goodbye Chris.* I tossed the final available link I had to him into a nearby garbage can. I didn't look back—*couldn't* look back.

My heart ached—oh, how my heart ached, but I stood strong knowing I'd made the right decision. I had the ring on my finger and my two precious gifts walking beside me as proof that sometimes in life, you just love someone so much it hurts.

Epilogue
-Chris-

I love my life. Really I do. I mean, who wouldn't love the life of a rock star? I'm a world traveler. Everyone kisses my ass to try to get a taste of riches and fame. Women clamor for a piece of me, but I never have to put forth much effort for a piece of them, that's for damn sure. *Never.* They just throw themselves at me like greedy, money hungry, fame seeking, attention whores. It's like an endless buffet of ass, just waiting for me at my beck and call. And, the shows…The flashing lights, the thumping music, the billowing smoke effects—it's all a trip! I fucking love it. I never get tired of hearing my name being chanted among the crowds. *Chris King! Chris King!* God, that never gets old. I'm living the dream life. This is what I live for!

"Shit, who am I kidding?" I grumble as I toss the latest tabloid magazine in the garbage. That shit's not me. That's not who I am. No one knows the real me. That self-absorbed rock star shit is just an act. Yeah, I have women throwing themselves at me, and occasionally I take the bait—mostly out of loneliness than anything else. But, everything about me runs much deeper than a quick encounter with some groupie chick willing to put out. No one will ever know the real me. No one, but *her*.

The bump and rattle of the tour bus, as we travel down the highway, reminds me of my grandfather's old Cadillac bouncing down the road to his weekly bingo games when I was a kid. I remember lying across the backseat. I was just long enough to fit, head to toe, across the seat. The constant hum of the car usually put me to sleep. Maybe that memory is why I am able to sleep so soundly on this piece of shit tour bus. Endless miles, to nowhere special, leave me feeling a sense of loss for *home*. There is no *home* on the road—only hotels. There is no stability—only a different city every night. I miss home. I miss stability. I miss her. *God, I miss her.*

I never thought I'd see her again. But, there she was, walking around in that grocery store with her kids. Her *kids*. The big kid, Eli...I remember her talking about him on our first walk together on the beach, when I found out she was married. She said she had a kid. Hell, at that time, kids were the very last thing on my mind! I'm older now. I'm almost too old for this nomad's life on the road. There are much younger, shit for talent, but popular teenage heartthrobs making their way to the big stage. I just want to go back home—back to my roots. Not necessarily her town, but somewhere I can call home. Maybe back to the beach. That's the place I was the happiest, writing songs and playing gigs on the weekends. That was the life—not this shit. This life is the pits. My agent's riding my ass all the time. I never truly know who my real friends are, or I'm wondering if they're using me as a stepping stone or whatever. Media pulls me in all different directions, harassing me for interviews and shit. Hell, I'm ready to settle down and possibly even entertain the idea of having kids.

Speaking of kids, there's that little kid. What was his name? Ethan? Oh yeah. Cute kid. Brown hair, brown eyes…God, I felt like I was looking in the mirror. Could he be mine? He definitely looked like he could be mine. Well, I guess technically it *is* a possibility. I mean, it was about six years ago she and I…well, yeah. I've had very few regrets in my life. I'm not saying she's one of them, but I know what we did was wrong. I fucked up. I don't screw other guys' chicks, especially married ones. That's messed up, but damn I loved her. I loved her more than I have ever loved any woman in my life, and I don't even know why. I can't explain it. We were young, so young. Maybe it was because we knew we couldn't be together. Maybe we had this crazy, cosmic soul-connected energy between us. Hell, who knows. All I know is I fucking loved her. More than life. More than *anything*.

It was just my luck; I walked around the corner, and there she stood, looking more beautiful than ever. But sad. Or regretful. Or scared. Hell, I don't know. I just wanted to hug her. She looked like she might bolt at any minute, or throw up. I just wanted to grab her and hug her like I did six years ago, or eight years before that. If I think hard enough I can still remember how she felt against my body. That woman did things to me I can't even explain, and I don't mean sexually either. I mean she messed me up inside—messed with my head. I could barely function when I got sent back to juvie. And, I don't think I slept for weeks after she left the beach six years ago. Ten pounds isn't a lot to lose, unless you lose it all in a week's time because you can't fucking think straight over a girl.

I saw the sadness in her eyes when she saw me, but I watched her before that. I watched the way she interacted with her kids—the way they adored her. The way her husband smiled at her, she was happy. She *is* happy. He's a good man. I remember that dude from high school. Math class fucking sucked, and there was that awkward, nerdy kid who sat in front of me. One time I slammed my fist into my desk, frustrated over some stupid fucking equation. He didn't even flinch. He didn't cower like most of the other country club douche bags in that class who had nothing better to do than call me a loser. He just turned around in his desk and asked if I needed help. He broke it down, explaining the equation to me in a way I could understand, and suddenly, it clicked. Dude was a saint—a damn genius! She got herself a good man, I'll give her that. I can tell he loves her. I can tell he'd do anything for her, just like I would if she were mine. But, she's *not...mine.*

Dammit! I don't know what the hell I was thinking giving her my phone number. What did I think she was going to do? Leave her husband and kids to come find me? Bring her kids on the road with me? Be willing to have every aspect of her life scrutinized by the tabloid media? Hell no! I love her, but I love her too much to drag her name through the mud and air her dirty laundry on the front of every magazine cover. No, I would never do that to her. I need to let her live her life, happily, with her husband and her two kids. I want her to be happy. She *deserves* to be happy. I know she still loves me. I have no doubts of that. I could sense it in the way she stared at me, smiled at me even, in front of the cereal aisle. I love her too, *still*, after all these years. I would do anything for her. Anything. *Anything.*

I never stopped loving her, or maybe it was the idea of her, I don't know. But, I've always loved her so much I can barely breathe just thinking about it, but...*I have to let her go.* Her family needs her. Her kids need her. She needs them. She doesn't need me and the life I have to offer. She has a husband who would walk across the desert for her. She's happy. She deserves to stay that way. She doesn't need me.

Taking out a pen, I scrawl a handwritten letter. My manager has connections I couldn't dream of having. I know the letter will get to her. I have no doubts.

Dear Kaitlyn,

I don't even know where to start. Seeing you in the grocery store, so happy with your family, brought a true smile to my face, one that hasn't been there in quite a while. I'm so glad I got to meet your children. Eli is such a fine young man. And Ethan, well I don't even know what to say about Ethan. He's adorable. I couldn't help but think of the possibilities when I looked at him. That's why I'm writing to you. I couldn't just walk away from those possibilities, but at the same time, I don't want to interfere with your happy life. Your boys look so happy. I could never rip their family apart and erase those sweet smiles from their faces. I saw them laughing as your husband teased and saluted you, and I knew then he was the man for the job that I know I could never do justice—not with my lifestyle. He's a good man, Kaitlyn. You both deserve all the happiness life has to offer. I want to do something for your family- for your boys. Consider it a gift. Consider it my contribution to a role I know I could never play in your lives, unless of course, you decide it's something you want. But, I love you enough to let you go, for now, knowing it's probably in everyone's best interest. Although if my assumptions about Ethan are true, I can't just walk away from that. If the only peaceable part I can play is to ensure their future education, then so be it. See the attached documents for details of this contribution. Please accept it with the understanding that I never expect anything in return, except knowing you and your family are happy together. Take care of yourself. Take care of your boys. Live well.

Love always,
  -C

I stare at my phone, pleading silently for it to ring, hoping she'll be on the other end begging me to come back and get her. But, I know my wish is hopeless, foolish even. I love her so much it hurts right now, but I know what I must do—what I *need* to do to make things right. I swipe the screen of my phone and call my manager.

"Beverly, I need a favor. I need you to contact my financial advisor. I want to set up an educational trust fund. I'll give you the rest of the details later. But, just get the appointment booked for now, okay?…Uh huh…Yeah…Thanks."

Listening to her jabber on and on about this or that is mentally exhausting. Most of the time I'm on the other end saying "uh huh, yeah, uh huh, right," while she sounds just like that teacher from the Peanuts cartoon. *Wah, wah, wah.* I don't even know what she's ranting about today. Something about a switch in venues for an upcoming concert. I'm a go-with-the-flow kind of guy. It doesn't affect me when or where I sing. Just give me a mic and a guitar, and I'm good to go! After a few minutes of drowning out her endless chatter, I finally manage to squeeze a word in edgewise. "All right, Bev, I need to ask another favor."

I know I have to follow through on my decision, but I know what the outcome will do to my heart. Regardless, it's the *right* thing to do. *Jesus, help me get through this.* "Listen Beverly, promise me there will be no questions asked about my next request, okay?" With a contemplative pause, I wrestle with the next few words, but manage to spill them out knowing my heart's in the right place—I'm doing this for *her.* "I'm gonna need you to change my phone number."

The End

Are you or a loved one a victim of domestic/dating violence? You are not alone. You can break the cycle!

Domestic/Dating violence is the willful intimidation, physical assault, battery, sexual assault and/or other abusive behavior perpetuated by an intimate partner against another. It is an epidemic affecting individuals in every community, regardless of age, economic status, race, religion, nationality, or educational background. Violence against women, often accompanied by emotionally abusive and controlling behavior, is part of a systematic pattern of dominance and control. Domestic violence results in physical injury, psychological trauma, and sometimes death. The consequences of domestic/dating violence can cross generations and truly last a lifetime.

- One in every four women will experience domestic violence in her lifetime.

- One in three teens and young adults experience some form of dating abuse

- An estimated 1.3 million women are victims of physical assault by an intimate partner each year

- 85% of domestic violence victims are women

- Historically, females have been most often victimized by someone they knew

- Females who are 20-24 years of age are at the greatest risk of non-fatal intimate partner violence

- 58% of college students say they don't know how to help someone who is a victim of dating abuse

- Most cases of domestic violence are never reported to the police

For more information or to get help, please call:
The National Domestic Violence Hotline at
1-800-799-7233

The National Sexual Assault Hotline at 1-800-656-4673

The National Teen Dating Abuse Hotline at
1-800-331-9474

Additional information, please visit:
http://www.ncadv.org
www.breakthecycle.org
www.loveisrespect.org
www.rainn.org

Acknowledgements

To my readers: THANK YOU! Words cannot express my gratitude. When I first started writing this book I never imagined the first person would read it. I'm so thankful that you have picked it up and given it a shot. I couldn't do this without the support of my readers and fans! You make this whole process worth every minute!

To my husband: Thank you for always supporting me. Thank you for being such a good sport about listening to me drone on and on about my story even though you have no interest whatsoever in romance novels. Thank you for your patience when I locked myself up in our bedroom all day to write. Thank you most of all, for three beautiful children, twelve amazing years, and your unconditional love! I love you!

To my parents who have always been there for me: Thank you for your love, support, and encouragement throughout my life. Whether it was at the bowling alley, the Soap Box Derby hills, the recital stage, or watching from the stands while I cheered, you have always encouraged me to reach for the stars. Thank you for providing me with the opportunity to attend college and get my degrees. Thank you for supporting me when I made the decision to stay home with my children. Thank you for being the best parents a girl could ask for, and the best grandparents to your grandchildren! No matter what, you have always been there for us. I love you both so much!

Thank you to the ones in my life who inspired my characters for this story. I truly believe you were each placed in my life for a reason, and I'll always be grateful for that. You have all touched my life in one way or another. I have been thoroughly blessed with love, friendship, and guidance through the years. While some of you might never cross my path again, the influence you had in my life will forever remain in my heart.

To my early readers and supporters, D.B., A.T., A.M., C.S., D.S., S.R., S.B., B.H., L.O., S.R, and V.R.: Thank you for encouraging me to keep going! Your ideas and feedback were invaluable!

To "My Girls": Thank you for not telling me I was crazy to think I could publish a book! Thank you for your support and encouragement the past seven years! In one way or another you guys helped me get through the tough stages of the terrible-twos and potty training. You loved me when I was a sleep-deprived maniac, and encouraged me to get out for play dates even when sitting on the couch in my pajamas all day sounded more appealing. You have no idea how all those early morning mall walks and lunches in the food court got me through those rough days of having three little ones at home. You all deserve a medal of honor! But, for now, a tiny blurb in my acknowledgements section will have to do. I love you girls!

To my "Indie Chixx", my "Indie Gals", and all my girls in between; you girls welcomed me into the Indie Author world with open arms: Thank you just doesn't seem like enough. I stepped into the Indie world, scared and alone. Thank you, *JC Isabella*, for encouraging me to take that first step and for always taking time to answer all those long elaborate messages I sent to you. Thank you, *Nichele Reese*, for welcoming me, introducing me to your circle of friends, giving me amazing feedback, and showing me the ropes! (And yes, I still use way too many exclamation points! Haha!) Thank you, *Kim Karr*, for believing in my story, taking a chance on me, and publishing my first chapter in the back of your debut novel. Thank you *Nacole Stayton* for reading my book and being huge encouragements to me when I was so close to hitting that delete button! I appreciate your friendship so much! Thank you, *Kimi Flores*, for being my personal cheerleader, with constant encouraging messages just to check up on me. I enjoyed every Vox conversation and every marathon chat session. I'm stockpiling beef jerky now for when I come to visit you. :) I can't wait to see the giraffes by the ocean! Love you bunches! Thank you for your friendship! To *Elaine Breson*, thank you for the many hours of chats that kept me smiling. Thank you for the beautiful photo mat and tote bag! To *Erika Ashby*, thank you for the many laughs and your hilarious sense of humor. Thanks for always being just one chat session away and for always answering my silly questions with such honesty. To *JL Brooks* thank you for those random, but strategically perfect, phone calls that talked me down off the "delete ledge." Your support and encouragement are some of the reasons why *So Much It Hurts* is still here today. Thank you, *Tania Hernandez*, for making my amazingly beautiful and heartrending book trailer! To *JL Mac*, thank you so much for your adorable videos! Not only did they keep me in stitches, but they were also so incredibly helpful to newbies like me. To *Lisa Harley*, thank you for taking time to read my story and provide me with such wonderful feedback! I really appreciate all your encouragement! To *Rebecca Shea*, thank you for offering to meet me, a perfect stranger, on your business trip through town. I never imagined I would meet a total stranger and not stop talking until I said goodbye three hours later! I know I've found a lifelong friend in you! To *Jennifer Wolfel*, thank you for beta reading and giving me some great feedback! *E.K. Blair*, thank you for opening my eyes to something I hadn't given much thought to. You may not even know it, but a single comment changed the course of *So Much It Hurts* for the better. To *Beverley Hollowed*, we still need that Skype date! Thank you for always being quick to encourage and keep me sane! Thank you, *Megan Hand*, *Ana Zaun*, *Jaime Guerard*, and *Laura Howard*, for the many late night conversations and for answering my infinite supply of questions. Thank you, *Kelsie Leverich* and *Jessica Louise*, for helping me with my blurb for my back cover of my paperback! You girls are amazing with words! Thank you also, *Mel Ballew*, whose friendship and feedback have been invaluable! I'm so incredibly grateful to you for publishing my first chapter in the back of your book and for combing through my manuscript with a fine toothed comb, pointing out all my overused words! The hours we've spent on the phone have meant more to me than you can imagine! Thank you to *Jenn Besterman* for swooping in to beta when I was feeling defeated! Your feedback was so helpful and encouraging as well! Thank you to *Amanda Stone* for always being there to reply to any questions I had. I appreciate all of your honest answers and feedback! To *Anne Leigh*, you were a new author on the scene who always popped in to ask me about my day or give me encouragement. Thank you for reading my manuscript and supporting me with such an amazing review! Thank you *Lynetta Halat* and *Heather Gunter*, my newest author friends who are just all-around awesome! I love you girls like the day is long!

Thank you, Katie Mac of Indie Express, who spent hours supplying me with invaluable feedback over the phone and on the internet. I'm so thankful our paths crossed on Facebook, even though I feel certain we may have crossed paths another time in our lives while living in the same small town. ;) I'm so thankful to have found such a wonderful, talented group of writer friends!

Thank you, Jim McLaurin, for your keen eyes and attention to detail. You helped me tremendously! Not only did you make loads of corrections, but you lifted my spirits as well. Even though my book is what you affectionately called a "girlie book," I'll never forget your kind words: "...a good tale is a good tale." Thank you for your support and for your boost of confidence!

Thank you to my final beta crew: Debi Barnes, Danielle Plane, Elle Wilson, Mindy Stickels, and Teri Page. You girls were my last minute betas who kept me motivated to perfect and polish my book. Your encouragement and support were phenomenal those final weeks before publishing! I look forward to working with you ladies in the future!

Thank you to Brett Fabrizio, with the help of his sweet and beautiful bride, for making my book cover more gorgeous than I could ever imagine!

Thank you to my amazing editor, Kathleen Lilley, who spent hours combing through my manuscript for every misplaced comma and grammatical error. I enjoyed working with you and spending time on the phone chatting about my book. Maybe, just maybe, I might have added a few things after you did my final edit. So if there are any mistakes, they're not your fault. After all, I'm a tweakaholic who just can't stop!

Thank you, blogger Kim Box Person of Shh Mom's Reading, for hosting my cover reveal for *So Much It Hurts*! Thank you for taking a chance on a newbie like me and helping to get my cover out to so many other bloggers. I appreciate your humor and all the hard work you put into blogging and reviewing! I hope you love my rockstar, Chris King! ;)

Thank you, blogger Holly Malgieri of I Love Indie Books, for hosting my blog tour and for always being one click away with all my messages. Thank you for answering all my questions and for being patient with a newbie like me. I know how much time and effort goes into planning a blog tour. I appreciate everything you're doing to help me.

Thank you to all the bloggers who have agreed to take part in my blog tour and who have agreed to read and review my book. I'm so thankful for everyone who has taken part in getting the word out about my book. Thank you for everything you have done and continue to do for indie authors! We appreciate you!

Thank you, Angela McLaurin of Fictional Formats, for making the interior of *So Much It Hurts* so incredibly stunning! You have a gift for creating beautiful masterpieces! Thank you for your friendship, also! I knew the moment we met at Book Bash that we would be great friends. I appreciate everything you've done for me. You are such a beautiful person, inside and out! I look forward to working with you in the future and hanging out with you at future book signings… you know, since you did volunteer be my assistant and all. ;)

Last, but certainly not least, thank you so much to my children, whom I adore with every fiber of my being (most of the time). They had to put up with a lot of pizza and takeout, which I don't think they minded much. They were very patient with me when I holed myself up in my bedroom writing with that 'Mama's got crazy eyes' look. They didn't tear the house up…too much. And, while sometimes they drive me BSC, I still love them more than life!!! (Psssst….if any of my kids ask, BSC stands for Banana Split Crazy) ;)

About the Author

Melanie Dawn is a thinker, a dreamer, and a hopeless romantic. When her head isn't in the clouds, she spends her time as a jack of all trades to her family. Melanie resides in the hills of North Carolina with her husband, her three children, and her cat. She enjoys lazy summer afternoons cruising around the lake on the pontoon boat with her family.

Melanie graduated from UNC-Chapel Hill with a BA in Psychology and earned her MA in School Counseling from Appalachian State University. She spent the first six years after graduate school as a middle school counselor. Those were years she deems as some of the best years of her life. That is, until she had children of her own. The last seven years have been spent as a stay-at-home mom. She has learned some tough life lessons, like what the inner absorbent pellets of a diaper look like scattered in the washing machine. She has also learned the strength of the willpower of a two year old lacking a nap. Through it all, Melanie has learned how to roll with the punches and appreciate the time she has been able to spend at home with her children.

Now that her last child has started Kindergarten, Melanie is ready to add a new chapter in her life. That chapter begins with her debut novel—So Much It Hurts.

Let's stay in touch:

Facebook: www.facebook.com/AuthorMelanieDawn

Twitter: www.twitter.com/MelanieDawn1

Email: melaniedawnauthor@gmail.com

So Much It Hurts:
PLAYLIST

Is There Life Out There by Reba McEntire
I Can't Do That Anymore by Faith Hill
And Still by Reba McEntire
Weak by SWV
Wonderful Tonight by Eric Clapton
Boys of Fall by Kenny Chesney
Face Down by Red Jumpsuit Apparatus
I Hate Everything About You by Three Days Grace
Bleed for You by Hidden in Plain View
Everything by Lifehouse
Hey Ya! by Outkast
Iris by GooGoo Dolls
Jumper by Third Eye Blind
Numb by Linkin Park
Jar of Hearts by Christina Perri
Mean by Taylor Swift
She Will be Loved by Maroon 5
U Got It Bad by Usher
Crush by David Archuleta
All I Want by Staind
The Dance by Garth Brooks
End of the Road by Boyz II Men
Here Without You by 3 Doors Down
You Found Me by The Fray

Bring Me to Life by Evanescence
You and Me by Lifehouse
I Don't Wanna Miss a Thing by Aerosmith
Collide by Howie Day
You're Beautiful by James Blunt
What Hurts the Most by Rascal Flatts
Fix You by Coldplay
Bleed Together by The Autumn Offering
Just Give Me a Reason by Pink
Unanswered Prayers by Garth Brooks
Blessed by Martina McBride

Continue reading for a sneak peak of:

Searching for Tomorrow

Coming Soon
A Contemporary Romance novel by
Katie Mac

What happens when you find the one person who completes you, and then life conspires against you? How do you set your grief and anguish aside? How do you pick up the shattered pieces, put those pieces back together again, and try to move on?

Katie and Tripp met on the playground the first day of third grade when Tripp tried to rescue Katie from Zack, her twin brother. A lifelong friendship that later blossomed into love began that day.

Broken beyond her own ability to repair, Katie boxes her grief up and attempts to raise her three girls the best she can on her own. As time slowly passes, Katie relives her times with Tripp while struggling most days to even get out of bed. She is reminded of him at every turn.

Zack is Katie's twin brother and was Tripp's best friend. Having lost his own love, he dedicates himself to helping Katie put her life back together. Throw in a mother-in-law who torments at every turn and poor Katie can't even find a chance to breathe, much less a desire to somehow search for tomorrow.

Excerpt from:

Searching
for
Tomorrow

Who is Tripp, you ask? Well, that is fairly easy to explain. Tripp was my best friend, my lover, my confidant, my soul mate. He was the salt to my pepper. He was the peanut butter to my chocolate. He gave me love and hope and joy. Together we created our three beautiful girls and together we looked at the world as ours to conquer. In short, he was my other half; the part that completed me.

Tripp and I met in 1992. It was the first day of the new school year and we were starting the third grade. Mom had made me wear this frilly pink dress and these hideous pink and white ribbons in my hair. During recess, all the kids went out to the playground for recess. The tire swing was my favorite thing to play on. Tripp saw me fighting with a boy who was trying to take the tire swing from me and decided he would come rescue me. He had no idea that the boy he rescued me from was my twin brother Zack who was quite used to trading punches with me. He quickly learned that fact when I joined forces with Zack to 'take that little twerp down'! From that day forward Zack, Tripp and I were inseparable. Like Tripp always said, "If you can't beat them, join them!" He introduced himself to us as Channing, and we let him keep that name for a short while. The change from Channing to Tripp was just the beginning of the start of our new life together.